THE QUICKENING

BOOK TWO IN THE
SISTERS OF SPIRITS TRILOGY

By the Author

Sometime Yesterday

The Sisters of Spirits Trilogy

The Awakening

The Quickening

THE QUICKENING

BOOK TWO IN THE SISTERS OF SPIRITS TRILOGY

by

Yvonne Heidt

2014

ISBN 13: 978-1-60282-975-6

This Trade Paperback Original Is Published By
Bold Strokes Books, Inc.
P.O. Box 249
Valley Falls, NY 12185

First Edition: January 2014

CREDITS
EDITORS: VICTORIA OLDHAM AND CINDY CRESAP
PRODUCTION DESIGN: SUSAN RAMUNDO
COVER DESIGN BY SHERI (GRAPHICARTIST2020@HOTMAIL.COM)

Acknowledgments

Once again, I get to thank all who are involved in the creative process. How cool is that?

To Radclyffe and the entire gang at Bold Strokes Books—my appreciation for all you do is immeasurable. Meeting several members of the BSB family has been one of the major highlights of my year!

The last twelve months has been a journey of extreme highs and unimaginable loss. Through it all, I have met some wonderful people—thank you for your support.

Shelia Powell, thanks for burning the phone lines with me, literally! Any theoretical errors are completely mine. I shall call it—creative license.

Jove Belle, Stephanie Keeler—best beta readers ever! Thanks for the advice and encouragement—even when I didn't like it. I know that going through my creative process was crazy for you at times.

Sheri Milburn, thanks for making me laugh and holding my hand when I needed it.

Maralee Lackman for being the best friend in the universe. You and Sandy are the reason I believe in soul groups.

For my parents and family—thank you for loving me just the way I am. Every family needs the hippie kid to make life interesting. Even if it's for nothing else but something to talk about at the holiday gatherings. *Where do you come UP with this stuff, Yvonne?*

To my amazing editor, Victoria Oldham. Thanks for showing me how to weave rather than juggle too many balls in the air. I appreciate your time and patience. I don't think I've lost more than a tiny handful of hair this time around!

To my readers—thank you for filling me with joy on a daily basis. I appreciate and thank you for your continued support.

Dedication

For Sandy,
My very own warrior

PROLOGUE

Tiffany Curran raced down the driveway and reached the car before her mother could catch her. She slammed the passenger door and turned to her best friend, Sunny Skye. "Drive!"

"Don't you want—?"

"No. Go, Sunny."

Tiffany peered into the side mirror and saw her mother standing in the middle of the street, shaking her fist at the retreating car. The only part of the tirade she caught before they turned the corner was "hell!" She closed her eyes and rested her head on the seat. Why did her mother have to be so difficult?

Sunny glanced over at her, her expression amused. "Tiffany, are you still in league with the devil?"

"Apparently." And because she knew that Sunny could feel her emotional pain, Tiffany made an effort to tamp it down. She'd become very good at that particular trick over the last five years. "Where's Shade?"

Sunny was quiet for a minute. "She's running late. She's going to meet us there."

"What's wrong with her?"

"She's fine." The answer was short, almost curt, and didn't invite any further conversation.

Tiffany didn't want to intrude. When Sunny wanted to talk about it, she would. But Tiffany still wished she could offer some comfort or something to lighten Sunny's mood.

But unexpectedly, Sunny began to talk. "Her mom is trying to get her committed again to Western State in Tacoma."

"So she wants to dump her so she can take off with some guy again?"

"You know the routine, Tiff."

Yes, she did, and it royally pissed her off. Whenever Shade's mother got itchy feet, she had her committed. "She could pretend she doesn't see the dead people, and then her mother wouldn't have an excuse."

"Shade's too proud for that."

"I know," Tiffany said. At least her mother never had her locked up. No, she just dragged her to the church where the priests prayed and threw holy water at her. She had counted three new crucifixes hidden in her bedroom over the last week. She couldn't wait to turn eighteen and get out of the house.

"Only two more years," said Sunny.

Tiffany smiled. "I didn't say anything."

"Since when has that mattered?"

Tiffany reached over to take Sunny's hand. "If it weren't for you and Shade, I don't know what I would do. Life would be unbearable with her."

Sunny pulled into the full parking lot. The energy emitting from the teen club, The Punk Palace, vibrated the car windows. Several groups of young people grouped together around different vehicles. "I hope there aren't any fights tonight."

"You and me both. It's crazy here. How are we going to find Shade?" Most of the people there were wearing black and looked alike in the dark. But before Tiffany finished the sentence, Shade appeared at Sunny's door to open it for her. "Well, never mind. How silly of me."

They walked into the building and were blasted by music. Heavy bass pressed against Tiffany's chest, altering the beat of her heart and speeding her pulse. People were dancing and body slamming in the pit. She wanted no part of it. Why people would hurt each other on purpose was beyond her.

Tiffany scanned the crowd. "Oh look, there's Mark!" She had to shout to be heard above the music.

Shade sneered. "So? What do you see in him anyway?"

Tiffany sighed. "Look at him. He looks just like Brad Pitt in the movie, *Legends of the Fall*."

As if he knew she was watching him, Mark gave her a quick nod that tossed his hair back from his face. God, he had such beautiful blue eyes. His smile lit a path through the crowd to warm her face. "He's *so* fine."

"Whatever. Where did Sunny get off to?"

"She's over there talking with Suze." She pointed to the area, and when she looked back, Mark was gone. Disappointed, she began searching the crowd again. Tiffany saw the flash of hurt before Shade turned to go to Sunny's side. It was almost uncomfortable, Shade's constant flash of hormones. She wished that Shade would just make a move on Sunny and get it over with. She startled when someone came up behind her and wrapped arms around her waist.

"Been waiting for you. What took you so long?" Mark whispered in her ear.

Tiffany felt herself flush and shivered at the contact. His hot breath warmed her neck. That he was interested in her always surprised her. Little internal bells and whistles went off whenever he was around, a roller coaster rush of emotions that thrilled her. "Oh, you know," she tried to sound casual. "The flight in from Paris was delayed."

"I hate it when you're late." His voice sounded tight, but his hands ran along Tiffany's sides, warming her body against his, melting her. "I missed you. Let's get out of here and go somewhere, and you can make it up to me."

Sunny and Shade came out of nowhere and flanked her. "We have to go now," Sunny said.

"Right now." Shade extracted Tiffany from Mark's grip. "Say good-bye." The look on her face was serious. Sunny appeared frightened.

"Wait," Mark said. "What the hell? You just got here." He grabbed her elbow to keep her from moving.

"Let her go," Shade said and grabbed her other arm. At her touch, Tiffany could feel Shade's temper simmering. She also felt panic, which was scary and puzzling. She knew she'd better go with her friends and see what it was about. Mark, on the other hand, didn't want to release his hold.

"I'll take her home. She can stay here with me." Shade tugged on one arm and her new boyfriend tugged on the other. Suddenly, she knew what the rope in a tug-of-war felt like.

Sunny interceded and tried to talk in a soothing voice over the loud music. "It's an emergency. We have to take her home."

Shade took the lead and half dragged Tiffany to the door. "Let go of her, asshole."

Tiffany managed to step away from both of them. "You're hurting me."

"Wait. Are you really going to leave with them?"

Tiffany nodded. "I'll see you tomorrow after school."

"Whatever," Mark said. "There's plenty of other girls here."

The words, along with his building black rage, crushed Tiffany, and she wavered on her decision to leave. Before she changed her mind, Sunny herded her through the door and toward the car. "Please, Tiff. Get in."

Sunny got into the driver's seat and peeled out of the parking lot.

"Does someone want to tell me what's going on here?"

Shade turned in the passenger seat to look at her. "You can't see him anymore."

"What?" Tiffany was shocked, then angry. Who the hell was Shade to tell her what to do? She got enough of that from her mother and the priests.

"Tiffany," Sunny said. "He's not good for you. Listen to Shade."

"Why are you guys ganging up on me? He's the first boy I've ever liked." *And that ever paid attention to me.*

"We're not ganging up on you. You can't see him anymore."

Tiffany could feel her own temper building, adding its energy to Shade's, and the atmosphere snapped inside the little car. She felt the telltale tingling on her scalp that meant Shade was trying to get in her head. "You fucking stop that. Quit trying to read my mind." She knew her tone was venomous, but Tiffany felt almost outside herself, powerless to stop the words she was throwing out in her angered state.

"Tiffany, please calm down." Sunny spoke quietly. "What we want to tell you is for your own good."

"No. I am not going to calm down. Stop giving me the psychic eyeball. I'm tired of everyone telling me what to do." Tiffany narrowed her eyes and pointed at Shade. "She's just jealous."

"Jealous? Of what? I have no interest in that dick." Shade gestured angrily.

"No, you're just pissed off because Sunny doesn't want you and you can't get laid."

Dead silence followed. It stretched into long, awkward minutes and sucked the air from the enclosed space.

Tiffany wanted to take back the words, but the negative power of them echoed back to her. Shade had told her in confidence how she felt about Sunny, and Tiffany had sworn she'd never tell her. She wanted to apologize, but her throat felt tight. Instead, tears gathered in the corner of her eyes. She hated to cry when she was mad. And that just pissed her off more. After all, it wasn't as if Sunny didn't know Shade had a major crush on her; she was a psychic empath for God's sake. She was tired of being in the middle and not having someone of her own to love.

Sunny stopped at the curb in front of Tiffany's house. "We'll talk when everyone has calmed down."

Tiffany hesitated before opening the door. "Shade—"

"I don't want to hear it."

So now everyone was mad at her: her boyfriend, her best friends, and oh, goody—her mother who was waiting inside to punish her for leaving.

She had been looking forward to this night all week. How had things fallen apart so quickly? Tiffany walked up the driveway and forced herself to not look back. The porch light came on before she reached the house, and her mother opened the door.

CHAPTER ONE

Thirteen years later

Tiffany paid the babysitter and locked the door behind her when she left. She rested her forehead on the doorframe and finally drew her first deep breath of the evening.

After finishing her nightly routine of checking the windows and double-checking the locks on the doors, she checked in on Angel. She kissed her forehead and tucked the comforter under her chin. "Sweet dreams, baby."

It wasn't until she got to her own room that she began to replay the evening and her reaction to Jordan's reporter friend, Katerina Volchosky.

The woman was tall and stunning, in a beautifully masculine way. Her short, spiky blond hair suited her perfectly, and her dark eyes appeared to hold invitations and secrets. Tiffany inhaled sharply, reacting to an instant rush of heat. Every instinct in her had told her to move, to get back on that elevator, but instead she had stood as still as the proverbial deer in headlights while her pulse raced and her throat closed. Butterflies circled in her stomach as the woman approached.

Tiffany had automatically zeroed in on the odd look on Sunny's face as Kat's long legs and strong, stalking pace brought her to Shade's side. She couldn't quite put her finger on what her reaction was based on, so Tiffany had put up all her psychic guards and shut down.

"Hi, Tiffany, I'm Kat. It's so nice to meet you."

Tiffany ignored the outstretched hand and kept her hands at her sides. The woman's dark eyes were too intense. There was something behind her voice, an undercurrent of emotion being withheld, and it made her nervous. She mumbled a greeting, made excuses, then left. She had felt the stunned silence behind her as she quickly left the gathering.

Okay, Tiffany admitted as she burrowed down in her bed. *I ran away*. She had been frightened of Kat, and she didn't know why. She'd never met her before, which was kind of odd in and of itself, being that she was Jordan's friend and Jordan was *her* best friend's partner.

She would have to talk to Sunny about it and maybe ask Shade to peek for her. There was something about Kat that hit her psychic notes, and she needed to know why so she could protect herself. That her own apprehension had kept her from being able to touch or read Kat for herself was a little disconcerting. Not that it was unheard of—sometimes she simply couldn't read some people. They could fall into two categories, gifted individuals who had psychic blocks in place or someone who had something to hide. Which category did Ms. Volchosky fall into?

Tiffany forced her thoughts from the strange encounter and focused on traveling to her safe place. She deliberately slowed her breathing, imagining a waterfall cascading down a rocky cliff to fall into a pool surrounded by ferns and lush plants. She saw herself sitting on a slick, flat rock just outside the reach of the spray of water in the moonlight, while crickets sang in the distance behind her. It was the comforting meditative vision she created to calm her mind before falling asleep.

Thunder growled through the sky and rain fell in sheets, blinding her. Tiffany blinked in an attempt to clear the water from her eyes while she shivered in the cold wind that whipped through the small valley, adding to the destruction the small army had left in its vicious wake.

Bolts of jagged lightning lit the sky, illuminating the carnage that surrounded her. Dead. They were all dead. Blood ran in rivers through the rain-soaked ground. The smell of scorched flesh burned her throat, and the only sounds she heard were the sizzle of water on the huts and the beating of her own heart.

The sky continued to roll with anger, shaking the ground beneath her, and in the flash of more lightning, she could make out a fast approaching horse galloping straight at her. The rider bent low over the horse's neck, and mud and water sprayed from under the hooves. Terror held her still and time slowed to a crawl. A scream sounded somewhere behind her, but before she could turn, it was silenced. She was terrified and knew she no longer had the strength to fight, run, or hide. She fell to her knees in the mud and covered her eyes with her hands. She didn't want to see the deathblow coming from the rider's hand as he bore down on her.

Tiffany jolted awake and pushed her hair out of her eyes. The nightmare had stalked her sporadically for years. The terror in her throat and chest lingered, and in her mind's eye, she could still see the horse and rider bearing down on her in slow motion. It took a full minute to calm her pulse and untwist her legs from the tangled sheets. Her nightshirt was damp and stuck to her skin.

Tiffany stood under the hot spray and tried not to think about why it had come back after so many years. It was always the same, right down to the last detail. The storm raged, the screams of women echoed around her, and the rider, always the rider, who bore down on his massive horse to kill her.

She hated the helpless feeling of dread the nightmare left with her. She didn't have time to try to analyze why it had returned, damn it! She had to make breakfast, get her daughter ready for daycare, and she had three clients scheduled today. She also had to go buy groceries, pick up her daughter, and a mountain of laundry to do.

God, she was tired, and she hadn't even started yet. *Suck it up, princess. You made your bed; now lie in it.* She may have made the bed, but she sure didn't have *time* to lie in it. Would she ever get rid of that harping voice in her head? Her mother lived three hundred miles away, but she still managed to infiltrate Tiffany's mind when she was at her most vulnerable.

"Good morning, Mommy."

Tiffany's heart swelled when she heard the little voice. And just like that, all was right again in her world. Her daughter stood in the doorway in her little pink footie pajamas and her baby fine hair ratted up from sleeping. She was the most beautiful little girl in the world to her. Tiff drew strength from that magic place that good mothers had, and finished getting ready for the day.

❖

Kat Volchosky sat on her deck and watched the first gray streaks in the sky turn red, then orange in a brilliant sunrise that promised a beautiful day in the city of Seattle. She looked down at her empty glass before setting it aside.

She was numb and couldn't recall when she'd finished the drink. How long had it been since the ice cubes had melted? Four hours? Five?

She was still in shock.

From the instant Tiffany had stepped out of the elevator, she'd recognized her. From her dark red hair, to every freckle, and her sea-green eyes. She'd *known*.

Kat had loved her through a thousand dreams and knew every nuance in every expression. The way her eyes lit when she was full of joy or the spark of temper, the way her lips softened before a tender kiss. She was the woman who lived in Kat's spirit. She was flesh and blood, instead of unobtainable desire from a life lived in another time.

Through the years, she continued to search the crowds for her, but eventually, she'd given up. Kat had almost convinced herself that her visions were the psychological fantasy of an adopted child searching for an identity. But deep down, she knew her dream woman was out there, waiting for her. She just had to find her.

How could it be anything other than destiny that her friend Jordan met and fell in love with Sunny? Kat had heard of Tiffany and her daughter, Angel, for months, but for some twists of fate, she hadn't been able to meet her until the night before.

She still felt hurt, remembering how Tiffany had turned and left her standing there. She hadn't appeared to recognize her. In fact, she'd appeared almost…frightened. That her lover from the past wouldn't fall into her arms and weep with relief at the sight of her had never occurred to Kat at all.

The sun's rays crested the horizon and made her squint through the alcohol-induced haze. Now what? It was a hell of a way to start her vacation, sitting in one spot all night drinking her confusion away. What she really wanted to do was drive to Bremerton and chase Tiffany down. But after the shock and the less than inspired reception, Kat didn't think that would be her smartest move.

She rose and stretched before stumbling over the iron leg of the chair. She supposed getting some real rest should be at the top of her priorities. She set her empty glass on the sleek granite counter and continued to her room.

A large mural on canvas nearly dominated the entire wall across from her bed. A female warrior seemed to rise from the edge of the frame in the forefront. She posed with one arm holding her blade, the other held in a defensive stance across the front of her body. Her biceps bulged with the controlled posture. She wore a leather tunic that hit mid-thigh. Her blond hair was held in place with an etched silver headband that allowed the long tresses to cascade down her back.

A little behind the warrior and to her left was a circular hut. Wood smoke rose from the chimney and the front door was open to the day. Purple heather bloomed amongst the wild fuchsia and pansies in the front yard.

The art had hung on her wall for well over a decade, but walking by it repeatedly for years had rendered it near invisible. Kat inhaled deeply, hoping to catch the scent of a past she only knew in her dreams. When it eluded her, she finally allowed herself to look at the small, white-robed woman who sat near the warrior with three puppies frolicking around her in the green grass. An unseen breeze lifted her red hair away from her heart-shaped face. Her sea-green eyes shone with love; she was clearly delighted in the late afternoon sun while she played with the dogs and watched the warrior move through sword practice.

Other huts dotted the landscape and more women in flowing white robes were captured in different positions of the idyllic slice of life depicted in the painting. One hung sheets in the breeze, another carried water alongside her partner who carried firewood. It was a snapshot of a different life and ancient time that Kat had painted from memory. The warrior guarding her priestess and home, as she should have been on that day.

That day.

She hadn't been crazy after all. Here was the proof her dreams had been real.

Kat thought about heading into the bathroom to splash water on her face and form a plan, figure out what she should do next, but after sitting on the soft bed, she fell onto her side and promised herself she would only close her eyes for a second.

Tiffany's new office at the Haven still smelled like fresh paint. She was early so she took the time to unpack her scented candles. She lit the last one and looked at her clock. Her first client was late. She sat in the room's armchair and stared out the window. It seemed like the first moment of real peace she'd had in weeks.

She watched the soft rain gather on the window, forming tiny streams that ran down the glass. The light from the clear crystals on the wide ledge sparkled and lit a single drop, just one out of the thousands falling.

Suddenly, in the face of a million tears streaming from the sky, coming together and drifting apart, Tiffany felt lonely. She loved Angel beyond measure, but sometimes she ached to have someone significant in her life. Sunny had Jordan. Shade had, well, Shade had whoever she wanted. They may have been superficial, but at least she was keeping warm at night. Tiffany hadn't been on a date in well over a year. It just wasn't high on her list of priorities. Not to mention how awkward it was to explain what she did for a living to any would-be suitors. Even if anyone was interesting enough to try, they had to pass Sunny's and Shade's approval. The last time she ignored their warnings had dire consequences for her. In the end, dating wasn't worth the trouble. She simply wasn't attracted to anyone and it certainly wasn't worth hurting herself or Angel in the process.

She turned when she heard the soft tap at the door. "Come in."

Sunny's head poked in. "Mrs. Larrick cancelled her appointment."

"Did she say why? If she isn't feeling well, I can go to her house."

"Her daughter flew in from Cleveland. She rescheduled for next week."

"Oh, okay." Tiffany turned back to the rain.

"You want to talk about what's upsetting you?"

Tiffany sighed. Lately, there was always something in her life upsetting her. She was too weary to put up any blocks against Sunny's inquiring mind. It wasn't that she wanted to shut her out, or that she didn't love her. It was that Tiffany was so *damn* tired of being the needy one of the trio. Sunny was brilliant and confident. Shade was fearless and grabbed the brass rails of any task in front of her. Tiffany felt like the weak link.

"Tell me," Sunny said. "Where are these dark thoughts coming from? I think you're the strongest person I know."

"How can you say that?" She should have known that Sunny could directly read the heart of the matter.

"Tiffany, you've risen above every challenge life has thrown at you. You're loyal, sweet, funny, and you go out of your way to help people."

Tiffany's throat tightened and she felt the tears building behind her eyes. "I don't feel strong, Sunny. I'm scared most of the time. Oh, let's be honest. I'm usually scared."

"Get a little perspective here. You deal with spirits on a daily basis. Sometimes even with a side of demon, sprinkled with a little a poltergeist activity. That's not exactly flowers and sunshine."

"The nightmare is back again."

"The one with chanting, red-robed tribal witches dancing around you?"

Tiffany shook her head. "No, the other one."

"Well, no wonder you're full of uncertainty today. A little massacre is enough to put anyone's morning off." Sunny reached for Tiffany's hand, and the contact sent a little burst of white energy through her system. Tiffany welcomed Sunny's comfort.

They were interrupted by a short, sharp squeal.

"What was that?" asked Tiffany.

"It came from reception." Sunny bolted for the door with Tiffany right on her heels.

At the bottom of the stairs, Agnes stood with her hands covering her mouth.

"What happened?" Sunny rushed to her.

Agnes pointed to the phone. "The caller said he sees dead people and they're coming this way."

"Oh, honey," Tiffany said. "It happens all the time. Didn't you see the movie, *The Sixth Sense*?"

"Oh. Little bastard." Agnes straightened her tie-dyed shirt and primped her curls. "It's not nice to mess with old ladies."

Tiffany bit her lip to keep from laughing. "No. It's not. Where's Aura?"

"I came in because I was in the neighborhood and she said she had an important errand to run. I took messages like she showed me. I was doing a great job too."

"It's all right, Agnes. Don't let them scare you. Do you want me to take over?" Sunny asked.

Agnes stalked back to the reception desk in her purple high-top tennis shoes. "No, I'm ready for them now. I promised your mother. Go on with you; go back to work. I got this."

Tiffany caught Sunny's eye. They hurried back to the stairs and waited until they were upstairs before giggling.

"Oh, I should be ashamed, but the look on her face!" Tiffany put a hand to the stitch in her side. "I haven't seen that expression since we did the investigation for her last year."

"Poor Agnes. She's not cut out for this work. I'm surprised she agreed to answer the phones at all, she's so scared of anything paranormal. Which reminds me, Mom said something the other day about permanently hiring a new receptionist."

"She did? Why?"

"She's tired, Tiff. She said she's ready to retire from the whole thing. I know that she's earned it, but I'm not ready for her to leave."

"Me either. Who's going to keep everything straight?" Tiffany felt a moment of grief. Aura was always there for comfort, strength, and advice. She was the mother she'd always wanted. She depended on her. "I love Agnes and all, but—"

Sunny laughed. "I wouldn't worry about it. Agnes is temporary for now. You know Mom wouldn't leave us with anyone who couldn't handle it."

Tiffany knew she wouldn't, but that didn't mean she wouldn't miss her terribly.

Sunny's head tilted a fraction to the right. "My appointment is here. Let's meet up later, okay? Then you can tell me why you ran away last night at the opening." She left before Tiffany could argue with her.

"How come you always get the last word?" Tiffany muttered to the empty hall. She went back into the room, curled up in the soft armchair, and waited for her next client.

Kat woke slowly, aware her cheeks were stiff with dried tears. The emotion she wouldn't give in to while she sat on the deck the night before had snuck out while she slept.

Coffee would give her a needed boost, and time to form a plan. She'd just stepped out of the shower when her phone rang; it was her editor, Liz. Kat debated letting it go to voice mail but picked it up anyway.

"Kat."

"What?"

"Where are you?"

"Home."

Liz sighed. "That's not here."

"You do know my vacation starts today, don't you?"

"I'm sorry. I must have missed the e-mail. Do you want to call me back later?"

"No. This had better be good. What's up?"

"I received a phone call this morning, and I think you're going to want in on this."

"What do you have?" The last thing Kat wanted to talk about was work when she felt hung over, but habit had her grabbing a notebook from the counter, and she sat at the breakfast bar to take notes.

Liz paused a moment, then continued. "One of my contacts at the Seattle Police Department called. He wants to keep this on the down-low."

Kat felt a little prickle of interest. She was an insatiably curious person, and anything that someone wanted to be kept secret was usually interesting and worth looking into. But damn it, she didn't want to get sucked in. She needed time off to get herself sorted out. "And?"

"Well, he wants to talk to you about the article you did on that ghost hunting crew who found the murdered teenagers. What's their name again?"

"Sisters of Spirits. SOS." Kat heard a slight ringing in her ears. There was no such thing as coincidence. Hadn't she just been trying to figure out how to get back to Bremerton and Tiffany? Now she would have a legitimate reason to contact her. "Why?"

"He wants to try having them work with some cold case files, and maybe get some input and new leads to follow."

"Why doesn't he call them himself?" Kat asked. *And how fortuitous for me that he doesn't.*

"It's complicated."

"How so?"

"Spoken like a true reporter. I asked him the same thing. He said he didn't want to go into it over the phone. He wants to meet with you in person."

Kat glanced at the clock. "Okay. Give me his number."

Liz gave her the information and hung up. Kat made the call, dressed, and was out the door within a half hour. She circled the parking lot until she finally found a spot. When she went in the building, she went through the motions and exchanged small talk with officers at the security checkpoint. Her mind wanted to race on two different tracks. The professional side dealt with possible stories and angles, but the emotional side, the tired and lonely one, still reeled from her meeting with Tiffany.

She looked down the ugly concrete hallway, and the green rolling hills of her ancient home superimposed over the cement floor. *Maybe I shouldn't have gotten out of bed after all.* She didn't want to crack up at the goddamn police station.

With what felt like massive effort, she pulled back mentally and focused on the door in front of her. She willed the sounds and smells of the police station to flood her senses—to keep her in the present. She wondered which of the myriad of scents lingering underneath the smell of sweat, stale air, and burnt coffee represented despair. Gradually, she felt more centered, more present, and able to concentrate on the task at hand. She knocked on the door.

The man who answered was dressed in plain clothes. He poked his head out, craning his neck, as if he were looking to see if anyone noticed she was there. That he was nervous was obvious to Kat, but she dismissed it. If he was so worried about what he was doing, he should have met her for coffee somewhere. Not her concern. He showed her in, and pointed to the one visitor chair in front of his desk.

"Detective Parker," she said and gave a short nod before sitting and retrieving her notebook from her briefcase.

"Please keep this off the record," he said.

"I've already told you I would. These are for my use."

A moment of silence stretched between them. Kat decided she would take the lead. "So, you're interested in working with SOS?"

Parker nodded. "I am. But you have to understand my position."

Kat heated with a flash of protective anger. "What? Is the problem that you're working with psychics, or that the department still wants to keep some distance between itself and Jordan Lawson. Which is it?" Kat was pissed that Jordan's integrity was in question at all. She'd blown dirty cops out of the water and been shot. She was a hero, not a snitch.

"I'm going to be honest with you. It's kind of both." He held up a hand to stop her protest. "Personally, I know that most of us here think what Lawson did was admirable. We don't hold an official or serious opinion on psychics. I may be grasping at straws here, but after reading your story on how this SOS group solved the missing runaways' case, I thought it was worth a shot. I'm getting some flack over it. But I want to know for myself that I've done everything in my power to solve these cold cases. The victims deserve that. I want to see if this group can open new leads for me." He stopped talking and looked at her expectantly. "But it would be easier to work through you. We know you, and we know you're good and honest. You don't mess around. If you work with them and feed the information to me, I can keep some distance but still get the answers I'm hoping for. I'll meet with them myself if I feel it's necessary, but this way would be more...diplomatic."

Kat decided to cut him a break; he looked and sounded sincere enough. She gave him some credit for trying to peek around the thin blue line, even if he wasn't willing to cross it openly. "Let me see what you have to work with."

❖

Tiffany's cell phone buzzed on the table. She startled and realized she had dozed off while waiting. She must have needed it. The melancholy she'd felt earlier had subsided for the most part and she felt almost refreshed. "Yes?"

"Shawna Waters is here."

Tiffany smiled. Agnes's voice was prim. "I'll come down and get her. Thank you."

She passed the mirror in the hall and grimaced. Her eyes were slightly puffy from her impromptu nap, and she tried to put some order into her wild curls, but changed her mind when they refused to cooperate. Instead, she pulled the hair band from her wrist and pulled the mass into a high bun, out of her way. She smoothed her sweater over her jeans and called it good.

Shawna smiled at her from the staircase and met her halfway up. "I'm so happy to meet you. I've heard so many wonderful things about what you do."

"Thank you, I'm flattered, and also glad you're here." Tiffany directed her into the room and shut the door. "Please sit down. Our first visit is short, simply one to get to know each other. I'll be happy to answer your questions or address any concerns you might have."

"I appreciate it." Shawna sat on the edge of the chair. "I don't know much about this, but my friend Carly comes here and she swears it's changed her whole outlook on life."

"Oh yes, Carly. I'm glad she's doing well." Tiffany loved that client. She'd come in after a nasty divorce and she'd been working with her for the last few months, clearing the negative energy, and balancing her emotional well-being. She took a few seconds while Shawna talked to assess her while she was listening.

Shawna's aura was threaded with several different shades of pink. The dark spots dispersed throughout the colors of her loving, gentle energy showed that Shawna suffered from headaches and other stress related problems. Tiffany's immediate assessment would be that they needed to work on the presence of a near-transparent hue of pink in Shawna's aura that indicated to her that Shawna was emotionally exhausted and giving too much of her energy away without saving any for herself. Tiffany didn't detect any other physical problems that would be of concern.

It was an aura pattern she knew well, as she had it herself. Shawna also had a spirit with her, but she wasn't here to address a psychic reading. The maternal energy that hovered wasn't interfering in any way with her. Tiffany blocked it from her mind and concentrated instead on the questions she could hear coming from Shawna's psyche, discerning why she had come.

Sometimes clients weren't sure of their reasons. The urge to make an appointment came from a place they weren't usually aware of, in the form of intuition or an impulse seemingly out of nowhere. The most prevalent reason Tiffany could sense from her was genuine curiosity and a willingness to try new things. "So," Shawna said. "I know a little about what goes on from Carly. But I would really like to know more about what you do."

"No problem. But why don't we start with what you want out of this."

Shawna laughed nervously. "I'm not entirely sure. I mean, I'm not sick or anything. My husband thinks I've lost it because I've been researching everything I can get my hands on about Universal energy, and how we create our reality by our thoughts. Ever since the movie *The Secret* came out, I've been searching. The subject matter resonated with me and I wanted to go deeper than the surface message I got from it. I've had too much time on my hands since the kids left. I guess I just want to...*know*."

Tiffany nodded. "You get what you put out into the world. Thoughts attract those like themselves, like magnets."

"Exactly. I don't know where I've been all my life. How come I didn't know all this Universal law stuff before? I've heard of chakras of course, but I didn't put any real value on the information. And really, who had time for meditation? I was raising my kids." Shawna's eyes filled and she wiped at them. "I'm sorry for being so emotional."

"It's fine," Tiffany said. "Of course you're searching."

"It's like I have all this empty space in me and I don't know who I am anymore. I know how to be a mom. I'm damn good at it, but they don't really need me anymore."

"I get that. Being a mother was your identity and purpose." Tiffany leaned forward. "We have to define who you are today and discover your current passion."

Shawna looked relieved. "I thought you were going to tell me I was just having a midlife crisis combined with an empty nest syndrome."

Tiffany smiled. "Well, it's both in a way. But we're going to use semantics and call it a spiritual awakening and emerging into your power. It's not a crisis but a symptom of change."

"Oh, I like that. That sounds so much better."

"I feel like it's a time that comes to all women. A knowing of sorts, when women who were once caretakers find themselves at a loss, somewhat empty, and full of longing."

Shawna placed a hand over her stomach. "And searching for something to fill that void that's deep down here."

"Yes, that hole in the sacred chakra. And do you know what I think they're searching for? Divine feminism. I believe it comes in a time of their life when women are pondering their faith, redefining what they believe, simply because they finally have time to. Up until then, they have been juggling a career, marriage, and children. In some cases they've also been helping elderly parents. And if that's not enough, on top of that, all the household duties required. It's as if their own soul's resonance remains dormant until then."

"You're talking about the Wise woman as an archetype."

"Yes, exactly." Tiffany was pleased. "The Wise Woman, or Crone, is the third aspect of the Mother Goddess. The first being the Maiden, the second is the Mother, who is the bringer of life. When all the clamor of the outer world finally dims, you're more receptive to transcendent experiences and value them more. You're ready to continue into the next cycle of life, one of spiritual growth."

"That makes so much sense." Shawna looked thoughtful. "You make it sound so reasonable."

Tiffany laughed. "Don't get me started on the patriarchal religions that suffocated women for centuries. It's important for us to understand that the masculine suppression was to have power over us, not that we didn't have any ourselves. We are born knowing differently, but forget while being raised with our parents' beliefs. The historical inferior status of women is what we're taught, *not* who we really are."

"But isn't that changing?" Shawna asked. "With the Internet and all the knowledge available at our fingertips?"

"Yes, of course it is. That's why you're here. You have the answers inside; you know you do. But you're afraid and unsure to voice them because you've given your power away for so many years. I'll bet you've had all kinds of spiritual insights, a sense of knowing there's more to this universe than you've been taught to believe."

Shawna nodded. "Yes, I have. But I can't talk to my husband about it. He thinks I need some kind of pill or something to make me the way I used to be, back when I didn't question everything."

Tiffany felt a moment of anger for Shawna. Why was it so often the case when women wanted to change and grow bigger than their expectations of them, the people around them thought something was wrong and rushed to push them back into their tiny boxes?

It must have showed on her face because Shawna hurried to continue. "He's not mean about it, really. He's just perplexed and struggling to understand. He's not keen on change, and I've uprooted his orderly life, changed the status quo. But he loves me and wants me to be happy."

"I'm sorry," Tiffany said, "It's one of my issues, for lack of a better term."

"That's interesting," Shawna said. "Don't you all heal yourselves and each other and live in spiritual bliss all the time?"

The remark startled a laugh from her. "Wouldn't that be awesome? I suppose in a perfect world, we could." *In a perfect world, I would have listened to Shade and Sunny's warnings about Mark so many years ago. But I wouldn't give up Angel for the world.*

"Is it a case of 'physician, heal thyself'?"

"Pretty much. We certainly help each other, but we're still learning. Life is an experience and a journey. We have to experience the entire human spectrum, or we don't grow spiritually."

Shawna nodded. "That makes sense. I've heard you each have different gifts here at Sisters of Spirits."

"That's right, but we overlap in several areas. We can all see Spirit in one form or another. For example, Sunny Skye is a psychic medium. She can also work with the body's chakras and use healing energy to correct imbalances, but her greatest strengths are empathy and communicating with Spirit that has passed."

"You're talking about ghosts?"

"Yes. Then there's Shade, who deals with the negative energies. She prefers the title Necromancer."

Tiffany noted Shawna's shiver. They all did that when Shade's gift was mentioned.

"Kind of like a spiritual warrior?"

"She would appreciate that likeness." Tiffany smiled. "And me, I have clairvoyance, the ability to hear another's thoughts. I prefer healing, but I can also see and hear Spirit. My strongest gift is one of reading residual energies."

"I've read about that. Psychometry. It's like seeing the past, like a recording, isn't it?" Shawna looked fascinated.

"Yes. It's also known as retrocognition."

"How did you all meet and start Sisters of Spirits?"

"Sunny's father was a renowned psychologist. Shade and I were both patients of his as children. He wanted to do a documentary on kids who had special abilities. We were eleven when we all first met. Sunny's mother, Aura, is also a skilled psychic medium and taught us how to use and live with our gifts." Tiffany smiled at the memory. "Sunny took over the day-to-day business when she graduated from college. Later, she invited Shade, and then me, to join her."

"That's so cool. Do you still have a copy of the documentary?"

"I'm pretty sure both Sunny and her mother kept a copy." Tiffany hadn't watched it in years. Sometimes, she found it too difficult to reconcile the wounded child to her adult self.

Physician, heal thyself.

"I heard you also do location investigations like *Ghost Adventures*."

"We do," Tiffany said. "But without all the fanfare."

"And that you solved a murder case in Seattle about missing runaways about a year ago?"

"We did. But in a way, we were only the conduit. The spirits were very strong. They gave us the information needed to pass on to the detectives who solved the case."

"I read an article about that in the *Seattle Times*," Shawna said.

Kat's face swam into focus in Tiffany's mind's eye. Her dark eyes looked penetrating and sharp, as if she were looking back at her. Tiffany redirected her concentration.

Shawna looked at her watch. "Wow, time flies and all that. I have a lunch date with my husband. This is all fascinating. I've truly enjoyed this meeting, and I would love to make another appointment with you."

"Of course, let's go talk to Agnes and schedule you."

Tiffany booked Shawna for the week after next. After she returned upstairs, she thought of Kat again and decided to talk to Shade. Maybe she could tell her what was going on with her and why she was reacting so strangely.

The door to the new war room was closed, and Tiffany knocked before opening it. It was dark and the computer screens were off. Shade was late again. She walked over to her massive desk to check her calendar. Tiffany's concern grew when she saw there were no appointments scheduled.

She returned to her own office and dialed Shade's cell phone, but it went directly to voice mail. She knew something was off, but unless Shade wanted to share what was going on with her, no one but Sunny would be strong enough to get past her extreme psychic blocks, and she wouldn't cross that line anyway.

Sunny and Shade were both her best friends, but sometimes the undercurrents in their relationship could be so awkward. She was happy that Sunny had found love with Jordan, but she continued to worry about Shade. The last year she seemed to go downhill. Partying nonstop and jumping from one woman's bed to the next, even before the sheets they'd slept on were dry. Though Sunny and Shade's relationship ended nearly eight years ago, the women Shade picked seemed to be cheap carbon copies of her first love, Sunny.

She couldn't help but feel they were all growing apart, and it made her sad. She made a decision to sit Shade down and encourage her to open up about what was going on with her.

Before it was too late.

Kat tapped her pencil on the closed tablet. She couldn't remember a time when her so-called personal life was more on her mind than her career. She knew she wouldn't rest until she got to the bottom of the mystery visions that haunted her most of her life. Now that she knew her dream woman was real and not a figment of her imagination, she was determined to figure it all out. The cold case files came with perfect timing as an excuse to see Tiffany again.

It was too late to drive to Bremerton tonight and request a meeting with the team at SOS, but she did leave a voice mail for Jordan to call her.

Kat opened the file in front of her and began writing notes. Unfortunately, the door she'd opened in her memory stayed open, and she had a hard time concentrating on the details. Frustrated, she shoved her chair back and walked to the window.

The afternoon sky was dark. Storm clouds had rolled in and obliterated the sun. From her vantage point in her high-rise condo, Kat watched the cars begin to back up in rush hour traffic on the street seventeen floors below.

It was muggy and she opened the sliding door to let the breeze in. She heard sirens in the distance. She hoped it wasn't for anything nearby because even if they wanted to, the commuters would find it nearly impossible to move over for the emergency vehicles.

She scanned the area with the binoculars she kept handy, looking to find which direction the emergency vehicles were headed, and wondered what was going on. There were too many sirens for the call to be something routine or simple. The commotion seemed to be coming from two streets over. She could see an ambulance break through the traffic and then stop before two men jumped out.

Kat held herself still. *No. I'm on vacation. I need a break.*

Curiosity battered against her flimsy excuses until Kat couldn't stand it anymore. She ran for her raincoat and headed out the door.

Without a car to hinder her, she made it quickly to First Street. Crime scene tape already stretched the boundary to preserve the area for possible evidence and keep out curious onlookers. *And reporters, apparently.* Kat felt the thought drip with sarcasm. She was tired and supposed to be taking time off. What was she doing here anyway? It's not as if there wouldn't be another murder next week, and the one after that. She thought she was jaded enough to not feel the drama anymore.

Just the facts, ma'am.

Seven units lined the street with their lights flashing, circling round and round, silent sentries that cut through the rain, illuminating the parking lot like a demented carnival.

She searched the crowd and spotted a uniform she recognized. Her height enabled her to cut a path directly to him. "Liam—sorry, Officer Murray."

"Not now, Kat. You know I can't tell you anything."

"Have you identified the victim yet?"

"Kat. What did I just say?" Officer Murray asked.

Spotlights lit the area, but the officers first on the scene had hung tarps for privacy. The coroner's van had just arrived and was currently backed into the small tented area. The police closed ranks, and Kat knew she wouldn't get any more information from them tonight. She felt a tingle on the back of her scalp and searched the crowd. She caught a glimpse of a man standing at the back edge of the crime scene. She didn't know why, but he looked out of place. Going with her instinct, she tried to focus on him, but when she blinked, he was gone.

But she did see Rob, her biggest competition at the paper, inching his way over to the covered tarps. When he glanced up and saw her, Kat saw his face flush. She stared him down until he gave her a smarmy grin and disappeared behind the barrier.

Kat knew he was gunning for her job. Normally, she would take it as a challenge and beat him into the dust, figuratively anyway.

She reminded herself even though he'd stolen assignments from her in the past, this was actually his story that she was encroaching on. It wasn't her style, and she needed to back off.

She was tired and rummy from the lack of sleep. Kat knew she needed to go home and sort out her complicated emotions. It wasn't every day that you found someone you'd fallen in love with in a previous life. Although it was exciting as hell, it was also confusing, and emotionally draining. The whole situation was enough to put anyone off their Wheaties.

CHAPTER TWO

Tiffany finished with her last client and drove to Sunny's for the afternoon meeting. She let herself in and found Sunny in the kitchen. "I've missed working here," she said. She loved Sunny's old Victorian house. It had never felt like working when she was there. Not that the new offices at the Haven weren't beautiful, just that the homey atmosphere wasn't as prevalent. She'd spent so much of her life in this old house.

Sunny sat at the long, polished table and smiled. "You're a bit early."

"I have to pick up Angel soon. So, what's on the agenda?"

Jordan looked up from her file. "Where's Shade?"

"She still has a few minutes before she's late."

"Speaking of which," Jordan said. "That's been happening with more frequency lately. Is there something going on I should know about?"

Tiffany glared at her. She liked Jordan, she really did, but defending Shade would always be her first reaction. "Why would you say that? Do you have any idea what she goes through for us?"

"Whoa." Jordan held up her hands. "I'm just saying. I recognize the behaviors."

Tiffany didn't hear Shade come in until she entered the room. The bell over the door had been removed when they switched their offices to Haven. Shade looked rough, and her eyes were bloodshot.

"What happened to you?" Tiffany tried to touch her, but Shade sidestepped to avoid her and sat in a chair directly across from her at the table. Her aura was dark red and muddy, showing her emotional turmoil. It was clear she wasn't getting much sleep.

"Not now, okay? I don't want to talk about me." Shade's tone was mild, but her body language was stiff and unyielding. "Let's just get on with it."

Sunny set down her tea. A sad look crossed her features before she nodded slightly. "Is there any old business or concerns anyone has that need to be addressed?"

Tiffany shook her head and glanced at Shade who didn't bother to look up from the table.

"Is everyone doing okay at the Haven?" Jordan asked.

"Just dandy." Shade sighed and rolled her shoulders. "Can we skip to new business? I have another client."

Sunny nodded. "I've set an appointment for Bristol Terrace."

Tiffany's stomach turned. She didn't want to do an investigation in that location. Not only did the place used to be a former hospital and morgue, the corporation that owned it previously had turned it into cheap apartments that were eventually overrun by junkies and gangs. It had been empty for two years and the new owners wanted to renovate the building into high-end condominiums. She couldn't imagine a more spiritually active building in Bremerton. An investigation there wasn't going to be pleasant. Any effort they would make to contain the negative energy would be like trying to shove a forest into a pinecone.

She tucked her feelings behind a façade so Sunny wouldn't pick up on them. Shade appeared to perk up a little at the prospect of spending a night in the horrible place. She wouldn't have noticed Tiffany's reticence about it even if she hadn't blocked it.

"This job gets a paycheck," Sunny said, then named the figure.

Tiffany straightened in her chair. Her little house was in a constant state of repairs. Her furnace was on its last legs, and she really needed a new roof before the winter set in. As tired as she was, the thought of being able to replace them in one shot was a bonus she couldn't pass up. "So, what are the owners reporting?"

"The whole nine yards—voices, shadows, and overall creepiness. They've had two other amateur ghost hunting groups come in and they weren't happy with the results."

"What did they find?" asked Shade.

"One group ran out in the middle of the night and refused to come back. The other didn't even make it two hours."

"Pussies." Shade laughed.

Tiffany ignored her. "Did they report anything at all?"

"I asked them not to tell me. I want to work without outside influence and do a cold investigation. I also really want to take extra precaution on our spiritual protection with this one."

Jordan wrote something down on her file. "With the building's history of drug and vagrant activity, I'd also like to bring another person for security."

"We did just fine before you got here," Shade said.

Tiffany watched Jordan's jaw tighten while she held her breath for a few seconds. But she didn't rise to the bait.

Sunny looked around the table at each of them. "So we're set on Bristol Terrace? Good, it's next month."

"Can't wait," Shade said.

"Let's move on to the next thing on our list. Jordan?"

"Yes." Jordan stood and walked to the head of the table. "Okay, so last night I received a call from Kat."

At the mention of her name, Tiffany looked up sharply.

Shade kicked her under the table. "What's wrong with you?" she whispered.

Tiffany ignored her, but not before she kicked her back, and felt some wicked satisfaction when she heard Shade's hiss of surprise.

"What are you, twelve?" Shade asked.

"Shut up."

"Stop it, you two," Sunny said.

Jordan began writing on the white board. "Can we focus, please? Kat called me with a request for help from the SOS team."

"An unusual request," Sunny added.

Tiffany waited for Jordan to answer. She'd learned that Jordan had a tendency to pause for effect when she talked.

"Well?" Shade asked. "Spit it out."

"Kat had a meeting with Detective Parker at the SPD this morning. He wants to work with SOS and see if you can raise any new leads on some cold cases."

Tiffany pointed at Jordan. "How do you feel about this?" She recalled Jordan's exit from Seattle's police force after being shot and the long internal investigation that followed.

"Putting personal feeling aside, isn't this more about the victims than how I feel about the department?"

"Of course the victims matter, Jordan. But we won't do anything that makes any of us uncomfortable." Sunny's tone was soothing.

Jordan cleared her throat. "Actually, he wants Kat to be the liaison."

Shade snickered. "She's a reporter. Don't cops hate reporters?"

"Generally," Jordan agreed. "But Parker sought her out, as he knew she had contact with SOS. Also, Kat has a good reputation with the force because she plays by the rules."

"I bet he's getting shit over this. Cops and psychics don't get together as a rule either," Tiffany said. "Present company excluded and all."

Jordan smiled and glanced at Sunny. "I'm sure that's why he wants us to work with Kat, rather than directly with him."

"When does he want to start?" Sunny asked.

"Wait," Tiffany said. "Are we going to do this? Just like that? No discussion, vote, or anything?" Psychometry was her specialty and the majority of the work would fall to her.

"You have to admit that it's an exciting opportunity." Jordan placed her hands on her hips.

Tiffany simply stared at her. It might be exciting for them, but they weren't the ones that had to relive the murders. But she was too tired right now to argue with Jordan. She needed to leave to pick up Angel from the daycare. "Look, you guys do what you want to. Let me know what you need me to do later." She grabbed her purse and left the room before Jordan, Sunny, or Shade could protest.

It wasn't until after she got in the car that Tiffany tried to define the low-level anxiety that buzzed along her nerve endings. They had done hundreds of investigations over the years, so it wasn't the Bristol Terrace job, which wasn't scheduled until the following month anyway. Was it that she didn't want to let anyone down while working on cold case files? Being a parent herself, there would most likely be an emotional attachment to the results, and that implied a huge responsibility. Tiffany also wondered if her reluctance might be the prospect of seeing Kat again. She still had her unresolved reaction to consider.

Before she got any further with that line of thought, she arrived at the daycare and put her questions and doubts away. This was Angel's time.

❖

Kat pulled up every scrap of information available on the Internet she could find on SOS. She found several scientific articles about Sunny's father, and a bibliography of his books, but nothing substantial on any of the women, or their investigations.

Tiffany was nonexistent on the computer. Kat couldn't find anything on her. Why hadn't she thought it was weird when she ran the story on them last year?

That was so unlike her. She researched everything down to the last detail. It was in her nature. She would have never run a story about Sisters of Spirits if she hadn't been able to verify the facts first, even if Jordan was her friend. It made no sense, no matter how hard she tried to remember her process when she'd written the article.

Sharp pain began throbbing in Kat's temples, making it difficult to read the screen. As soon as she closed the search engine, the discomfort subsided.

It was odd and it added one more needle to the haystack of mystery she'd encountered over the last couple of days. She went to the kitchen and took some aspirin for the headache that remained.

After she sat back down, she intended to make her list of priorities on the case files, but her attention was drawn to the window instead. Outside, the moon hung in the sky. Kat felt goose bumps rise on her arms. On impulse, she grabbed her laptop and went out onto the deck. Seattle's lights drowned the blanket of stars, but Kat could draw from her memory their places in the sky.

She felt a sense of urgency, a calling from deep inside. For once, Kat didn't question the reason behind it.

It's time.

Kat was excited and nervous. The idea she had kicked around for years came to the surface. Maybe it was meeting Tiffany that drew it out, the actual physical proof not everything in the world was black and white. Not that she doubted herself or her visions. She had always known at the deepest level they were real. It had just been convenient as an adult to put them away when they suddenly stopped. Easier to conform to the beliefs others held about reincarnation and, in essence, to bury a piece of her soul, the part that echoed with grief and loss.

Easier to live with the pain.

Then again, maybe it was stopping at that latest murder scene and sensing the bone-deep awareness that she was done. She was finished with the damn politics and violence of the city.

Maybe—for once—she didn't *have* to know why.

Kat created a new document, inserted the date, and tried to put her journalistic style of writing out of her head. Where should she start? Reporting was very different from writing a story; there were emotions involved, imagination.

A small thread of doubt snaked its way through her usual confidence. Wasn't this different? The stakes were so high. If she started this venture, she knew her life was going to change. She couldn't go back to the compartmentalized way she'd been living because seeing the woman in her dreams, in Tiffany's body, had opened a door that had been shut for a very long time. She felt pumped but raw at the same time.

Kat took a deep breath and typed her name.

Tanna.

The dam that held her emotions in check began to crack, widening the fissure that appeared when she'd sat out here the other night in shock. Kat allowed the dual aspects of time that had been shifting for two days to focus on the dreams that began when she was six years old.

The heartbreakingly beautiful rolling green hills of home spread as far as the eye could see from an aerial view. Thick forests and ribbons of rivers passed beneath her as she flew toward her memories and willed herself to clearly see the past.

Back to the beginning.

The air was filled with the scent of sweet, fragrant flowers. Kat took a careful step in the shallow water, then another. She didn't want any splashing to disturb her prey. The morning sun sparkled off the river's surface and a squirrel chattered in the tree to her left.

"Hush with you now," Kat said, "or you'll be meat for my mother's pot." She pushed away a long strand of hair that fell across her face.

She held her body taut, ready to spring. She slowly inched farther ahead. She was just inches away from catching it and was precariously balanced on the toes of one foot, when a voice sounded from behind her.

"What are you doing?"

Kat lost her footing and tumbled into the water. She came up sputtering, furious at the interruption that allowed her target to flee. She wiped the water from her eyes while she coughed. "You made me lose my frog!"

"Are you always this clumsy, then?" The girl laughed and held out her hand. "Come on, I'll help you."

The sun in her eyes made it difficult for Kat to see much of the interloper beyond the wild red curls that fell around her shoulders. It wasn't until she climbed to the bank and into the shade that she saw her clearly. The small heart-shaped face was sprinkled with tiny freckles, and her green eyes still held gleeful amusement. Her pink lips turned up at the corners. Then she smiled just as a beam of sunlight moved through a blowing branch, backlighting her in an almost divine halo.

Kat's heart nearly stopped. She felt a funny tightness in her chest. "Who are you?"

"Tanna, and you?"

"They call me Kat."

Tanna stifled a giggle. "Because you're so full of feline grace?"
She tried to repair her shattered dignity. "It was your fault."

"Yes, I suppose it was."

"Well, then." Kat didn't know what to say. She gawked at
Tanna, who stared right back at her.

Several long moments later, a wicked gleam sparkled in Tanna's
eyes. Before Kat knew what was happening, Tanna had turned and
jumped into the river from the bank.

Ripples of water marked where she'd gone in. Kat laughed
while she clapped her hands together, delighted with the impulsive
move. She waited for her to come up.

And waited.

She counted sixty heartbeats, then counted them again.

She'd been under the water for too long. Maybe she hit her
head on a rock. Panic began to beat in little flutters in her belly. Kat
rushed to the edge and threw herself into the water. She opened her
eyes to try to find Tanna in the crystal water.

When she surfaced for air, she spotted her back on the bank,
braiding her wet hair, as if she hadn't a care in the world. As if she
hadn't scared Kat to death.

Kat pulled herself from the river and shook like a wet dog. Then
she stalked over to Tanna. She wanted to be angry, she really did,
but she was more impressed at how long she'd held her breath and
stayed under. She flopped next to her on the grass where they lay in
the sun to get warm.

A loud horn sounded from the street below her building,
bringing Kat out of the memory. She'd gone so deep into the past
she'd lost all sense of the present moment.

Kat could still feel the sun from that afternoon on her face.
Every detail of the first dream she'd experienced as a young child
felt vividly real. She took a deep breath and began typing what she'd
just remembered, without cutting any of her thoughts or opinions.
It was going to take some practice. She was used to deleting herself

from the stories she reported. The way she felt, or wanted to feel, hadn't been important when she turned in articles for the paper.

She was hoping to change all that. With this first rough scene written, the sense of excitement she felt earlier was still present. It felt wonderful. Kat didn't realize how much of her identity she'd buried until she lifted the wall and saw through the rationalizations and justifications she'd made over the years.

Kat saved her document, turned off her computer, and went inside. It was late and she wanted to make sure she was well rested for her trip to SOS headquarters tomorrow. Hopefully, between now and the morning meeting at SOS, she could come up with a logical way to approach Tiffany. To try to figure out what the hell was going on.

The thought of seeing her again sent a thrill through her.

CHAPTER THREE

Tiffany was buckling Angel into her booster seat when her phone rang. She kissed the top of her daughter's head before answering it.

"Good morning, Aura," she said.

"Back to you, sweetheart."

"What's up?"

"I received a call from my cousin, you know, the one who lives in Ocean Shores. She's invited me for a visit."

"That's nice. It's beautiful down there." Tiffany wished she could drop everything and go too.

"I was hoping that you'd let me bring Angel with me."

Tiffany smiled. The request wasn't unusual. Aura often took Angel on trips. She considered her an honorary grandchild, and Angel adored her. As always, Aura had been able to read Tiffany like a book. Her invitations coincided perfectly with Tiffany's need to refresh and regroup. She didn't know what she would have done without her since Angel had been born.

"Beach, Mommy!"

Tiffany was aware that Angel hadn't heard the conversation, as she was standing outside the car, but her daughter knew. That was the other benefit of Aura helping her; she knew what it was like to raise a gifted child.

"I'll take that as a yes, then?"

"Well, okay. When do you want me to drop her off?"

"Now's good."

"She's not even packed."

"Of course she is, dear. I have a suitcase for her right here. What she doesn't have, Nana will buy for her."

Tiffany laughed. "Of course you will. You know, one could say that you two planned this already."

"One could, but one won't," Aura said. "I'll see you shortly. Thank you, Tiffany."

She hung up the phone and peered over the seat at Angel. "Sneaky, Angel. I guess you're going to the beach with Nana."

Angel clapped her hands and smiled radiantly. "Let's go!"

Tiffany called the daycare to let them know that Angel wouldn't be attending for a few days, and then headed to Aura's house. She made a mental note to take a vacation soon. She would love to go play in the waves herself.

When she entered Aura's foyer, she wasn't surprised to see the packed bags by the door. Angel squealed and gravitated straight for the beach toys.

"You'll spoil her."

"Nonsense," Aura said. "That child doesn't have it in her to be spoiled. Come into the kitchen with me for a moment."

Tiffany followed and sat in the chair that Aura was pointing at. "What?"

"There are changes coming for you."

A small chill settled at the base of Tiffany's spine. "And?"

"And I'm not being shown anything concrete and clear."

"Please don't be all cryptic on me. What do you see?" Tiffany asked.

"I just want you to be aware you have some choices coming. Honestly, there are two paths twisting together. The vision wasn't clear on which is the right one. "

"They usually aren't." Tiffany regretted the sarcasm in her voice, but really, hadn't she made enough bad decisions in her life? Wasn't there a quota somewhere?

Aura looked to the right, her eyes glazed over a bit. "You'll need your strength and courage. Something that looks threatening, isn't. Another looks innocent, and isn't. Neither are what they appear to be."

"Oh well, that helps." Tiffany gave up quickly. There was no way to interpret that statement with any real logic at the moment. Riddles and warnings always raised questions but provided few answers until you looked at them in hindsight.

"Be on your toes, Tiffany," Aura said. She laid a gentle hand on Tiffany's forehead. "You are loved and precious to me."

Tiffany felt the warmth of her words surround her heart. "I love you too. Thank you for everything."

Aura smiled. "Go to work. Angel and I are off on our trip now."

"I don't have any appointments scheduled. I'm hoping to get some paperwork done." Tiffany hugged her and then pulled Angel close. "You be good for Nana, okay?"

"Okay." Angel's arms came around her neck. She covered her face in tiny kisses. "Love you, Mommy. See you."

Tiffany left them at the door, grateful that her daughter was secure in the love that surrounded her. She must be doing something right.

The ferry that crossed to Bremerton wasn't too crowded this time of morning, as most of the traffic was coming into Seattle, not going the other direction. Kat pulled her car behind a bright yellow Hummer and turned the engine off. She went to the upper deck in search of coffee. After standing in line, she found a bench seat by the window and stretched her legs out.

Someone from an earlier run had left a copy of the *Seattle Times* on the seat in front of her. Kat reached for it, curious to see what kind of article Rob had written about the body in the alley. Her fingertips grazed the edge of the paper before she changed her mind. Today, Kat would leave the ugly headlines alone. Old habits were hard to break, but she was willing to try.

She was on vacation and on her way to see Tanna. *No, her name is Tiffany.* She must learn to think of her as Tiffany. Kat had formed a thousand questions in her mind, but found few answers that satisfied her. She was restless and almost couldn't control her legs, which bounced with suppressed energy. Finally, she couldn't stand it anymore and went out to the rail of the boat.

Hundreds of jellyfish floated in the water below amongst the green algae and seaweed that covered the surface. The wind was chilly, smelled of pungent salt, and cut straight through her light shirt. Kat shivered but stayed on deck. The rocking of the ferry seemed to help with her need to pace, almost soothing her.

Almost.

❖

After she parked at Haven, Tiffany received a text from Sunny to come over to her house instead. Tiffany was content to leave the undone paperwork on her desk for later. She turned the car around and made the short drive to the Victorian.

She felt a slight alteration in the air, a feeling akin to déjà vu. A quickening of the spirit when you know something shifts in your conscious. Once she tried to concentrate on the feeling and grasp the meaning, it slipped away from her.

When she let herself in the front door, the comforting smell of sage and herbs greeted her. Sunny's warm energy reached Tiffany, and she smiled. She didn't care why she was here; she was just happy to come.

"Good morning! I'm back here." Sunny's voice sounded from the kitchen.

Tiffany joined her and poured herself a cup of tea before sitting at the table. "It's beautiful out, isn't it?"

"Mmm." Sunny tilted her head and stared at her.

Tiffany felt her energy bump up against her psychic shields. "What are you looking for? You know, if you asked nicely, I just might tell you."

"Not always, Tiff. You want us to *think* everything is well and good. You're gifted enough to even make us believe it most of the time."

"Why are you trying to get into my head?"

"You look tired."

Tiffany rolled her eyes at her. "That's just a nice way to say I look like crap."

Sunny smiled. "I think you're spread too thin lately. You should take some time off."

"I was just thinking that before I dropped Angel off at your mom's. However, it's not feasible right now. I don't have any choice but to keep working."

"You need to recharge, Tiff, or you'll burn out."

Tiffany studied Sunny's expression, the "I'm done being reasonable and I'm going to get my way" look. It was better to give in now and renegotiate later. Say, after she got some solid sleep. Then she caught a trace of Sunny's thoughts. "You already cancelled my appointments?"

"Yes." Sunny's firm tone transitioned seamlessly to soothing. "I checked, and none of them for the next week are your regulars or favorites."

"Isn't that kind of presumptuous?" Tiffany knew Sunny was trying to help, but it irked her nonetheless. Her independence had been so hard won. She despised it when others tried to take over or tell her what to do, even if they were her closest friends. She needed to make her own decisions.

"The fact you are projecting such a defensive emotion tells me I'm right. But I also have a proposal for you."

"You know I can't afford to take time off." Even as Tiffany's irritation began to rise, she felt Sunny's calm energy butt up against it.

"You haven't listened to the rest of my proposal yet."

Sunny was right. Tiffany sighed. She was exhausted and couldn't work up enough energy to argue. "So you and your mom planned this whole thing."

"Pretty much."

Tiffany got up to refresh her tea. "Because you love me, blah, blah."

Sunny laughed. "I knew you would listen to reason. Now, here's what I'm suggesting. At our last business meeting, we discussed working on cold cases with Kat."

Tiffany pointed at her. "You talked about it. I left."

"In any case," Sunny continued, "we're all convinced that you're the best qualified for these. And I also know working on them is going to cost you the most emotionally."

"Thank you for acknowledging that, but realistically, both you and Shade can do it as well."

"Yes," Sunny said. "But you're better at reading photos."

"Didn't you just say that I needed to rest?"

"From the healing sessions, yes. The cold cases are different. You're not attempting to change the physiology or genetic imbalances of someone who is ill."

Tiffany didn't mind donating her time to people who needed it, such as their clients for paranormal investigations. She also didn't mind working with people who couldn't afford to have sessions at the office. In fact, she considered it part of her sacred duty, her life's path. But she needed those formal appointments for her livelihood. Keeping a house and raising a young daughter by herself wasn't easy. There were always unexpected expenses. Tiffany chose her words carefully. "Let me see if I have this right. My schedule is cleared of *paying* clients, so I can work on cold case files. Is that correct?"

"Absolutely." Sunny beamed at her. "But I'm not done yet."

"Please go on." Tiffany waved her hand. "Because I'm confused."

"Well, Jordan and I have decided since this is a personal project, and you're the best to have working on it—we want to pay you a salary. This is your first paycheck. We'll see if you want to continue with the cold cases after the week is over." She passed a check across the table.

Tiffany was shocked and shook her head. "This is too much." She wanted to cry.

"Actually, it's not, honey. I've done some research on what other paranormal professionals make in various fields. Apparently, we don't charge enough."

"It's not about the money for us. It never has been," Tiffany said.

"I know that. But when we took over, we kept my parents' business model. We never adjusted anything for *ourselves*." Sunny leaned forward. "They were financially set because of my father's practice and published works. The paranormal investigative side wasn't their only source of income. This was a hobby for them."

"So what are you saying?"

"I'm telling you that Skye Trust will be paying you a salary, in addition to the money you make on your private clients—whether you like it or not."

"But that's the fund your father set up for your family."

"Hush. Listen to me. The money is also there to further my father's research, to extend his legacy. I don't mind telling you, there's plenty of it. You don't have anything to prove anymore, Tiff. You're worth every penny, believe me."

Tiffany took a deep breath. She could almost feel layers of stress on her shoulders begin to dissipate. "It still feels like charity."

"It's not. Why can't you let yourself want more, Tiff?"

"That's a good question. Let me think about it later because I'm a little stunned. We might have to argue later. I'm not sure yet."

Sunny laughed. "So, are we good?"

Tiffany nodded.

Sunny checked her watch. "Damn, it stopped again. What time is it?"

"It's almost nine."

"Great. Let's get set up in the dining room. Kat's on her way. She should be here any minute."

"Today? We're going to start now?"

"Jordan is going to be here later. She's interviewing a few certified counselors for the teen mentoring program at Haven this morning. Shade and I both have clients today that we couldn't reschedule."

"I feel funny doing this by myself," Tiffany said.

"Why? You're perfectly capable." Sunny turned and studied Tiffany. "Oh, that's right—we never talked about how nervous Kat makes you. Her energy is different isn't it? I can't quite put my finger on it."

"I didn't touch her. But when I came out of that elevator and saw her standing there? The reaction hit me instantly. My heart started pounding; my palms got sweaty. My first inclination was to run the other direction."

"Do I need to point out that's exactly what you did? Honey, there isn't anything dark about her that I can sense." Sunny put her file down. "Have you considered that you may be attracted to her? She's a tall, blond drink of fabulous, don't you think?"

After Sunny so casually said it, Tiffany felt an answering tug in her belly. If she went on pure physical appearance, Kat was certainly magnificent. "I haven't had sex with anyone in so long, I wouldn't know attraction if it slapped me upside my head. Besides, I can always live vicariously through yours and Jordan's trysts. Or, if I'm in a really adventurous mood, pop in on one of Shade's."

"Get out! You don't, really?" Sunny's cheeks flushed. "I didn't realize. I should have, but didn't."

Tiffany was mortified. "Crap! I didn't mean to blurt that out. Don't be sorry. It's not *all* your fault." She blew out a breath. "God, I'm embarrassed. Okay, I'll be honest with you. I can read Jordan's thoughts. She hasn't mastered her blocks yet. And since I can be a little voyeuristic sometimes, I didn't shut down right away."

"Pervert." Sunny laughed. "Stop it. I'll be more careful to shield in the future. And please, whatever you do, don't let Jordan know. She gets freaked out enough when she thinks that Mazie is around."

Tiffany knew Sunny was referring to her ghost in residence in the Victorian. "Does she still mess with her?"

"Yes, as often as she can. Now swear to me." Sunny held out her pinky.

"I promise," Tiffany said solemnly while she linked her finger with Sunny's. "I'll never let Jordan know, that I know you guys have wild monkey sex in the kitchen."

Sunny pinched the bridge of her nose and sighed. "God, Tiff."

The doorbell rang and Tiffany startled. "That's weird. I'm so used to just walking in, I never even think to knock."

"That must be Kat. I'm late, so I'll let her in on my way out." Sunny gave Tiffany a quick hug.

"Do we still have an investigation tonight?" Tiffany asked.

"Yes, the Wilson house. I've already done the preliminary interview. Don't worry about the cold cases. You'll do awesome. See you later; love you."

"I hope so. Bye. Love you back." Sunny left her standing alone in the room.

Tiffany felt dizzy for a second. There was that shift in the air again. Aura's words came back to her.

Something that looks threatening, isn't. Another looks innocent, and isn't.

So which one was Kat?

❖

Kat waited on the porch after she rang the bell. In a moment, she heard the sound of high heels approaching from the other side of the door before it opened.

"Hello, Kat. It's nice to see you again. Go on back. Tiff's in the dining room setting up." She pushed past Kat to go down the stairs.

"Wait. Aren't you going to stay?"

Sunny turned and winked. "I'll leave you in Tiffany's very capable hands. Jordan will be here in about an hour, and Shade and I will follow after our appointments. See you."

Kat watched her get into her car and drive off. While she was stoked to see Tiffany again, she was also uncharacteristically nervous. How was she going to layer how she felt about Tanna alongside having her first face to face with Tiffany, who looked exactly like her dream counterpart? She didn't want to look like an ass, or appear incompetent on this job. Kat detested being unprepared, and there was no way to know for sure how this meeting was going to go. Her racing thoughts stopped the second Tiffany stepped into the hall to greet her. Her hair was pulled back and her face scrubbed clean, making her appear much younger than the twenty-nine years Kat knew her to be. She looked shy and unsure. Kat's stomach muscles tightened, and she felt a definite increase in her heart rate. Kat dropped her keys, and the noise caused her to flinch when they hit the floor and slid across the polished boards under a table. She walked over and had to get on her knees in order to retrieve them.

"Um, hi," Tiffany said and crossed her arms. "I guess you're stuck with me today."

"Good morning." Kat's voice was hoarse and she cleared her throat before entering the dining room, taking note that Tiffany was careful to keep space between them as she finished lighting white and purple candles on the sideboard.

"What are those for?" Kat inhaled the smell of lavender.

"Purity and protection. Would you like some tea or coffee?"

"Coffee, if you have some. Black, thanks."

"I'll be right back. Please sit down." Tiffany left the room.

Kat's legs felt weak. She was grateful to take a seat. She rubbed a hand down her face. Her physical reaction was totally inappropriate for the situation. Desire hit her swiftly and without mercy. She couldn't remember the last time she'd felt it this intensely.

That's not to say she lacked female company. Kat had lovers, but they were essentially "friends with benefits" encounters. This ache was like falling into the ocean with no lifejacket or scuba gear.

Tiffany returned and placed a steaming cup in front of her. "Here you go." She walked to a chair on Kat's left. "I don't want to shout across the table. This is where I usually sit."

Kat felt blood rush to her eardrums and fill them with the sound of her rapid pulse. She searched Tiffany's face and eyes for any signs of recognition, but was disappointed. Her expression held what? Curiosity, perhaps. She knew Tiffany was gifted clairvoyantly, but could she read Kat's thoughts? Probably not, Kat decided, since she wasn't running away or covering herself.

"You really don't remember me?"

Tiffany looked a little bewildered. "No, I'm sorry. Where is it you think you know me from?"

Kat debated how much should she share. She felt a gentle tingle along the top of her scalp. "Can you read my mind?"

"No, I'm not getting any thoughts, but that's not terribly unusual. Some people have natural barriers. I can sense some basic intentions. Believe me when I tell you, it's much better for me when

I can't read you. I apologize for trying to peek. It's a habit. Though most aren't as perceptive as you are."

Kat wasn't in any way psychic like Tiffany, Sunny, or Shade. She was unable to connect with spirits in the present. But her sixth sense was heightened enough to let her know when people were trying to get in her head. "What can you see?"

Tiffany shrugged. "You're gifted, but I can't see what that ability might be, or if it's just undeveloped yet. You want something, but I can't tell what, and you're nervous."

The rising morning sun cleared the top of the houses on the other side of the street and shone into the dining room through the stained glass windows. There was stillness in the air, a sense of waiting, anticipation. They stared at each other until the space between them became charged, almost electric, and filled with unasked questions.

Tiffany tried to act cool and professional but was mesmerized by the colorful fire the sunlight created as it reflected off Kat's diamond nose stud and the several gold earrings she wore in each lobe. From the moment she'd arrived, Tiffany had felt the attraction. It only intensified after Kat crawled under the hall table to retrieve her keys, showing her perfect ass in designer jeans. But that was nothing compared to the heat that reflected in Kat's dark eyes. It was a little nerve-wracking to be stared at like that, as if she were being hypnotized. As if Kat wanted to swallow her whole.

Uh uh. While she thought the look was sexy as sin, it was starting to make her feel awkward. She broke eye contact and took a drink of water.

"So," Kat said. "Uh, Jordan told me you would be best for this job."

"That's flattering, but we can all do it. The three of us just take different paths to the information."

"My mother always told me there was more than one way to get to Cleveland."

"Mine only had directions straight to Hell." Tiffany cringed when the remark fell out of her mouth. She'd better get down to the business at hand before any additional stupid comments fell out. "I'll answer your questions and then we'll get started, okay?"

Kat nodded. "How does this work?"

"Sometimes when I touch an object, it's like I'm seeing a movie of the energy that remains embedded in it. Other times, I see still pictures of a person, or places that might be attached. I might also see symbols, which are meant to remind me of something, and then I have to decipher what they might mean."

"Like a symbol of fire might mean something different to you than it does me."

Tiffany was relieved that Kat understood quickly. It made her job easier. "Yes, just that. One could be fascinated by it, and another person scared to death. So the symbols I see could very easily be misinterpreted by me. That's one of the reasons why legitimate mediums might be accused of being frauds. It's not an exact science. Psychometry is only one of the psychic tools through which we can look at things from a different, outside perspective."

"It sounds fascinating. What else happens to you?" Kat asked.

"I often see flashes, or x-rays, is a better word, of what's remaining of the past in a particular location. I can receive echoes of what they felt during their trauma. Normally, I try not to open to that much emotion. It's too draining for me and can be dangerous. If you want more of a personal connection to the negative energy, you'll have to ask Shade. But if there is an actual spirit that does come through, I can let you know what they're trying to communicate. Again, I can only tell you what I see, or rather, my perception of it."

"That works for me," Kat said. "So where do we start?"

"I'm going to enter a slight meditative state. Give me a minute." Tiffany began to take deep breaths. One by one, as they surfaced to clutter her mind, she shut her thoughts out, imagining them being placed in a strong box at her feet until gradually, she felt lighter, free from present distractions and ego.

I am a messenger of love and peace. Please help me to focus on that which was in the past. Please shut out my personal feelings and judgments. I only want to be an observer. Let me stand surrounded with love and light, and protect me from any energy that holds harmful intention. Help me to find the answers that are being sought. Thank you.

Tiffany remained silent in the spiritual aura for a few moments before she opened her eyes. "I'm ready."

CHAPTER FOUR

K at placed a photograph facedown in front of Tiffany and then turned on her recorder. Fascinated, she watched Tiffany's features soften until her expression was nearly blank as she placed her fingertips on the photo.

It took all her willpower to keep from touching the hand on the table to see if it was as soft as it appeared. Tiffany's eyes opened and looked straight into hers. It was an otherworldly glare, pinning her, catching her. Fathomless. It was a heady feeling to be on the other side of it. She was disappointed when it shifted to the left, somewhere on the wall behind her.

"Don't tell me anything unless I specifically ask for clarification," Tiffany said. "I'm seeing an average-sized woman. She's young, in her twenties maybe? She has light hair, light brown—no—hazel eyes. I'm getting that her name starts with a hard J, but it's short. Joy, Jay, Joan? Joy." Tiffany's voice was firm.

Kat didn't have to look at the file to know she hit it on the head. She was enthralled already by Tiffany's nearness, and the reading itself was off to a great start. Still, she couldn't help but see how different researching was from actually witnessing psychometry in action.

Tiffany turned the picture over to look at it. The corners of her mouth turned up slightly as she seemed to acknowledge she knew she was correct on the details. "I'm tuned in on her energy. She feels happy. Oh, it's her birthday. She's picking up some last-minute items at the store for the party. Balloons, wine, and her cake."

Kat struggled to keep her reaction neutral. There was no way in hell Tiffany could have known that Joy had icing in her hair when they found her body.

"She's smiling as she's walking to her car. I can see her putting things in the trunk, but she's also struggling with the helium balloons. She doesn't notice the man coming up behind her. I can't see his face; he's wearing a ski mask. His hands are white, blondish hair on them, his nails are clean."

That's a good detail, Kat thought. She wrote it down carefully.

"Yes, it's very clear. They're soft hands, not a man that works with his hands much. His clothes are dark. He hit her on the back of the head, and she fell into the trunk. I can see him tying her hands behind her back, but she's not struggling. She's out cold."

Kat realized that Tiffany had answered her thought, not anything Kat said out loud. As fascinated as she was with the process, she knew she would have to be careful with Tiffany's clairvoyance as well. She didn't want to taint the reading by unwittingly giving her information telepathically. This could be harder than she first thought. Kat shut the file and decided to listen instead of analyzing the details yet. "Can I ask a question?"

Tiffany nodded. "Sure."

"How come when you talk about Joy, you seem connected with her emotions? And when you mention the killer, you relay his actions, but you're disconnected?"

"Shade can link with the bad guys, but I refuse to connect with any dark energy. It's much safer for me not to try."

"That makes sense," Kat said. "Sorry for the interruption."

Tiffany nodded and continued. "When she wakes up, she's very scared. I can smell her blood. She's confused and crying. All she wants to do is go home."

The sadness in Tiffany's voice caused Kat some anxiety. It made her realize how different it was to report just the facts. She had been allowed a small distance from the horror, only learning the details after the crimes had already been committed. It hadn't, in any way, given Kat the emotional connection that she was experiencing now—to actually feel as if she were there, witnessing it. She felt a slight chill in the air. Kat didn't know if it was because of her proximity to Tiffany, or because of the otherworldly feel to the session.

"I get the impression they drove for a while because there is a blank spot in the energy. She must have lost consciousness. Now she's awake and has to go to the bathroom. I feel her bumping all around the trunk. Maybe they're on a dirt road? God, this is awful. She's lying on top of her birthday cake. How horribly sad that is. There isn't any hope in her. She's saying her good-byes to her family because she knows she's going to die." Tiffany's breath drew in sharply several times.

Kat's shoulder and neck muscles tightened. She couldn't bear the thought of Tiffany suffering Joy's experience. She was about to end the session, but Tiffany's soft voice continued.

"She felt terrible fear when he opened the trunk and forced her out. I'm trying to pull back from the violence because I'm connecting with the attacker as well. He's powerful, and their energy is becoming intertwined. I'm having a hard time separating the two. It hurts."

The air was charged in the room, and she wanted to get up and pace the anxiety off but didn't want to interrupt what Tiffany was doing. "We can stop," Kat said.

"No. He hit her, and she fell to the ground. She tried to fight at first, but he was too strong and full of rage. He yelled at her. Worthless, hate her, hate her, cheating bitch."

The hairs on the back of her neck rose with Tiffany's venomous tone. Kat opened the file and checked the notes for a boyfriend or husband as a suspect. It was getting harder to keep an objective perspective.

As if she could read Kat's question, Tiffany went on. "No, he doesn't know her. He's thinking of someone else."

"Can you see who?" Kat asked. This was something that wouldn't be in the evidence, looking out from the killer's eyes. It could provide new clues.

Tiffany shook her head. "No, not clearly. It was a brief flash of a woman with long reddish hair. Here's the thing, he's not thinking logically. He's bat-shit crazy. I still can't see him clearly. I'm sorry, but I can't get any more than that."

Kat jotted the detail down. There was a definitive heaviness in the air, but she didn't know if that was her imagination or because of Tiffany's state.

She didn't appear to notice that Kat was even there. Her gaze remained unfocused as she continued with the reading. "He's going to kill her. He's going to teach her a lesson, the unfaithful bitch. God, it's like listening to a beehive in his head, the buzzing of his hatred." Tiffany shivered and crossed her arms. "It's so cold in here."

Kat didn't agree. She was perspiring from nerves and concerned about the effort and toll the reading appeared to be taking on Tiffany. "Didn't you just say you didn't want to interact psychically with the killer?"

"I can usually distance from the actual pain. I'm having a hard time with this one, and I don't know why."

"I don't know what I was thinking. I had no idea it would cause you this much discomfort when the police suggested we work together."

Tiffany smiled weakly. "I want to skip the gruesome details because I don't want to walk through the actual murder; is that all right?"

"That's fine." Kat sincerely regretted that she put that photo in front of her. What she had thought was a good excuse to get near Tiffany turned out to be a hurtful one. She never wanted to see a moment of pain on her face. And yet, she'd asked her to experience a woman's torture and murder? How fucking stupid could she be? "We can stop now."

"No," Tiffany said. "I'll finish it, but I'm going to skip to the end. He left her broken there, and he's gleeful about it. Talking to himself about how he showed her." Tiffany's voice cracked a little. "He took some of her hair, just whacked it off. He has no regrets over what he's done."

Kat felt the hair rise on her neck while she wrote that detail down. It wasn't in the file she held, but she felt almost positive it would be in the official one. "Do you see where he's going when he leaves?"

Tiffany closed her eyes. "No. I'm not sure. This is really weird. It's as if his energy trail starts and ends in the same place. Who he became in that car, isn't who he appears to be normally. It's like he's created in the moment he stalks her, then dies when he leaves the victim. Does that make sense?"

"A split personality? Someone who leads a double life?"

"I'm trying to remember if I've ever felt this before, and I can't. We'll have to ask Shade. I'm sorry I couldn't help more."

"No, I'm sorry. I had no idea what it would be like for you."

Tiffany took off the throw. "I need to use the restroom upstairs."

"Of course. Can I get you anything?" *Can I hold you, take away the horror you've just seen?* Kat wanted to wrap her up in her arms in a protective cocoon.

"I just need my bag." Tiffany picked it up from the hall floor before she disappeared.

It seemed like she was up there for an eternity, but when Kat checked the clock, it had only been ten minutes. What was she doing in there? "Are you all right?" Kat hovered at the landing, lingering to make sure Tiffany was well, but not wanting to appear overbearing.

A door opened on the second floor and Tiffany came back down. "I'm okay," she said. "I needed to cleanse myself psychically to break the connection."

Kat noted the slight bruising under Tiffany's eyes. She felt horrible about it.

"I'm fine, really," Tiffany said. "I need some air."

"Sure. I'll follow you."

Tiffany led the way through the kitchen of the Victorian, down the back stairs, and through the glass doors onto the large walkout patio. The large area overlooked the water flowing under the Manette Bridge. Tiffany leaned on the stone wall, took her hair down, and lifted her face to the sun.

She looked so delicate standing there, Kat wanted to kick herself again. She'd been so sure when she found the reincarnation of Tanna, everything would fall into place and they'd live happily ever after. She had to remind herself that those were the wishes of a young girl, a fantasy she carried around in her own head. She felt clumsy and heavy. What exactly should she say? "Hi, honey, I'm home?"

Instead, she crossed to the wall, stood beside her, and looked over. "That's quite a drop."

"I just love Sunny's yard. It's always felt magical to me, and at night the lights across the water are stunning."

Kat wanted to touch her, but Tiffany sidestepped a pace. There was clearly sparks between them, but Tiffany acted as if she were scared of her. She braced herself. *Here I go.* "Why do I make you nervous?"

"I don't know why. *That* bothers me. All my internal bells and whistles are going off."

Kat's heart skipped. Maybe Tiffany did remember her, even if it was subconsciously. "Really?"

Tiffany nodded.

"Is your heart speeding up?" Kat cautiously closed the small distance between them. Maybe if she kissed her, she'd remember. When Tiffany held her ground, she leaned in closer, making sure to give her time to back away if she felt she needed to. "How about now?" Kat tilted her neck and then touched Tiffany's lips, featherlight, against her own. They were just as soft as they'd been centuries ago.

Tiffany's body stiffened at the contact. Though it cost her, Kat kept her arms at her sides. The green scent of damp forest reached her, and she heard the crunching of crisp autumn leaves. Inexplicably, a spectral gray fog emerged from the ground, swirling between and around their ankles.

Tiffany gasped and pushed Kat away. "What is that?"

"What did you see?" *Please let her remember.*

Tiffany took a step back and held up a hand to keep the distance between them.

Kat was disappointed but didn't press her advance.

Tiffany looked perplexed. "What was that mist?"

Hope flared in Kat's chest. If she could see the fog, then there was a possibility she would remember her. "Time," Kat whispered. "Can you go back? To when you knew me?"

"No," Tiffany said without hesitation. "I can't do this right now. I have to think." She turned around abruptly, made a beeline through the glass doors, and disappeared inside. A moment later, Kat heard the front door slam shut and listened to Tiffany's car drive away.

Kat stood at the wall. She was torn and didn't know what to do next. Tiffany had just shut her down in her tracks. She knew that Tanna lived on in Tiffany's spirit, had felt the connection in her very being.

Now what? She'd prematurely played her first card and Tiffany ran away. Kat was used to going after what she wanted with a vengeance, and it had served her well in the past. But that was for her career. She also couldn't recall the last time she chased after a woman, and it caused her to pause and consider where she stood.

Kat's instinct told her not to press the issue. Though it went against her nature to wait, what happened next was up to Tiffany. She would have to give her some space. The reading had seemed to fly by, but it had taken nearly two hours. Jordan or Sunny should be home at any time. Kat thought of a dozen tasks she could be accomplishing. But instead, she hopped onto the wall to sit and watch the water go by.

An hour had passed before Kat realized she didn't have her phone. She must have left it on the dining room table. That was surprising; most times it seemed the Bluetooth was as permanent as the row of gold earrings she never removed.

So much of her job required her to be plugged in and available to run at the drop of a hat. Kat loved technology and the rapid pace it developed. It was only recently she began to question the pros and cons of being *on* all the time. She wondered if it had anything to do with recalling the memories of her past life, when they lived in harmony with nature, and each other.

Kat entered the hall and heard running on the second floor. "Jordan? Is that you?"

Was that laughter she heard? The hair rose on her arms. "Sunny? Are you home?" Kat waited for an answer, but there was none forthcoming. A small bell tinkled nearby. She turned quickly and laughed nervously when she spotted one of Sunny's Siamese cats. It was either Isis or Ash; she couldn't ever tell the difference.

She'd just let out a sigh of relief when a voice whispered in her ear.

Katerina.

Her name was drawn out into four long syllables and scared the hell out her. Where the hell was Jordan? She hurried to the dining room to find her phone and called her.

"Jordan."

"I'm almost done. Sorry it's taken so long, I didn't expect so many people to show up."

"Jordan."

"What?"

"I think I just met your ghost."

"Oh, Mazie? She's harmless. At least that's what Sunny keeps telling me."

"Look," said Kat. "I'm here by myself. Sunny's not back yet."

"I was just getting ready to call you. She had a client emergency. Where's Tiffany?"

"She left." Kat didn't want to tell her she ran off because she'd kissed her.

"Why? Never mind. Can you meet me? I should be done by the time you get here."

"Sure."

"Lock the door before you leave. Later."

"Fine." Kat disconnected the call and turned the lock on the knob on her way out. *As if a lock is more of a deterrent than a ghost.*

Tiffany was proud of herself on the surface. Underneath, she knew she was a mess, but held herself together until she got home. She had willed herself to stay in the present moment, though she couldn't *un-feel* the sensation of Kat's lips on her own.

The kiss still sparkled along her nerve endings. The scent of cool water remained with her.

It caused her some consternation, knowing that she would have stepped into that kiss and melted against Kat. Oh, she wanted to. But she was a mother, not a harlot.

Harlot?

Oh geez, that was something her mother would say. Tiffany was almost amused.

Almost.

In reality, it had been the intruding vision that held Tiffany back. The full moon appearing behind Kat, the illusion of a strange mist, the feeling of falling sideways, all had been unexpected. Kat had called it *time*.

She needed to think. Although unusual, it most likely wasn't the mist or the vision that had her hitching. It was the loss of control. She hadn't allowed herself to lose it in a very long time. When she stepped outside the careful boundaries she'd built for herself, something bad always happened. She had responsibilities and Angel depended on her. Tiffany needed to be grounded at all times.

She needed to be safe.

There was nothing safe about Kat. She made Tiffany feel things that were better left buried, or better yet, dealt with in the middle of the night when she was alone. Even if she left the sexual attraction she felt out of the equation, thinking about Kat also made Tiffany feel sad, and that didn't make any sense at all.

She was drained from the cold case session and didn't have enough energy left in reserve to analyze her emotions right now.

Tiffany looked at the clock, deciding she had plenty of time for a long bath and a nap before she had to work that night. It had been a while since she had the luxury of bathing without interruption. As in love with her daughter as she was, occasionally, she needed some solitude and a rare moment for herself.

Tiffany grabbed her robe on the way into her bathroom. She let the tub fill while sprinkling sea salt under the hot stream. Because she was low on energy, she added a few drops of real carnation oil. Aura had gifted her with a bottle, telling her it was known to aid in healing and restore energy imbalances after performing a reading. She thought about adding some cinnamon to help her focus on her confusion about Kat and the way she felt when she kissed her, but decided not to when she remembered that it was a female aphrodisiac. Tiffany didn't need help with her libido right now. Instead, she added some hyacinth for peace of mind and relaxation.

The scent filled the bathroom. Tiffany closed her eyes and inhaled, drawing the aroma into her nose and lungs. When Kat appeared in her mind, beckoning her forward, Tiffany nearly fell into the water. She opened her eyes. Of course she was remembering Kat; she'd just been with her. *And kissed her.*

Great, now she was on edge again. She quickly dropped her clothes before sliding into the welcoming water. The very best thing she'd ever bought for herself was the giant soaking tub when she'd done a modest remodel in her master bathroom a few years ago. In her line of work, which could be draining and downright dangerous sometimes, it was almost a necessity to own one. It gave her some peace of mind anyway.

Tiffany let her back slide down the porcelain until she was completely submerged, cradled by the healing waters. She went limp and floated, letting her mind empty, seeking that place *between* thoughts, the spot where peace and love reigned. That space where her soul could just *be*, with no judgments, no reproach, and no expectations to crowd her consciousness.

There was a small part of her, in the back of her mind, that remained lucid, and watched while she began meditating.

She saw herself in the outer edge of a pool at the base of a waterfall, lazily floating in calm water, and looking into the blue sky. She was aware of the birds chirping, the warmth of the sun on her face. She felt happy and relaxed.

From her peripheral vision, she saw an intruder perched on the rocks, and she turned to look closer. No, there shouldn't be anyone here; this was her sanctuary, her place. The stranger took a dive, and the large splash filled her with anxiety. She began to backstroke, to retreat. But in her fear, she headed toward the waterfall instead of the safety of the bank. The pressure of the stream beat her under, rolling her, until she lost her sense of direction, and she began to panic.

A strong hand grabbed her ankle. As Tiffany screamed, water poured into her mouth, burning her airway and filling her lungs. The hand moved from her ankle, and an arm came around her neck.

She tried to scream again, and the effort snapped her back to the present. She inhaled deeply, but the feeling of drowning stayed with her. Had she slipped under the water while she was in her meditative state? She could still feel the iron grip of a hand on her ankle, so she lifted it out of the water to inspect it. Fingerprints.

As a paranormal investigator, she'd seen a lot of unusual things, but never this. She had never experienced this before. Tiffany dried off while she headed to her room. *Murder by drowning.* She didn't want to consider the implications, or attempt to guess what the dream might mean. She still had the Wilson investigation to do tonight and she could talk with Sunny about it during that time.

Sleep. She needed a nap. Everything looked better after some rest. It was an indulgence she usually didn't have time for, either financially, or when Angel was home. She was still on the fence about how she felt about her new salary. She was extremely grateful for the increase in her finances, but somehow, it still felt like a handout. Tiffany had worked hard to make sure she never needed to depend on anyone else again.

She knew better than most how someone you loved and trusted could turn on you. Even as the thought came, she knew it to be ridiculous. This was Sunny; betrayal would never come from her direction.

But there was still that belittling voice in her head, playing old tapes from her past, telling her she was a burden, and not worthy of anything good. Tiffany put the pillow over her head.

Shut up!

What was up with the emotional backsliding? These were things she hadn't told herself in a very long time. She had, in fact, worked with a therapist before Angel was born to banish these kinds of thoughts. Tiffany turned over in the bed and doubled her effort to enter a meditative state again, but it took a long while for her to fall asleep.

❖

Jordan was waiting for Kat outside Haven's front door. She hopped into the passenger side. "Thanks, I walked over this morning. Go straight down until you hit the light and then turn left."

Kat pulled into the traffic smoothly. "I saw your fancy gym downstairs today. Do you even use it?"

"Sometimes, but I still prefer walking to work. It's not that far." Jordan looked at Kat and grinned. "So you met our Mazie."

"Pretty much. I still can't believe you hang out with ghosts now."

"Right?" Jordan jabbed Kat's shoulder. "That's what I'm saying. It's pretty much impossible not to when you live with a psychic medium."

Kat noted Jordan's laid-back attitude and warmed. It was so nice to see her happy. Jordan had lived on the dark side for so long, Kat hadn't held out much hope she'd ever see her relaxed. "How did the interviews go?"

"Pretty well. I have several applications to go through. I'll pick out the promising ones and then make calls to check references." Jordan laughed. "I had to remind myself to pull back on the first interview. It started out as an interrogation. I think I scared the poor woman."

Kat was amused. "Once a cop, always a cop. It's the same thing with me. I'm on vacation but can't turn off the reporter in me."

The applicant I felt best about was pretty young and not very experienced. Still, there was something about her that I felt would fit into our little circle."

"Do you think you're becoming psychic by osmosis?"

Jordan laughed. "Maybe. Turn right at the next corner. The restaurant is halfway down the block."

After Kat parked and they went in, the hostess led them to a table by the window.

"We missed the lunch crowd," Jordan said. "Or we'd have never been able to sit here." She motioned to the waitress. "Just bring us two specials."

"You're ordering for me? I didn't even read the menu yet."

"Trust me," Jordan said. "I eat here a lot. You'll love it."

"What is it?"

"Patty melt, potato salad, and fat fries."

"Isn't Sunny a vegetarian? I thought she would turn you into one."

Jordan grinned at her. "That's why I eat here several times a week. And don't let her fool you. That woman can put away a steak faster than I can when she has a craving for one."

"I'm fine with the special," Kat said.

"Okay. Now tell me why Tiffany left early."

"She said she was tired; the session wore her out." Kat wasn't lying exactly. She was omitting. As much as she trusted Jordan, she felt her first conversation about her dreams should be with Tiffany. She was the one who had the starring role in them.

"That sounds about right. The readings seem to affect her most out of the three of them."

That peaked Kat's curiosity. "Do you know why that is?"

"You know, I've never really asked. It's been that way since I've known them. Shade and Sunny pretty much close ranks around her. They're very protective. I kind of just fell into doing it as well."

"Is she that fragile?"

Jordan shook her head. "I don't think so. From what I know of her past, she's had a rough time of it."

"Care to elaborate?" Kat hoped her tone was conversational.

Jordan stared at Kat. "You're fishing for details. Ooh, and your face is turning red."

Damn it. Kat should have known Jordan would pick up on her curiosity and get to the point. There was a time when they were younger that Kat could have had Jordan singing like a bird for crackers. Apparently, their roles had reversed.

"I'm going to take your silence for assent," Jordan said. "You're walking on shifty ground there, my friend. As I told you, Sunny and Shade would just as soon bury you than have you mess with Tiffany." Jordan's expression tightened. "And as much as I love you, I'd have to help them."

The remark stung a little, but why wouldn't it? Tiffany was Sunny's best friend. Not only did Kat not have a great track record, she didn't have *any* record at all. Since she'd met Jordan several years ago, Kat had never had any kind of permanent relationship. The last thing she wanted to do right now was try to convince Jordan that Tiffany was a reincarnated version of her past life lover. She hadn't sorted it all out for herself yet. "We're working together, that's all." Kat was saved from having to elaborate when their food arrived. Before they began eating, she pulled out the file from her briefcase, effectively changing the subject to something safer.

For her.

CHAPTER FIVE

"Tell me exactly what happened," Sunny said.

Tiffany relayed the details of the dream while she raised the leg of her jeans to show the red marks. "It doesn't hurt anymore, but it was scary at the time."

Sunny's touch warmed her skin and Tiffany felt her uneasiness settle as the bruise faded.

"After you got out of the bath, did you sense anything in the house?"

Tiffany shook her head. "Not spirit, but the house felt *off* somehow. It's hard to explain. It's like there was an empty space, an echo of something that used to be there, but isn't now. I've never felt anything like it before, even with the kind of readings I do."

Sunny looked thoughtful. "Missing energy maybe?"

"Kind of, but more somehow."

"Oh, that explains it. Not."

Tiffany laughed. "Should I be worried?"

"I don't know the answer to that question. I'm not getting any indication of malicious intent, and I don't sense the presence of *other* around you. The only thing that I can tell you is that it doesn't feel like an attack to me. What was going on before all of this happened?"

"She kissed me."

Sunny blinked slowly. "Come again?"

"Kat. She kissed me, in your backyard, after the reading."

"And how did you feel about that?" Sunny asked.

"I was frozen, then I ran.

Sunny's expression tightened. "No wonder she and Jordan weren't here when I got home. She took advantage of you." She stood up. "I'm going to call her right now."

"No. Stop it. She didn't force herself on me. It's all your fault anyway."

"My fault?" Sunny looked stunned when she turned to look back at her. "How am I responsible?"

"Because this morning, you were all, 'isn't she a fine sexy drink of water' or something like that. Which got me thinking, yes, yes she is. So when she got here, I couldn't help but think about it. Kat smelled so good, I couldn't notice anything else *but* how gorgeous she was. Next, she dropped her keys."

"Your thought process astounds me." Sunny shook her head.

"I'm not finished. When she bent over to get them from under the table, I wanted to bite her ass. Where the hell did that come from?"

Sunny's eyes widened. "You weren't peeking again, were you?"

Tiffany laughed nervously. "No, and I should have never told you that. Forget I said anything."

"So did you?" Sunny asked.

"Did I what?"

"Bite her ass?"

Tiffany rolled her eyes. "No. Kiss, run. Keep up with me here."

"I'm trying, Tiff, truly I am. Let me get this straight. You're attracted to Kat, you wanted to bite her, she kissed you, but you ran?"

Tiffany was about to tell her about the strange mist, but Shade walked into the room. "What's up?"

Sunny motioned her to a chair. "Our Tiffany was just about to tell me she bit Kat's ass."

"What?" Shade asked. "What the hell did you just say?"

"I did *not*—repeat, *not*—bite her ass. I said I wanted to." Tiffany jumped to her feet. She should have kept quiet. Once again her mouth had moved faster than what was left of her remaining good sense.

"Okay, I'm completely lost," Shade said. "Let me buy a fucking vowel."

Sunny raised her eyebrow. "It won't help you, not one little bit."

"Geez, you guys. Can we just drop it now?" Tiffany said. "Oh, look at the time; we have to go, or we'll be late."

As she left the room, she heard Shade ask Sunny, "What's she on?"

Tiffany had just climbed into the passenger seat of Shade's van when her phone rang. The screen showed an unknown caller but she answered it.

"Hello?"

The sound of heavy breathing created a ball of nausea in her stomach. "Who is this?"

She disconnected the call when a high-pitched whistle nearly deafened her. She hated that her instant reaction had been one of fear. It took effort to convince herself it had only been a stupid crank caller, but she managed to. If she had to over think something as simple as a supposed prank, she needed to go back to counseling. Tiffany had thought the days of jumping at shadows and perceived threats were over.

Shade jumped into the driver's seat. "Port Orchard, here we come."

They hadn't gone a block yet when Shade looked at her. "You want to tell me what I was late for back there?

"I said I'm not talking about it."

Shade shrugged. "Okay, fine. But if you ever want to bite my ass, you better warn me."

"Seriously? Shut up." Tiffany looked out the window. "Turn on the radio, please."

Shade pushed a button and Katy Perry's song came out of the dashboard.

Tiffany gasped. "Are you flipping kidding me?" She reached over to shut it off, but Shade loudly sang the chorus while blocking Tiffany's slaps with her right hand.

"I'm trying to drive here." Shade laughed and finally turned it off.

"Oh, come on," Shade said, "That was funny, right?"

It really was, Tiffany thought. But she wasn't going to let her know it.

"Seriously, what happened with Kat today?"

Tiffany was careful to keep her shields in place because she could feel Shade's probing. "I wish you wouldn't try that," she said. "You're intruding in my private thoughts."

"Wow, that's calling the kettle black. I could say the same to you, Tiff."

"You knew?" Tiffany was both shocked and ashamed.

"I had an inkling."

"I'm sorry. If it means anything, it was mostly accidental. I was so connected with both you and Sunny, I couldn't help it. Please don't be mad at me."

"We set the world on fire back then, didn't we?" Shade looked sad, as if she were briefly lost in the past.

Tiffany was so damn sorry she'd upset her. Shade's tough exterior slipped for a moment, and Tiffany could see the heartbreak that still lived and breathed in her spirit.

Shade closed her eyes. When she opened them, she put on her trademark smirk, the one that had scores of women falling to their knees in supplication. "Well then, we're going to have to set you up with an entirely new skill set."

Tiffany blew out a breath, relieved she appeared to be forgiven. "Deal. Learn from the best?"

"Fucking right. Let's go to work."

"Okay," Tiffany said. "But I really am sorry."

"We're not done with this conversation about Kat."

Tiffany got out of the van and looked at the restored historical house. It seemed innocent enough with its white wood exterior and blue shutters. But she knew better than most how deceptive outside appearances could be. Beauty could hide dark and twisted things. Sleek renovations could put lipstick on something hideous.

"Hey!" Shade said. "A little help here?"

"What? Oh, yes. Of course." Tiffany walked to the back of the van to help unload the equipment.

Sunny and Jordan arrived in time to grab the rest of the cases. It wasn't until Tiffany walked up onto the porch that her stomach began to churn.

There were secrets in the walls.

Tiffany finished setting up the night vision cameras around the interior of the house, making sure they had a good view of each room before she returned to the living room. "I'm finished. What do we have on paper?"

Jordan plugged in the last monitor and then handed the clipboard to Sunny, who began reading her notes. "Here we go," she said. "Mr. and Mrs. Wilson bought the house less than six months ago. He said the activity started the night they moved in. They began experiencing general uneasiness and a heaviness in the air. Then they began hearing a woman cry a few times a week. Mrs. Wilson started documenting when they heard it, and it was always within the eleven to twelve o'clock hour.

"Those are all classic signs of a residual haunting," Tiffany said. "The Wilsons didn't need an investigation for that. There isn't any surefire way to stop those. I mean, we can put quartz crystals around to purify and lower the frequency, but it either fades away over time, or it doesn't."

"I'm not done," Sunny said. "They've also reported cold spots, strange mists, and dark shadow figures, both in the back room and downstairs."

"Of course," Tiffany said. "It's always the fricking cellar."

"I don't understand why you're still uneasy about them. You've been doing this for years," Jordan said.

"I don't either, really. I know it's always been a long-standing joke, but I've never been able to be completely comfortable in them. I tolerate it when it's my turn, but for some reason, my aversion is getting stronger, not better."

"It's getting worse?" Shade asked.

"Yes, but please don't tease me about it. I'm all about facing my fears and all, but not if I feel so stressed about it all the time. Every instinct in me says to avoid the damn basement."

Shade's eyes narrowed. "Go with your gut. I'll take it this time, but remind me later we need to talk more about this, okay?"

Tiffany nodded, happy to drop the subject. God, she hated feeling weak. Worse, she hated them *knowing* she was weak.

Sunny pulled her to the side. "Let it go. We don't think that, and deep down you know it."

Tiffany sighed. "I know. Old tapes, but they still run now and then. For some reason, they're playing really loud too."

"When's the last time you had a healing session with my mother?"

"It's been a while."

"When she gets back," Sunny said, "Make sure of it, promise me."

"I promise."

"I'm keeping you to it," Sunny said. "Let's circle up."

Tiffany joined hands with Sunny and Shade. They asked for protection as they stood in the center of the living room, standing for past, present, and future, with Jordan rounding out the circle, representing justice. Tiffany was proud of her. She'd been one of their biggest skeptics before she and Sunny became serious. Over the last year or so, she'd become a valuable part of the team. She didn't have the psychic gifts the team did, but she was open to learning. Love, Tiffany thought, is a miracle worker.

When they were finished, Tiffany felt better. Her skin buzzed pleasantly with the energy they raised. There was no other rush like it, that punch of power she felt afterward, when they were all connected and protected. She was ready to kick ass.

"Can we use the voice box?" Jordan asked.

Shade sneered. "Still need your training wheels, Jordan?"

"Hey, I can't help that I can't hear voices in my head, *Lacey*."

"Don't start," Tiffany said after Shade opened her mouth to retort. "Geez, can't we all get along?"

"I was only joking," Shade said. "Don't get your panties all in a twist."

"Even if I wore them," Jordan said, "it would take more than a smart ass comment from you to knot them up."

Although Tiffany knew that the bantering usually started out as teasing, it occasionally had a tendency to get out of hand. It also upset Sunny, and when she was anxious, everyone felt it. The power of an empath worked both ways.

"Don't say ass around me. It's not safe." It was better to defuse them quickly before it escalated, even if it was at her own expense. It had the desired effect she wanted. Shade laughed.

Jordan looked puzzled. "What?"

"I'll tell you later," Sunny said, then winked at Tiffany. "Come on, Jordan. We'll watch the monitors from the van. We can take the second shift."

Tiffany saw a brief moment of pain cross Shade's face before she brought her expression back to neutral. Tiffany reached out tentatively and touched her back. She concentrated on sending a soft, healing light toward Shade's heart.

Shade closed her eyes for a second. "Thank you," she said before she deliberately took a step away.

"Why won't you let me help you more?" Tiffany was aware of the dark stains inside Shade's aura, and it made her sad. It had been a long while since Shade let her get that close to her without shutting herself off first.

"It's mine to deal with. Leave it alone."

"Why do you keep punishing yourself? It's not necessary when I can assist the process."

Shade pointed to the camera lens in the corner of the room. "Let's just get to work." She closed the discussion down for good when she put on her wireless headphones, which operated on a special frequency that allowed her to hear EVPs in real time. "Lights out."

"All right." Tiffany had forgotten that Sunny and Jordan would be able to hear and see them from base. She would have to let it go for now, but the knot of worry she'd felt for Shade over the last several months tightened further. They were due for a heart-to-heart. It had been months. Life just got so damn busy all the time. Shade was really good at deflecting with her "we'll talk later" excuses, but it was nearly impossible to pin her down when "later" came.

Tiffany flipped the switch, grabbed her handheld recorder, and sat on the couch. She would ask the questions while Shade listened.

She considered the energy for a moment before beginning. "Wilson investigation. Tiffany and Shade. Living room. First impression, I sense our clients use this room a lot."

She waited a moment and then began asking questions, leaving a fifteen-second pause between each of them for the recorder's sake. "Who are you? Can you come and talk with us? We're not here to disrespect or harm you in any way."

Tiffany didn't sense anything off. The silence wasn't heavy or filled with any tension; it was just quiet. "Hello? Are you here?"

"Did you hear a voice?" Shade asked Tiffany. "Here, hold on." She rewound the recorder and handed her the headphones.

Tiffany listened carefully. After she heard herself ask the questions, she could hear a heavy sigh. "Barely. But it's there."

Shade nodded before she took the headphones back. She replaced them around her neck.

"Marking heavy sigh heard, continuing EVP, and noting slight temperature change." She glanced down at the thermal gun she had pointed toward the hall. "It went from seventy-eight down to seventy-two."

"Shadow in the left corner of the room." Shade snapped a few pictures.

Tiffany had to wait for her eyes to adjust after the flash. By the time they did, the anomaly was gone. "I still don't feel much."

"I feel something. It's just under the surface, waiting, barely throbbing, kind of like a toothache in a small cavity. You don't always notice it until something gets inside it."

"Oh, that's a good one," Tiffany said. "Are you going to provoke?"

Shade nodded. "Quit hiding and come out where I can see you."

A loud thump sounded from the floor above. "What's up there?" Tiffany asked.

"The attic, I think."

The two-way radio on her hip crackled as Sunny's voice came through it. "Yes, it's coming from the attic. I heard it on the monitor."

Crap. They were almost as bad as basements. She nudged Shade. "I'll follow you."

Tiffany walked behind Shade until they were in front of the bathroom's threshold. She was aware of energy emanating from the open door. She stopped and tugged on Shade's belt loop. "Hang on a minute," she said. She took a deep breath and placed her hand lightly on the wood frame. "Someone died in here."

Shade peeked around the small room. "I agree. It feels sad and heavy. Do your stuff." She turned the viewfinder on the camera she was holding toward Tiffany. "You're on. Action."

"Wilson house, bathroom," Tiffany said. She pressed her hand firmly on the wall to receive and read the energy in the room. "There's a woman looking in the mirror. She's crying, sobbing. She's calling herself stupid, stupid, stupid."

"Young or old?" Shade asked.

"I'm going to say thirties, maybe? Dark, messy hair. She's wearing a long blue nightgown. She looks like she's been crying. Her eyes are swollen. Okay, she's opening the medicine cabinet now. She's pulled something out."

Tiffany turned toward the tub. "She's getting in the bath with her nightie on. Oh no, no."

"I smell blood," Shade said. "Mark the time, eleven oh two p.m."

Tiffany struggled to keep her gag reflex under control. "She's cut her wrists with a razor. The water is turning red really fast." She broke the residual connection by putting her hands in her back pockets. It didn't keep her from feeling the energy, but it did stop the movie in her head. "A woman committed suicide in this room, but I can't tell how long ago. I will say the slate tiles appear to be exactly the same."

"The stone could be holding it. Are they natural?"

"Yes," Tiffany said. "I think so, which is why the energy is still so strong in here."

"Maybe removing them will do the trick."

"Hopefully," Tiffany said. She was reluctant to touch the wall again to link up with the scene in the room. "Shade, do you see her at all?"

"No, I smell blood and feel the leftover desolation."

"Are we done here then?"

Before Shade could answer, a loud knock sounded on the other side of the wall.

"Never mind," Tiffany said. "Apparently not."

Shade went into the hall and toward the sound. Tiffany followed her to the back bedroom. She winced when she heard another knock, this one much louder than the first. "Can you see anything?"

"Just a trace," Shade said.

There was movement in the corner of the room. "Look!" Tiffany said. "The rocker is moving." She stared harder, to make sure it wasn't a trick of the light coming in around the curtain from the streetlight outside.

"I can see it through the night vision," Shade said. "Whoa. It just came right at me."

Tiffany felt the energy whoosh between them, back into the hallway. She gasped at the coldness of it. "I hate it when they do that," she said.

Shade pointed to the ceiling. "Ssh, listen."

After five heartbeats, Tiffany heard the faint footsteps above. Before she could acknowledge them, Sunny came up behind her and scared her. Tiffany placed a hand over her heart. "Jesus. Warn a girl, would you?"

Shade snickered. "Here, hold my stuff. I have to pull the staircase down."

"I came to help with the active spirit." Sunny turned on her handheld recorder. "Attic, Wilson investigation."

There was another loud thump overhead, followed by the sound of someone running across the floorboards.

"It doesn't want us up there." Shade unlocked the hasps on the portable stairs.

"Oh, goody," Tiffany said.

"Let's go up," Shade said. "Brawn before beauty. I'll go first."

❖

Kat was still seething hours after she returned home from Bremerton. How dare Parker give her a case file that had already been solved? She felt used and insulted. Not to mention embarrassed.

She'd barely gotten into the details over lunch with Jordan when she'd told her that she was familiar with the case file. Kat passed her the folder she'd made for the reading and let her read it while her temper grew.

Jordan was ticked off as well but brought a cooler head to the table. As a former police officer, she'd explained his need to have some kind of validation for using the resources. In this case, SOS. Even though this had been a test, Tiffany didn't have any prior knowledge of it, and she'd gotten all the details correct, right down to the icing in Joy's hair. She just hadn't seen the killer go to jail.

Kat didn't feel as generous. Though she understood the need for factual validation, she felt awful that Tiffany had walked through that crime scene for her, and all for nothing. She left a message for Detective Parker to call her. When he hadn't returned it as fast as she would have liked, she debated going to his office, but office hours were over. Instead, Kat decided a cooling off period would probably be better than stalking into a police station with her temper as it stood.

After she'd been home and calmed down considerably, she sent an e-mail to him, outlining the Fisher case, and sent a copy of the recorded file. She managed to keep her tone professional throughout her letter, but just barely.

She knew her anger had much more to do with how the reading affected Tiffany, rather than the perceived insult from Parker.

How did she really feel about Tiffany? If she was honest with herself, and she always tried to be, she didn't know her as much as she would have liked. Yes, she may have appeared to be a twin of Tanna's, but she wasn't the same person. She actually knew very little about Tiffany, even if she felt like she knew everything. It was surreal enough to keep her unbalanced.

Her cell phone rang, and she winced when she heard the Amy Winehouse tune that announced the caller, Valerie, Kat's ex-girlfriend. Well, if you could even call her that. Last year, they were exclusive for a few months until Valerie's budding acting career took her to Los Angeles.

They were so busy with their respective careers, their relationship status fell into a casual one. Valerie's work occasionally brought her to film in Canada, and she usually took the opportunity to call Kat when she was in town to visit her family. Kat remained very fond of her, and more often than not, cleared her schedule to make time and see her.

"Hi," Kat said.

"Hello, sweetheart. A slot just opened on my dance card. Interested?"

"I'm sorry, not in a dancing mood."

"Oh, you want me to come over there for a night in?"

Kat heard the suggestion in her silky voice, but her emotions had taken a ride on a roller coaster the last few days. Not only was she taking time off work, apparently, normality had taken a vacation as well. She didn't feel like she would be very good company. "Can we meet somewhere for a drink and talk?"

"Sure, no problem. Where?"

"How about the Alibi Room?"

"On Pike?" Valerie asked.

"An hour good for you?"

"Sounds good. See you soon."

Kat hung up and went to her room to change. On her way to the closet, she passed the mural. She had a tiny second of hesitation. She felt guilty, which was kind of ridiculous when she thought of it. Even if she believed Tanna was reincarnated in Tiffany, the fact remained she'd run from Kat twice now. They were different people, in a different time, and maybe she needed to accept that.

She needed a distraction, and time with Valerie was better than drinking alone on her balcony while she drove herself crazy with currently unanswerable questions.

❖

Kat turned the last corner and saw Valerie waiting outside the bar for her.

Valerie smiled while she waited for Kat to reach her. "Hi," she said softly, then kissed her cheek.

"Thanks for meeting me." Kat led her to a small table near the back of the bar. The place was well on its way to being packed, and the waitresses looked swamped. It would be easier to muscle her way to the bar herself. She was already uncomfortable; she didn't want to start the conversation just to be interrupted.

Valerie sat and tossed her hair back. "I'll have a tequila sunrise tonight."

Kat was surprised. "No white wine?"

"After seeing that look on your face, I have the feeling that I'll need something a little stronger."

So, Kat thought, she knows. She nodded. "I'll be right back."

When she returned, Valerie took the drink and waited until Kat sat across from her. The music was loud, but the table they were at was small enough so she could be heard. "It's okay, really. We had a good run, didn't we?"

"I haven't said anything."

"Kat, darling. I know you. When you answered the phone this evening, your voice was different. Usually, it drips with sexy come-on-over vibes. I knew something was up. Then I saw you, and I can read the end in your eyes, babe."

Kat didn't know what to say. She knew that Valerie would be gracious, she was that kind of person, but she hadn't expected her to be so perceptive up front. "I'm so sorry."

"So am I," Valerie said. "Who is she?"

Kat shook her head. "Let's not go there, please. I want you to know how much I enjoyed our time together. You are so beautiful, both inside and out. I'll always smile when I remember you."

"Those are pretty words. I'll take them, thank you. Can I still tell you I wish it were me?" Valerie looked wistfully at her. "At one time, I thought it was me in that painting."

Kat had always known that Val wasn't the one, but she'd tried to convince herself of it for a while. Yes, she was a beautiful redhead, had a sweet disposition, and there was an incredible physical attraction. But the soul connection, the recognition of spirit, wasn't there. "You're an amazing woman, and I wish only the best for you. One day, you'll find someone."

Valerie laughed. "Oh, honey, they'll find me. Don't worry. I'm not looking to settle down anytime soon. I'm having too much fun." She stood. "I'm going to go now."

"I'll walk you out." Kat followed her. When she was near the door, she felt a chill run down her back. She turned to search the crowd.

"What's the matter?"

"I don't know. Someone just walked over my grave."

"You know I don't believe in that stuff." Valerie waved her hand to dismiss the comment. "Kiss me good-bye and watch me walk away, like in the movies."

Kat held her close for moment and kissed her. "I'll be seeing you on the big screen one day," she said.

Valerie waved. "Of course you will, and then you can pine away for me because you let me go." She turned away and walked down the street, making a perfect exit.

"Good-bye," Kat said softly. She watched until she turned the corner before she headed for home.

She had a feeling something was off. She kept hearing footsteps behind her, but when she turned to look, she couldn't see anyone. There was a couple walking on the other side of the street and a few stragglers way back. Not close enough to put her guard up. Regardless, Kat quickened her stride and reasoned it away. It was a little foggy out, and she'd been under stress the last couple of days. It was amazing what your imagination could do under the right circumstances.

She recalled the recent murder in the neighborhood, and shifted her thinking. It didn't pay to be too careless. She ducked into a vestibule of a closed store and waited. If there were someone following her, they were going to get the surprise of their life. Kat took her hands out of her pockets, shifted her weight to the balls of her feet.

She was ready.

After five minutes, several people had passed her, and none of them looked at all threatening. She stayed quiet and still for a few more moments. When nothing jumped out at her, she began to feel a little stupid, and then continued on her way home.

Still, her instincts were on high alert, and she couldn't shake the feeling of being watched. Kat searched the street at the entrance to her building. If someone *was* following her, they were damned good at it, and remained hidden from her.

❖

Tiffany screamed while she wiggled and jumped up and down. "Get it, get it, get it."

"I will if you hold still. It's just a little one," Shade said.

"Check my hair, now!"

Sunny patted her down. "Calm down. It's gone. We got it."

Tiffany shuddered. "I hate spiders. Why do they always jump on me?"

"Because you despise them. They lay in wait, just for you, my pretty." Shade set the spider on a windowsill. "Can we continue, please?"

"Yes. I'm sorry, guys." Tiffany quickly snapped her recorder on again. "Continuing Wilson investigation. Sunny, Shade, and Tiffany in the attic."

"I feel a masculine presence," Sunny said.

Tiffany paused for a second before gravitating toward the back of the room. She hesitated only briefly before she touched the wood. "There's, um, somebody hanging from the beam. God, this is so sad, two suicides in the same house. But I don't feel that they're related. There's a time span between them." Tiffany flinched. The hanging wasn't as messy as the first death she'd witnessed earlier, but it didn't make her stomach hurt any less.

"He won't talk to me," Sunny said. "He's not even projecting a vision of himself. He's showing me an empty black hole."

Tiffany put her hands back in her pockets. "Shade?"

Shade nodded and approached the beam. She sat on the dusty floor, closed her eyes, and lay her hands palm down on her knees. Shade's brow furrowed while she concentrated. He wasn't making it easy for any of them to make contact. They sat in silence for several minutes while Shade attempted to meet him on the astral plane.

"Finally," Shade said. "I've got him, but he's not happy about it."

"Tell him we're just trying to help," Sunny said.

"I'm trying, but he thinks we're evil witches come to take him to Hell."

"What?" Tiffany felt the pang of a momentary flashback involving her mother. "Why?"

"I can feel traces of his fear and anguish," Sunny said. "He's scared to death. Oops, sorry, no pun intended."

Shade was quiet for a moment before she continued. "His name is Bob. He either won't tell me his last name, or he's forgotten it. Hang on. He's coming forward."

"What's he saying?" Tiffany asked. "I'm only catching the past loop."

"He's breaking my heart," Sunny said. "He's saying he can't go. He killed himself. That's a deal breaker, and there is no moving on."

Tiffany automatically knew why. Suicide was a big fat no-no in most religions. "Will he tell you why he did it?"

Shade looked thoughtful. "There's something bad here. Bob is telling me that he lost everything—his wife, his job, and the house itself. He says there's a demon in the basement. That it made his life unbearable."

Sunny was surprised. "Why haven't we felt it?"

Shade shrugged. "Tiff, remember the undercurrent I felt downstairs? If it's able to hide that well, it's going to have some serious intelligence."

"Yes," Tiffany said. "Do you think that's why two separate owners committed suicide? Now that I know what I'm looking for, it will be interesting to find out if I can find articles when I research the property."

"There are multiple layers of desolation here," Sunny said. "It's entirely possible they could have been coerced by a dark energy, especially if they were susceptible to suggestions and easily manipulated."

Tiffany shivered. "You're talking oppression?"

"Bob's freaking out," Sunny said. "Let's concentrate on him right now."

Shade pulled two more white candles out of her bag and lit them before joining hands with Tiffany and Sunny. "It's long past his time to go home."

Tiffany closed her eyes and drew energy from the circle. She concentrated on conjuring a bright ball of light in the corner of the room.

Sunny continued to soothe Bob in a soft tone of voice, encouraging him to trust her, to take a chance. Tiffany lost track of time and she even grew a little sleepy. Sunny implored him to go into the light.

The sad, heavy feeling in the room faded gradually. Bob's spirit took a hesitant step out of the dark when the light shifted. The joy on his face when he felt it envelop him brought tears to her eyes. Tiffany waited until the light faded. "Rest in peace," she said.

Sunny had also shed a few tears. Shade wasn't crying, but Tiffany could see there was a touch of tenderness in her expression that hadn't been present for a while. She felt drained. It had been a long day, but this was what she loved most about what they did as a group. Shade and Sunny were quiet as they picked up their equipment in order to go back downstairs, and Tiffany didn't want to break the hush of silence.

She tried not to think about their unfinished business in the basement.

CHAPTER SIX

Kat couldn't quite shake the feeling of being followed home. It gnawed at her nerves, and she paced her hallway while she drank a glass of wine.

What she needed was to concentrate on something else. It was late, but the time wasn't an issue for her. She'd always been a night owl. After she retrieved her laptop from the living room, she continued into her bedroom and then set it down on the dresser before she went into the large closet.

All the way in the back on a top shelf was a metal box. She took it down and blew the dust off. Inside were the carefully packed journals that chronicled Kat's parallel lives.

The dreams had been as authentic to her as her waking life was.

Kat had always known she was different. As far back as she could remember, she'd had another person's memories—the memories of a woman who had lived centuries before. As a child, she never understood why no one else had a sister-self that they saw at night. While she was growing up, she felt as if she lived two lives: the one in the past through her dreams, and the one in the present. It had been that way all her life and she'd learned to shut up about it to avoid the teasing. Not that her parents were mean, they simply didn't understand. Her friends just thought she was a freak, so she kept quiet.

Her visions stopped the year she turned twenty. The year she thought she might die from a broken heart.

When Tanna was murdered.

Kat gulped a swallow of her wine, took a deep breath, and finally opened the case. The covers of the diaries were all different and were numbered on the spines. She chose one she'd written when she was a teenager. Here we go, she thought, as she flipped it open. On the title page, inside of a heart, and written in curly handwriting were the words:

Dream Journal
Kat and Tanna
A long, long time ago...

On the next page, on the very top line, was the date, January 26th.

Tanna and I were at the river, just hanging out. The sun was very bright in the sky, and it was hot. Too hot to lie on the bank, so we went to the rocks lining the big pool around the waterfall.
It felt like a lazy day, you know? We were talking, I can't remember about what. Then Tanna stood up and took off her robe, saying she had to cool off. She had a funny look on her face...

Kat looked up from the page and smiled. It hadn't been the first time she'd seen Tanna naked. But while reading her entry here and now, as an adult, it was clear to her that budding sexuality was the topic of that particular dream.

Kat remembered the way Tanna's hips sashayed, the way the sun streamed from behind the trees to spotlight her as she stood with her arms above her head, almost posing for her, inviting her to look.

Kat turned to the next page to continue reading.

My stomach felt weird. I just stood there and watched the spot where Tanna went into the water. When she came up, she floated on her back. I could see the tips of her nipples just breaking the water line before she did a back roll, giving me a full view of everything. And I mean everything.

When she surfaced again, she laughed at me and told me I should see the look on my face.

I asked her what she thought she was doing, and Tanna tried to look all innocent. She asked me if I was stupid in addition to being clumsy.

I told her I wasn't stupid and dove into the water to try to catch her. I knew it wouldn't be easy; Tanna swims like a fish. I went back under and opened my eyes, but I couldn't see her anywhere...

Kat recalled the frustration she'd felt, followed by the panic when she saw Tanna go under the falls. She had swum as fast as she could to pull her out, diving again and again until she was finally able to grab her ankle and get an arm under her, to tow her out. In her panic, her fingernails had left bloody moons along Tanna's ankle.

She had saved her life. That time. Kat continued to turn the pages in her journal, skipping ahead to the part she was looking for. Ah, there it was. She remembered the fever her seventeen-year-old self felt after she had this particular dream of her first kiss. Beneath the trees, along the river, under the full Goddess moon.

She lay on her side and read the passage while she brought the experience forward, and set the stage to remember. Snapshot memories played in her mind, like flipping through a photo album.

The heavy beat of drums pounded in her chest. Two rings of women danced around a central fire. The red-robed warriors danced around the priestesses in white. A slow and sensual circle dance. Spin, clap, step—reverse—again. The flames sparked with every clap.

In the vision, Kat hadn't taken her eyes off Tanna, who was being initiated as a priestess. Her emerald eyes almost glowed while she held her glance. Kat had been hot, so hot. But she wasn't the only one; several of the young warriors who danced began shucking their clothes, leaving only leather loincloths. Their breasts were bared and bounced with each stomp they took to the beat. The priestesses encouraged them, and showed more and more skin, inviting them to feast with their eyes on the smooth skin beneath their robes.

The drums sped up, along with the sexual tension, until Kat thought her heart might burst with need.

The high priestess stood next to the drummer and held her hand up, stopping the rhythm, and all eyes went to her as she led Tanna to the front of the circle. "Who will step up and petition for this initiate's favor?" She paused. "Who will bend on one knee and give their absolute allegiance to the Goddess and worship her through her beloved priestess?"

Kat immediately stepped forward and dropped to one knee. "It would be my honor, Mother," she said. She and Tanna had waited so long for this ceremony, the rite that would make her union with Tanna official in the eyes of her sisters.

There was a low murmuring from the back of the crowd as another woman stepped up. "I give mine as well, Mother." The woman's bare chest glistened with sweat as she also knelt.

"There are two who want to claim you, Tanna. They must fight for the privilege. Kat and Maeve," Mother said.

Kat had walked to where she laid her sword before the tribal dance. The sharp metal sang against the scabbard as she drew it out, the fire bounced off the polish and reflected in her opponent's eyes. She snarled at the interloper. Kat had been so full of lust and adrenaline, she almost forgot that it was part of the ritual, and well prepared for in advance. In order for Kat to mate with Tanna, she needed to prove herself worthy before the tribe.

The women circled the opponents. The heavy drumbeat commenced once again, rhythmic enough to keep the energy of the women high.

They stood before the high priestess, kissed their blades, and offered them straight up to the sky for the Goddess's blessing.

"And so it begins," said the mother.

Kat and Maeve had circled each other, tested each other's reflexes. A small breeze kicked up sparks from the fire into the air between them, but Kat ignored the glowing embers and advanced toward her opponent. The quicker Maeve was on her back, and under her blade, the faster she could complete the ritual.

Sound had narrowed down to her breath and the stomp of their feet on the ground. Maeve swung first, but Kat turned the blade easily from her with her own. Again and again, Kat had deflected and parried with little effort.

Had Maeve sought to wear her down with child's swordplay? It was to be real battle, not pretend. Kat's anger had built, and with it, her concentration slipped just a fraction, enough for Maeve to draw first blood. A nick on her left arm bled.

Maeve bared her teeth. "Is that all you have, pup? I thought we weaned you."

The insult burned as the next slice of Maeve's sword opened a long, shallow scratch on her thigh. Kat felt moisture run down her leg.

The chanting and shouts from the watching women had encouraged Kat to regroup. She paused only for a second before she had gone on attack, surprising Maeve with a series of blows, putting her on the defense.

The steel blades clashed repeatedly, and the sound of metal scraping against metal set Kat's teeth on edge. She'd been slick with sweat from the fight and the heat of the fire at her back. Her sword arm felt the blows from her fingers to her shoulders each time they clashed. She'd felt her strength begin to wane slightly. It was time to put Maeve down and use the move she'd practiced for months. A move her sister-teacher hadn't expected from her.

Instead of blocking the next thrust, she helped the sword on its way, putting a barely perceptible pause in Maeve's balance, but Kat had watched for it. She crouched, ducked under the backhanded down thrust of the blade, swung her leg into Maeve's ankle, and knocked her off balance. She fell heavily into the sand. Kat placed a foot on her wrist and pinned the sword to the ground.

Maeve's blue eyes showed her shock at being bested, but Kat had also seen a reluctant pride.

She placed the tip of her blade to Maeve's jugular. "I claim this victory, Mother. I claim the rights for the priestess Tanna."

"Let it be known, the warrior Kat has earned her place at the Goddess's side on this night."

The murmur in the crowd grew louder as the women shouted and clapped and paired off. Maeve's partner had helped her from the sand while she laughed good-naturedly.

"Halt!" Tanna said, and the voices and drums stopped. "I demand the chase before Kat claims her victory." Her eyes had caught and held Kat's, as she stated her own challenge. "She has to catch me first."

The dance, fight, and chase were part of the ceremonies that had been passed down for generations. Kat had won the fight, proved she was worthy, but the ritual wasn't complete until the priestess let herself be caught.

Tanna had an hour head start, and she had known those woods as well as Kat had. She had moved silently like smoke through the trees as well as any trained warrior. If she hadn't been found before daylight, Kat's petition for union would have been denied.

It was the last page in that journal. Kat closed it reverently and held it to her chest while she curled onto her side. Emotions swirled along with the memories. This had been serious stuff when she was younger. Her real life had been boring compared to the ancient one she dreamt of at night. She was too tired to keep her eyes open, let alone look for the next book. She turned off her lamp and was quickly lulled to sleep by memories of sweat and love.

Tiffany felt bad for not staying at the Wilsons'. Shade didn't want her to stay while she investigated the rest of the house. She tried to argue, but Sunny agreed it would be best if she went home. It had become an unwritten rule after she had Angel that Tiffany would be excused from the worst energies. Since they didn't know exactly what was causing the haunting yet, and the house had already seen two tragedies, they ganged up on her and made her leave.

Tiffany had no real desire to go up against anything in the basement, so it wasn't too hard to convince her. Jordan offered to take her home. After Jordan's nasty experience with a dark entity last year, she didn't want to hang around either.

Tiffany packed her personal equipment and then met her at the car. "I should wait and help load up when they're done."

"I'll come back and do that." Jordan opened the trunk.

"You're going to drive all the way back here after you drop me off?" Tiffany probed her thoughts gently. "You know you have nothing to worry about, right?"

"Get out of my head, Tiff. I hate it when you guys do that." Jordan slammed the hatch and got in the car.

Tiffany sat in the passenger seat. "I don't mean anything by it. I'm only trying to help."

Jordan sighed. "I know. Sorry for snapping at you."

"S'okay." Tiffany closed her eyes and rested her head.

"How did you feel about the reading with Kat this morning?" Jordan asked.

"Damn, was that this morning? It feels like days. No wonder I'm exhausted."

"Kat said you left in a hurry."

"Did she tell you why?"

"Said you were drained."

"Ah," Tiffany said. "Did she say anything else?" She wondered why Kat hadn't told Jordan that she kissed her.

"Tiffany."

"What?"

"Is something going on between the two of you?"

"Why would you say that?"

"Because you're both acting suspicious."

"Did your secret spidey sense tell you?"

"I'm a cop at heart. I know when things feel hinky, and this feels hinky."

Tiffany laughed. "And you say you don't have any psychic abilities."

"Seriously. What's going on?"

"I don't know. I haven't figured that part out yet. Can we talk about something else?"

"Okay."

Tiffany loved that about Jordan. She didn't ever push an argument, and she never had to worry about her popping into her thoughts.

"I have something to tell you. That case you read this morning? It was a test. They already have somebody in prison for it."

"No, they don't."

"Joy Fisher's case has been solved for nine years. I read about it when I was a cadet."

"The man who did this crime is not in custody. And the more I think about it, the way his appearance was blocked from me? I think that he must have some sort of dark gift."

Jordan shook her head. "I'm sorry, Tiff. If it's any consolation, you got everything else right."

Tiffany didn't agree that the case was solved, but she was too tired to argue tonight. She yawned and her jaw cracked. "Excuse me," she said. "When is the next reading?"

"Can we do one tomorrow?"

"Sure, after I sleep in. Jordan, don't take offense, but it would be easier for me if you weren't there."

"Why not?" Jordan looked hurt. "You don't think I would be an asset?"

"See? You think I'm insulting you, but I'm not. It's that you haven't mastered your blocks yet. Your thoughts are all over the place, and I can hear them."

"I don't know what to say about that."

"You don't have to say anything. Of course you're an asset to the team. I just think it would be better for the situation if you wait until after I do my readings and then help."

"Can you hear Kat's thoughts? She was in the room with you."

I wish. "Just a trace, and once I told her I could, she shut down."

"How the fuck does she know how to do that and I don't know about it?"

Tiffany laughed. "I don't know. You'd have to ask her."

"You think you know a person." Jordan pulled into Tiffany's driveway and popped the trunk. "I'll walk you to the door."

"Thanks anyway." Tiffany hefted her bag to her shoulder. "I'm fine, really. I'll talk with you tomorrow."

"Good night." Jordan kept step with her up the path.

Tiffany was amused. She hugged her when they reached the door. "See? All safe."

"Later."

"Hey," Tiffany said. "You really don't have anything to worry about. Shade's doing the best she can, but I want you to know, she would never cross any lines with Sunny. Your relationship is safe."

"No, I know that. I trust her," Jordan said. "Underneath it all, I really like and respect Shade. It stings, the fact she's so miserable, and knowing I have a part in it."

"Sunny and Shade were over long before you came into the picture."

"I know that logically, and I'm sure on some level that she does too."

"There's something else going on with her as well. You just happen to be a good scapegoat."

"Baa," Jordan said.

Tiffany laughed. "Good night, Jordan. Thanks for the ride." She stepped inside, closed the door, and turned both of her deadbolts.

On her way down the hall, she stopped in the doorway of Angel's empty bedroom. The small bed was neatly made, her teddy bear dead center on the pillow. She missed her terribly when she was away.

She sighed and snapped off the light.

After her quick shower, she climbed into her bed and snuggled under the down comforter. She had just entered the floating state of her meditation when a noise from outside brought her back to awareness. It sounded like it was outside her window.

Her heart thudded while she strained to listen for additional sounds.

There it was again. It could be the raccoon that had been terrorizing the neighborhood recently. Now that she heard it, she'd have to check it out. She'd never be able to sleep well otherwise. With her light ready in one hand and her cell in the other, she walked quietly down the hall, keeping in the shadows. When she reached the kitchen, she peeked through the glass in the back door. Streetlights illuminated the backyard, and she could see it was empty.

The clatter of garbage cans almost stopped her heart. She gathered her courage to look again and saw the large dark shape dart across the lawn. She let out a nervous laugh. It was the raccoon. Now she felt silly for being so scared.

She shook it off and returned to her bedroom, still a bit shaky but determined not to be afraid. She heard a few more noises, but dismissed them. She was tired and sleep came easily.

She was kneeling in the mud.

She felt the ooze under her bare knees, smelled the smoke, the copper, and felt the crushing panic in her chest. Purple heather and fuchsias smoldered on the ground next to her. She could see the green and brown ridge of the mountains on her right, the forest in front of her.

Not again.

She looked to the left, knowing she would see the large horse bearing down on her, the rider bent over its back with his bloody sword extended. She forced herself to stare him down and try to remember the details. The rain and screams made it difficult to concentrate on him.

The man had long yellow hair, and it blew in streams behind him. His teeth were bared, his aggression thick and heavy in the air. The closer he got, the more she could see. Tiffany forced herself to stay this time, to face her fear, rather than wake up like she always did.

The horse's hoofs sprayed mud into her face, but she looked up at the rider. She wanted to see who her murderer was. Blue eyes glared down at her, the whites bright against the dirt. Even in her dream state, this wasn't right.

He wore Mark's face.

Tiffany's eyes snapped open, and she forced herself to breathe. She felt sluggish and heavy. It took some effort, but she was able to turn on her nightstand lamp before falling back against her pillows.

She struggled to connect with reality, to keep herself awake until the dredges of the nightmare receded. She was hyper-aware of her rapid pulse, her panic at seeing Mark's murderous face above her.

Not real, it's not real.

Tiffany knew it had to be her subconscious playing tricks on her. Mark was in prison. She was safe. More importantly, Angel was safe from him. She still had no idea why these issues were surfacing so often lately.

She concentrated on her waterfall, bringing herself to her safe place, but it was a long time before she fell back asleep.

CHAPTER SEVEN

Tiffany woke to the sun streaming through the gap in her curtains. She frantically glanced at the clock and kicked off the covers, thinking she was late. The next second, she remembered Angel was at the beach. *Lucky girl.* She stretched and thought about lying in bed for a while longer, just because she could.

It was no use. Her thoughts began racing with to-do lists and odd errands she should run while she could. Hadn't she also told Jordan last night she would do a cold case reading today? Oh, and she should call Shade or Sunny to ask how the Wilson investigation went.

She sighed, got out of bed, and headed to the bathroom to take a shower.

After the coffee was started, Tiffany went outside to right the garbage cans the raccoon had knocked over. She noticed areas where the grass was lying flat by the house. Damn, it was big. No wonder it made so much noise.

She heard her phone in the kitchen and ran for the back door to answer it. "Hello?"

"There's been an accident," Sunny said.

"What happened?" Tiffany's heart sped up. She knew she should have stayed last night.

"I'm not sure of all the details yet. Some woman named Beenie just called me and said that Shade was in the emergency room. They were attacked early this morning."

"Oh my God! Is Shade okay?"

"I'm on my way to the hospital now," Sunny said. "I'll meet you there."

Kat got up before dawn. She spent the early hours of the morning reading some of her early journals then carefully translated her child's point of view before she began typing them into her new manuscript. With each new line, her excitement grew.

When she finished the chapter she was working on, she opened her e-mail and saw that Detective Parker had responded. He apologized for the deception, but he wanted to make sure the resource was accurate before proceeding.

Resource? His choice of words pissed her off even more. Her jaw tightened, but she read on. Could she please contact him at her earliest convenience?

Kat felt her temper build then checked herself on it. This was a job, and it was out of character for her to take things so personally. She knew it had everything to do with Tiffany and Kat's past memories of her. She was used to having a level head in any situation. Having her emotions so close to the surface was going to drive her off the edge if she didn't find a resolution one way or the other.

Screw Parker. First things first. She needed to call Jordan. While she waited for her to answer, she decided she wanted to have a long talk with Tiffany. It was time to get things out in the open. Kat wouldn't accept anything less than complete disclosure, because waiting for Tiffany to recognize her hadn't helped.

"Hello?"

"Jordan, what time do you want me to come over today?"

"We're going to have to reschedule, Kat. We're on our way to the hospital."

"What's going on? Is anyone hurt?" *Please don't let it be Tiffany.*

"Shade was jumped this morning."

Kat was ashamed she felt so relieved. "Is she going to be okay? Do they know who did it?"

"Negative. I'm going to get more information when I get there."

"Is there anything I can do for you?"

"Not that I can think of. I'll call you later."

"Okay. Please keep me updated."

"I will."

"Later." Kat disconnected the call and began pacing. She liked Shade and sincerely hoped she was all right. Tiffany must be scared to death. Kat was aware of how close they were. She tried to settle down to write some more, but she couldn't sit still. She went out on the deck; she came back in, repeating the pattern. "Hell with it." She grabbed her keys. She didn't want to be stuck here across the water from where she wanted to be. She was going to catch the next ferry to Bremerton.

Tiffany hit the double glass door entry at a run. She went directly to the front desk where Sunny and Jordan were talking with the receptionist.

"Have a seat. It's going to be a while before you can go back."

Sunny looked worried. "Can't we—?"

"No, I'm sorry." The receptionist looked to the man behind Tiffany. "Next!"

Sunny grabbed Tiffany's hand. "I'm so worried about her."

Jordan led them to an area that had three empty seats together. "Do you want something to drink?"

"Aren't you going to raise hell?" Tiffany felt a little hysterical. "Go be a hard-ass or something."

"Tiff, sit down," Sunny said. "It does no good to alienate the one person who has control over that door."

"But—"

"Trust me, that woman has a spine of steel, breathes fire, and she won't be giving an inch. We're going to have to be patient."

"Hey," Jordan said. She pointed to a pair of uniformed officers being ushered through the back door. "There's my old partner. Hey,

Vince! Wait up." Jordan sprinted to catch up with them, and then disappeared around the corner.

Tiffany felt helpless. She hated not knowing what was going on. "Are you getting anything at all from Shade?"

"No. I tried." Sunny put her hands over her face. "I don't know what to do."

"Have you called your mom?"

"I didn't want to worry her until I know what's happening back there."

Tiffany rubbed Sunny's shoulder. "Who's Beenie?"

"I don't know. I'm assuming she's one of Shade's friends."

"Call her back and get her to explain what happened."

"I tried, Tiff. She used Shade's phone. Now when I ring it, it just goes to voice mail."

"Oh. This sucks. Isn't there anything we can do?"

"We're already doing it. I hope Jordan comes back with some news."

"Can't you read Jordan? She's back there."

"I think I'm too upset. I keep seeing static." Sunny slumped back in her chair and crossed her arms over her stomach. "Please, Tiff, sit down. You're making it much worse."

"Oh, sorry." Tiffany made an effort to calm down for Sunny's sake. The energy overflow from the crowded waiting room had to be overwhelming her.

She heard the hiss from the hydraulic hinge on the doors. Most of the people in the room turned to see who was coming out, then immediately went back to their conversations when it wasn't who they expected.

Tiffany stared at the door like her life depended on it, willing it to open and give her some answers. Now she knew how her friends felt when she was lying back there. She ordered herself not to go *there*. She was a long way past the pathetic wreck she'd been.

Sunny's phone rang. "It's my mother. I don't know why I thought I could keep this from her. I'm going to go outside. There's bad reception in here."

"Tell her I'll call Angel in a little while, okay? After we find out what's happened."

Sunny nodded.

Great, now she was stuck here and waiting by herself. She hated hospitals, especially emergency rooms. She'd spent enough time in them making up excuses and lying to the doctors about how she'd been injured.

The doors opened and a disheveled blond teen came out. Her hair was tangled and her eye makeup had run down her face. She looked like she'd been in the same clothes for a week. Tiffany felt sorry for her. She stood still and searched the room as if she were lost. She turned and looked at Tiffany, exposing a bruise alongside her cheekbone, triggering sympathy pains, and a knot began forming in Tiffany's stomach.

The girl made eye contact then approached her. She could see the girl was older than she thought at first, maybe in her early twenties. "Hey, are you Tiffany?"

"Yes. How did you know?"

The girl ignored her question. "I'm Beenie. I need to give you some stuff." She dug in her purse, pulled out a cell phone to hand to Tiffany, along with a large plastic bag with a bloody leather coat in it. Shade's coat. "Oh my God," Tiffany said. "What happened?"

Beenie stared at her with empty eyes. "Look, I can't stay. I didn't see anything, get it?"

Tiffany grabbed her good arm, and dug her fingers in to keep her hold. Damn it, she was going to get answers one way or another.

"Let go of me!"

Beenie was stronger than she looked. Tiffany tightened her grip, but she broke free and pulled back as if she were going to punch her.

Her first reflex was to duck and protect her face, her next was raw rage. Tiffany stood up and balanced herself. She wasn't going to cower for anyone, ever again.

The clenched fist came at her but was stopped mid-air. Kat appeared at her side, towering over them both. "Problem?" she asked Tiffany, then stared Beenie down. "Back off."

"What's your fucking problem?" Beenie's voice reached a screeching volume.

"I suggest," Kat said quietly, "you leave right now."

"I can take care of myself." Tiffany was livid and felt her face burning with anger.

Kat moved to stand between her and Beenie. "I'm sure you can. But security is coming down the hall."

Tiffany turned to look. When she swiveled back again, the last she saw of Beenie was her back as she slipped out the door. She stared up at Kat, speechless.

Sunny appeared at her side and placed her hand on her back. Tiffany wanted to fight the calming warmth spreading through her, because the anger felt better than the fear. "What happened?"

"I had a hold of Beenie-Bitch and Caveman Kat here stopped me."

"She was going to hit you," Kat said.

"Oh Lord." Sunny led Tiffany back to the seats. "First, Angel is fine and having fun at the beach. Second, Shade isn't severely hurt."

"I saw it!" Tiffany said. "That woman set her up. Shade never saw the blow coming." She could feel the angry tears coming, and took a few deep breaths.

"Can you tell us what happened?" Kat sat next to her.

Tiffany was still mad at her and turned toward Sunny. "They were walking down a dark street. It wasn't Shade's neighborhood. I didn't recognize it. Some guy came out of the alley behind them and then hit her over the head with a pipe. She fell immediately. It was awful, seeing her going down."

Sunny gasped. "Oh no!"

"What makes you think she was set up?"

"Because Beenie kept looking over her shoulder. I saw a flash of money changing hands, and the dope she was going to buy with it. She *knew*."

"Wasn't she hurt too?" Kat asked.

Tiffany glared at her. "She talked with the attacker after Shade went down. She figured the amount she was receiving was worth getting beat up to avoid suspicion. I didn't get any more than that before you stopped me."

"I didn't mean to piss you off. I thought I was keeping you from a broken nose."

"Thank you," Sunny said. "Tiffany, she thought she was helping. She couldn't have known what was going on."

"I didn't have time to ask. All I saw was a fist headed toward your face," Kat said. "But I'm sorry if you thought I was out of line." Tiffany's anger abated. Of course she couldn't have known. She'd taken so many fists to the face that one more didn't scare her a bit. She'd lived with the devil for four years.

Jordan came through the doors. Tiffany jumped to her feet before she ran over to her. "I have something to tell you."

Tiffany explained what Beenie's thoughts had told her. "Go arrest her."

"I'm not an officer anymore, Tiff. But I will tell Vince." She paused. "The nurse told me Shade has staples for the gash in her head, but the scan didn't show any fractures in her skull. The doctor is going to admit her, but he says only one of you can go see her right now. She needs to rest."

Tiffany wanted to be the one to go back, she really did. But she turned to Sunny instead. "You go on in. I'll wait until they say I can go."

"Are you sure?" Sunny asked.

"Yes. Give her a kiss from me." Tiffany glanced at Jordan. "Okay, a hug. But tell her I'm here and waiting for permission."

"Thank you."

Tiffany wished she weren't so agitated. She could have sent some of that healing back into Sunny. There was no way she was calm enough to help anyone right now.

"I'm going to find Vince and tell him what you've just told me." Jordan bumped shoulders with Kat. "Take care of her."

Tiffany's adrenaline rush expired and her energy plummeted. She plopped down in the nearest seat with Kat doing the same beside her. She was exhausted and upset Shade was attacked. The psychic readings, late night investigations, and nightmares were taking a heavy toll on her. "You know, it's been a long couple of days, Kat. You have an agenda, and I would like to know what it is. But please, please, don't drop it on me right this second. I don't think I can take it."

"Okay," Kat said, then leaned back in her chair. "I'll just sit here with you."

Tiffany sensed the coiled tension in Kat, belying her laid-back posture. But she couldn't catch any thoughts or intentions from her. The hospital's residual energy was too loud. Because she wasn't having any success, she eventually stopped trying. Her head ached from the sensory overload.

Tiffany closed her sleepy eyes and let her thoughts take her to her sacred place where she saw herself sitting cross-legged in the grass.

Only this time, she wasn't alone.

She heard laughter, genuine jubilant laughter. It was a welcome noise, and she turned toward it while still in her meditative state.

Just then a shadow covered the sun. A tunnel of wind nearly knocked her over. The birds fell quiet and a sense of impending danger loomed.

Tiffany's eyes flew open. Kat was standing in front of her looking around the emergency room. A blur of movement caught her eye, and she saw a man disappear into the elevator. He didn't turn, and she didn't see his face, but the threat from his wake hung in the air.

The question was how did Kat know it? It didn't escape her notice that Kat had put herself between Tiffany and the implied threat. She was going to ask why but was interrupted by Jordan's approach.

"She's all tucked in now, room 334, bed A."

Tiffany nodded. "How's she feeling?"

"You know Shade; she's tough. She's already flirting with the nurses."

Tiffany grinned. "That's our girl. When can I see her?"

"Later tonight. And she insists that we all go home. She'll call if she needs anything." Jordan gestured toward the bag containing Shade's coat. "Give me that."

"I hate leaving her here alone."

"She's pretty looped right now. The nurses said they were finally able to give her something for the pain. She's under close supervision by the staff."

"Where's Sunny?"

"She's talking with the head nurse. After that, she's going to give her insurance information to the administration. She said to send you home and that she'll call you later."

Tiffany couldn't resist prodding Jordan's thoughts. She was telling the truth about what was said. Not that she thought Jordan would lie per se, just that she didn't want to be mollified, as if she couldn't handle the truth. The following thought was that she realized she'd encouraged just that behavior from her friends over the last four years. Yes, she'd come from a horrendous situation; she had needed time to heal. But she didn't need to be protected any longer. They didn't have to shield her from unpleasant information anymore. She could handle it. Well, except for the spiders. Definitely the spiders.

"Thank you for coming." she said politely to Kat and walked toward to the sliding exit doors. Kat kept pace beside her.

"Is there anything I can do?"

"No, thank you. I'm going home." Tiffany stood in the middle of the parking lot for thirty seconds before she changed her mind. "Yes. You can come home with me." Kat smiled and it hitched Tiffany's breath. "I meant to talk."

"You just said—"

"I know. Please, there's too much uncertainty swirling around. I need to get grounded, and to do that, I need answers."

"Okay," Kat said. "I'll follow you."

Tiffany felt Kat staring at her while she walked away, then remembered the creepy doom feeling she'd felt at the hospital. How could she have forgotten that? Complacency was dangerous. Apathy could be deadly.

Kat pulled in behind Tiffany's car. She was already waiting on the porch for her. The house was a mid-century modern ranch style on a street full of them. The yards were clean and maintained. She liked it. Kat had grown up in a neighborhood much like this, and it reminded her of home.

Tiffany unlocked a deadbolt, then another. It could be the smallest of details that told Kat about a person. Tiffany didn't feel safe.

"Come on in." Tiffany motioned her forward and then relocked the doors. "I'll be right back." She disappeared down the hall to a room on the end.

Kat stood in the living room and looked around. The house was tidy, but comfortable. It was nothing like her sleek, minimalistic, clean-lined condo. This home was lived in. The furniture looked soft and inviting. Everything from the biscuit color on the walls, to the honey toned hardwood floor, looked warm.

She walked to the wall lined with shelves. It was full of neat rows of books, charming fairies, geodes and crystals, and dozens of framed pictures. She looked at the photos of Sunny, Shade, and Tiffany, taken at various points of their lives, and a sweet-faced baby grew to a toddler in several more. Angel was beautiful and as aptly named as Sunny. Large cornflower blue eyes stared back at Kat, and she experienced a powerful flash of déjà vu. Recognition flooded her heart with love and sadness simultaneously. It was much the same that Kat had experienced when she saw Tiffany, but with a different intensity. If she doubted the connection even a little before, she was convinced now. Standing here in this energy gave her an overwhelming sense of homecoming.

A door closed in the back of the house and Tiffany returned. "She's gorgeous, isn't she?"

Kat nodded. "How old is she?"

"Four, and the light of my life. She's at the beach with Aura. They'll be back in a couple of days."

"I'm looking forward to meeting her. Jordan talks about her all the time."

"We're very lucky she has three aunties who love her to pieces. Let's go in the kitchen. I'm hungry."

Kat followed mutely. She knew whatever she said next could affect her destiny. One of those monumental moments you looked back on later in life and pointed to with a certainty—convinced it was the one choice you made that changed your path forever. The importance of it nearly paralyzed her.

"Do want some coffee or tea?" Tiffany asked.

"Coffee, please." She didn't know what to say next. She wanted to see where Tiffany led the conversation. Kat didn't want to screw up. She wasn't used to being nervous. How ironic, she thought, that a writer couldn't find her words. "Where is the restroom?"

"Down the hall, second door on the right."

Even the bathroom was warm, with earth tone tiles and stone counters. It made Kat's place look as sterile as a hospital. She splashed cold water on her face and stared in the mirror. She felt odd but didn't look any different. She combed her hair back with her fingers, tucking strands behind her ears. She needed a haircut.

When she returned to the kitchen, she saw Tiffany had put a plate for her on the table. A sandwich with the crusts cut off and apple slices. She smiled. "Peanut butter and jelly? Really?"

"Comfort food," Tiffany answered. "And I needed some. And don't be weird about the naked bread. It's a habit. I always do it for Angel."

Kat laughed. "It's fine. I haven't had it in years." She took a bite and relived the taste of childhood. Hot summer afternoons, swimming in the family pool, cicadas singing her to sleep. She'd forgotten how much she'd loved it. She tried to say thank you, but the peanut butter stuck to the roof of her mouth. She was hungrier than she thought, and she nearly inhaled her food.

Tiffany cleared the table and then poured them each a cup of coffee. "I really should quit drinking this," she said. "But I secretly enjoy it at home and make tea when I'm working at the office. I don't think that anyone's fooled."

"I love coffee; it's an essential food group."

"But we're not here to talk about beverages, are we?"

Kat's anxiety began to rise. No one had ever believed her story before, not really. They simply smiled and nodded, placating her fanciful imagination as they saw fit. Still lost on where to start the conversation, she simply shook her head.

"I want to start with the odd mist that formed when you kissed me, but let's go further back to when you asked if I remembered you. I got the distinct feeling you were hiding something."

Kat studied her expression. Tiffany looked receptive. She remembered her earlier resolve to tell her everything, but now apprehension and the fear of rejection had perspiration forming on her brow and upper lip. "Uh."

"See? You're doing it now." Tiffany looked exasperated.

Kat took a breath and tried to convince herself the situation was much like jumping out of a tree when she was a kid. It was always the fear of jumping that was much greater than the actual landing. "Do you believe in reincarnation?"

"Of course. It would be kind of senseless of me not to."

"I've dreamt of you." Kat wanted to reach out for her hand, but stopped herself. "I knew the moment I saw you who you were."

A look of sadness crossed Tiffany's features briefly. "But I didn't, and don't, remember you. I'm sorry for that."

"Are you absolutely certain?" Kat's stomach hurt. "I mean, have you done a past life regression? Do you all even do those at SOS?" She hadn't thought the dismissal would be so quick.

Tiffany smiled softly. "Yes, and the clients are usually mine. I've never done one on myself or asked Aura to."

"Why?" Kat was curious and hopeful. If she hadn't looked at her past, maybe there was still a chance she would remember.

"I've never shared the reason with anyone other than those in my close circle. Are we going to be friends, Kat?"

If Kat had her way, they would be much more than friends. But she knew Tiffany's real question was whether she could trust her. "Yes."

"Then we'll come back to that. First, tell me why you think I'm—what's her name?"

"Tanna, her name was Tanna."

"That's a beautiful name, but I'm not feeling attached to it." Tiffany rose from the table to refill her coffee.

While her back was turned, Kat got up to stand behind her. Tiffany turned slowly. "Please don't do that. I hate it when people sneak up behind me."

"I'm sorry. I didn't mean to make you nervous." Kat backed her against the counter slowly, and then gently cupped her hands on Tiffany's cheeks. "Let's try this again."

"I can't think," Tiffany said. "I want to talk, but I can't think with you this close to me."

"Then don't. Let me show you," Kat whispered. She flicked the tip of her tongue along Tiffany's lips to part them and followed with soft butterfly kisses. Kat was dizzy with wanting her. When Tiffany drew Kat's tongue into her mouth, wave after wave of feeling crashed through her, and her knees grew weak. Kat lifted her onto the counter with one swoop, and then put her arms around her, crushing Tiffany against her, lost in the passion they were sharing.

Tiffany put a hand against her chest and Kat felt a small push. Kat complied reluctantly, breaking the kiss and resting her forehead against hers.

"My God," Tiffany said. "I can't breathe."

Kat was having a difficult time herself. Her heart felt as if it were pounding out of her chest. She placed Tiffany's palm over it. "This is what you do to me."

Tiffany gripped her shirt and drew her back in. Kat's dreams had been amazing, but nothing prepared for the onslaught of the reality of kissing Tiffany. She wanted to peel off her shirt and pants, strip her bare on the counter, and worship every inch of her. But a little voice in her head said it was too soon. She wanted to ignore it but didn't. Her instincts were rarely wrong.

Kat brought her hands back to Tiffany's cheeks, and slowed the kiss gently, until she was breathing softly against Tiffany's lips for a moment before she held her against her chest. Kat ran her fingers through her hair, then down her back in slow strokes.

Tiffany's phone rang and they both startled. "It's Aura's ringtone, which means it's my baby." She slid off the counter and crossed the room to answer it. "Excuse me," she said. "I'm going to talk in the other room."

Kat used the time to calm down and go into the bathroom. She was a little light-headed and her slacks felt too tight.

When she returned to the kitchen, Tiffany was sitting at the table. "We have to talk," she paused. "About what just happened."

Kat sat down. "Yes." Tiffany's tone was serious.

"There's this crazy connection between us."

"There is." Kat almost held her breath, waiting for her continue.

"I'm relieved that Angel called because it reminded me there isn't just my desire here to consider. My daughter is my first priority, above all else."

"I understand that," Kat said. "And I wouldn't expect anything less from you."

"There's so much going through my head right now, Kat. I have so many questions, doubts, and concerns, that I can't sort them all out yet."

"Yet? So you're not shutting me down." Kat exhaled slowly.

Tiffany took her hand across the table. "My reaction to that sizzling kiss, which I loved by the way, took me completely by surprise and knocked me for a loop."

Kat was confused. "And that's a bad thing?"

"It's important for me to feel in control. Kat, you have me all off balance, and that scares me."

"Why? I'm not going to let you fall."

"But I don't *know* that, and even if you think you know me, you don't—not really. You're convinced that I'm Tanna."

Tiny beads of anxiety began to leak into Kat's confidence when Tiffany took her hand off of hers. "But—"

"So I'm not sure that passion was meant for *me*."

"I promise you, I have never had a kiss like you just gave me." Not in any life, Kat thought.

"I can't jump into anything," Tiffany said. "As much as I want to, I'm going to have to take a step back here and slow things down a little. Maybe we did know each other in a past life. But we don't know each other in this one. So we'll have to get to know each other before we go further."

Kat nodded. "If that's what you want. I'm not going to push you." *Much.*

Tiffany smiled. "Good, that's good. I thought you'd be mad."

"Not at all. Right now I'm grateful you didn't shut me down completely. The look on your face was so serious."

"I am going to ask you to leave, but only because I have to go and see Shade. There's a little crystal shop in the Pike Place Market that I would love to revisit tomorrow. Since I'll already be in Seattle, we can work the next case from Parker, and save you the trip over to this side of the water."

Kat's blood pressure spiked. "You want to come over?"

"Yes. Is that okay?"

"Absolutely, call me when the ferry comes in, and I'll meet you. I can drive you home later." Kat wondered if Tiffany had any idea what that innocent look in her eyes was doing to her.

"It would be nice not to have to worry about parking downtown."

"Aren't you upset that Parker tested you?"

"Not really. I'm used to dealing with skeptics. Normally, I would dismiss them, but this is important to me. I have to go visit Shade before visiting hours are over. We can talk more about this tomorrow. I'll walk you out."

Tiffany kissed Kat's cheek, then stood on the porch and waved.

Kat's mind and heart reeled with possibilities. She was exhausted from running the gamut of emotions since she'd arrived. She'd hit everything from elation to panic and then back to hope, and around again. Kat had turned her own orderly, organized world upside down to chase her dreams. She loved it.

She sincerely hoped she would survive the changes.

Tiffany crossed the threshold into the small room and stopped. Shade looked pale and lifeless in the hospital bed. No traces of her trademark eyeliner remained, and the colorless tone to her skin made the purple bruises under her eyes much darker, giving her a fragile appearance. Blood seeped through the white bandages on her hair.

The room itself held traces of pain, emotional stress, and grief. Tiffany attempted to block out leftover energy from previous patients and focus on Shade. When she got it down to a manageable level, she took a steadying breath and walked to the bed.

Tiffany was deeply unsettled. Shade had always been her rock. Seeing her in this condition broke her heart. She reminded herself of the promise she made to herself to come out from behind Sunny's and Shade's shadows and stand tall on her own. Now was the time. This was her first challenge.

Shade's eyes snapped open when Tiffany sat in the chair next to the bed. "Hey."

"Hey yourself. How are you feeling?"

"I hurt."

"I know, honey." Tiffany held up her hands. "May I?"

"You're not going to bite me are you? I'm kind of at a disadvantage here."

Tiffany laughed. "Do you want me to?"

"Not tonight, dear, I have a headache." Shade chuckled, then winced. "Ow, don't make me laugh."

Tiffany was glad to see her sense of humor was intact. She laid her palms gently on Shade's bandaged head, focusing white, healing energy into the wound. She drew as much of the pain from Shade into herself that she could for the next few minutes.

"Enough. Feels good." Shade broke the connection by removing Tiffany's hands gently. "That's almost the best that I've felt all day."

"What do you mean, almost?" Tiffany brushed Shade's bangs out of her eyes.

"The last nurse that was in here, leaned over to adjust the bed. Her boobs were in my face."

"You're incorrigible. Your distractions aren't going to work. I'm still going to ask questions."

"Let it—"

"No, Shade. I'm not going to let it go this time. You've put everyone off for too long. The 'later' that you always insist on, is finally here."

Shade looked at the ceiling, and Tiffany felt rather than saw the temper that was brewing.

"You can't put me off forever. I'm worried about you. We're all worried about you. So while you evaded and ducked us for months, right about now, I'm thinking our concerns were quite valid."

No answer.

"Beenie nearly got her ass kicked downstairs."

Shade glared at her then looked away. "Tell Jordan to keep out of my business."

"It wasn't her, it was me," Tiffany said. "I saw what happened to you and I was furious. What are you doing hanging out with her anyway?"

"Trust me, Tiffany, you don't want to know."

"Damn it, Shade! I love you."

"I love you too, Tiffy, but I'm not talking about this."

"You are so frustrating."

"It's part of my charm."

"No, it's not. I want to smack you right now."

"But you won't."

Tiffany sighed. "No, you're right. I won't."

"I'm okay. Please don't worry."

"Do you know who attacked you?"

Shade's expression tightened. "No, I didn't and I can't see him."

"Beenie did." Tiffany recalled the vision of money changing hands.

"I'll deal with her when I'm on my feet. Believe that."

Tiffany felt a small chill. The venom in Shade's voice was a little scary. Suddenly, she didn't want to talk about it anymore.

Shade's pain was evident in her eyes as she stared at Tiffany. "You stop that!" Tiffany said. "Don't you pull that mind persuasion crap on me."

"If my head didn't hurt so badly, it would have worked." Shade said. "Please, Tiff, I'm tired. This is not the place to go into all of this."

She's right. Tiffany's temper deflated instantly. "I'm sorry. I'm just so damn worried about you."

"I've got this. Promise me you'll be careful."

"Why?"

"Things are fuzzy right now. I just know that something that looks innocent, isn't. Something dark is coming."

"Okay, that's a little frightening. Aura told me the same thing before she left for the beach." The hair on the back of her neck raised and Tiffany rubbed her neck. "Can you see any more of my future?"

"No, my head hurts when I try."

"Of course it does. I'm sorry. I promise I'll be careful. You just get better, okay?"

"Kiss me and go home."

Tiffany leaned over and kissed Shade's cheek just as a nurse came in. Shade winked and mouthed the word, boobs. Tiffany pinched the inside of her arm.

"Ouch."

"You deserved it. Promise me that when you get out, we'll talk about what's going on with you, or I'll do it again."

"Do what again?" asked the nurse.

"Nothing," Tiffany said sweetly and smoothed the sheet. "Good night. I'll come see you tomorrow." She left the room and waited on the other side of the open door.

"Can't wait," Shade said.

"I heard that," Tiffany called.

"Go home."

CHAPTER EIGHT

Tiffany hopped the bus that would take her to the ferry terminal. She knew she could have asked Sunny or Jordan for a ride, but she didn't want to bother them with it. Besides, this way she didn't have to answer any questions. Sunny would have known in a second what happened with Kat last night, and her curiosity would have been greater than her usual tact she displayed when she felt other people's emotions.

The stale air on the bus reeked of misery, and Tiffany blocked it as best as she could. At the next stop, an elderly couple boarded and sat on the long bench seat behind the driver. They held hands and their auras were brilliant with a rainbow of colors. They had a deep, abiding love for each other.

As she stared at them, the gentleman looked at Tiffany and smiled at her. It was then she saw the dark mass in his colon and it pulsated with dark, poisonous energy. Being a healer was an innate trait in her personality, but she had learned long ago she couldn't save everybody. There were some things she just couldn't make better. She glanced back up to his face.

He was still smiling at her. *I've had an amazing life. Don't be sorry for me. It's my time, little one.*

Tiffany blinked, surprised the man spoke telepathically to her. She smiled back to let him know she heard him.

He winked at her, turned his smile to his wife, and his adoration for her lit up his face. Tiffany had longed for that look her entire life. She'd certainly never received it from her mother or her ex-husband.

Your daughter looks at you with love. Look forward. The answers to your past are in your future.

He was right. His words humbled her. *Thanks.*

She was getting off at the next stop. There was no need to ring the bell. Most of the passengers were exiting for the ferries. The couple stayed seated.

She couldn't resist. On her way out, Tiffany touched the gentleman's shoulder, sending a powerful burst of white light directly to the mass. It wouldn't cure it by any means, but she hoped it would alleviate some of his pain for the day.

She looked at him one last time before the doors on the bus shut with a hiss. It was his turn to look surprised. *That felt good. I should get out more often.* She'd insulated herself from the outside world for too long. The people she met on a daily basis came to *her* for help.

The crowd closed in around her and Tiffany quickly raised her mental shields. She'd forgotten it was like a cattle run, everybody rushing to the ferry to get to work in Seattle. She clutched her bag across her chest like a shield, caught up in the gauntlet.

The majority of the passengers rushed to the window seats, the rest to the onboard café for coffee. She just wanted to find an empty space to breathe for a few moments. The energy she'd given the elderly man and the mindset of the boarding passengers had made her a little nauseous. Tiffany dug in her large purse to find the crackers she kept stashed for Angel.

The fresh air would do her good. She reached back into the depths of her bag and found a hair tie she would need on the windy deck. She walked out to the railing and leaned out.

Tiffany looked down at the water and saw, through the wake and waves, hundreds of clear jellyfish. The houses along the sides of Puget Sound were gorgeous, with their long piers and docked boats. She wondered briefly what it felt like to live in one, to be able to sit outside and stare at the water every day.

Tiffany let the salt air refresh her. She was soon filled with happy anticipation. She was still stunned that she was so forward with Kat last night. The kiss, oh man, that kiss. She had no idea it would be so soft, so sensual. If she thought she knew what she was in for by peeking into someone else's trysts, she was dead wrong. Nothing compared to the reality.

She honestly hadn't known she even possessed that force of lust. Tiffany remembered Kat lifting her onto the counter. *How freaking sexy was that?*

After the kiss, she'd brazenly invited herself over to Kat's house. She didn't know where she'd found the bravery. Maybe it was the promise to herself she'd made to step out and up. She might not always make the best decisions, but at least she was now making them for herself.

The Seattle skyline drew closer and Tiffany left the rail to go to the restroom. By the time she fixed her hair and refreshed her makeup, they would be pulling into the dock. There was no way she was going to get in the middle of that crowd exiting to get to work on time. Late commuters could be brutal.

When she was done, she meandered toward the end of the line. Someone slammed into her. The force was strong enough to knock her into the wall. By the time she caught her balance, the person was a blur running along the exit. She couldn't see their face, and it wouldn't matter if she could. Some people were just that rude. It wasn't as if she could do anything about it, and she hated that it was the possibility of intentional violence she perceived first. *It wasn't personal. He was rushing to work, that's all.*

Still, she was careful when she exited into the terminal. She spotted Kat standing by the doors next to the street, and the sight of her took Tiffany's breath away. Her senses were hit with the smell of a rich, green forest and meadow flowers. Something teased the edge of her consciousness, but the harder she reached for it, the faster it slipped away. It was gone by the time she reached Kat.

She may have shown uncharacteristic forwardness yesterday, but now faced with Kat's magnetic smile and presence, Tiffany felt shy and unsure.

"Hi," Kat said. "You made it."

Tiffany nodded. "Hi."

They stood in silence though the terminal's activity buzzed around them. It was as if they were in a bubble, reliving the energy of their kiss the night before. Butterflies circled in her stomach and she was hyper aware of Kat's arm around her shoulder as she steered her through the exit toward the street.

"Are you up to walking or do you want to catch a cab?"

"Walking is good. With traffic the way it is now, a taxi would take longer." Tiffany's hand was enveloped in Kat's as they walked the distance to Pike Place Market. It felt…right.

Dozens of questions flooded Tiffany's mind along the way, but none would form clearly enough for her to articulate in this crowded environment. The sights and smells of downtown Seattle were distracting enough, and the thousands of stray thoughts from the people rushing around them had Tiffany struggling to focus on her feet, let alone on Kat beside her. But oddly enough, she felt protected, and none of her usual apprehension of being in large groups of people was present.

She loved the wide wooden planks in the building. She imagined it was much like being in a large pirate ship. Kat held the door for her and placed her hand on the small of Tiffany's back. Her skin instantly heated underneath her shirt.

Now that they were inside, the noise outside dimmed somewhat, making it easier to talk. "Have you been here before?"

Kat grinned. "A time or two."

The store welcomed Tiffany like an old friend. It was full of thousands of colorful minerals and stones from various regions. Giant boulder-sized amethysts lined the walls and crystals hung from the ceiling alongside fairies with multi-colored wings. Bronze and pewter dragons curled around faceted gemstone spheres. Everything seemed to sparkle with energy.

Tiffany felt drawn to the back of the store. There on the shelf was a beautifully detailed statue of a warrior maiden. She stood three feet tall and her hands rested on the pommel of her sword, which was stuck in a crystal at her feet.

"See something you like?"

She'd forgotten Kat was behind her, and she flinched when her question startled her. She'd been mesmerized by the bronze. She quickly recovered and hoped Kat hadn't noticed.

"She's stunning," Tiffany said. "She looks almost familiar."

Kat's breath was hot next to her ear. "Really? Tell me why."

Tiffany felt her face heat along with her back where Kat pressed against her. God, she couldn't think straight. She'd forgotten what she'd come to the store for. She knew she needed something, but it was lost in the rush of desire. Tiffany was about to tell her to stop teasing her but instead was struck speechless by quick stabbing pain to her temple. She put her hands up and cried out.

"What's the matter?" Kat caught her before she fell, ready to set her on the floor.

The pain was gone as fast as it appeared. Tiffany's legs felt shaky, but she refused to sit down. "I'm fine." She looked around the store, trying to find the source of the psychic attack but didn't sense any suspicious energy trails. It wasn't the first time this had happened in similar places. The energy stored here in residence could be used for good or ill, depending on the person who harnessed it. She should have been more careful. Kat's presence was thoroughly distracting.

"What do you mean you're fine? That was not okay. You were hurting."

Tiffany noticed Kat searching the room as well and it made her curious. "What are you looking for?"

"I felt something weird," Kat said. "It passed right through me."

"We should go now," Tiffany said. "I don't want to be here anymore."

"Okay. Are you still hurting?"

"No, but I am hungry." She was also mad that some power-tripping asshole ruined the trip to her favorite store. Tiffany tightened her shields.

"Where do you want to go and eat?" Kat asked. "I'll take you to brunch."

"Could we please go to your place?" Tiffany felt exposed. "I'd rather not be out right now. We could stop at the store and pick up something to make."

"I have plenty of food."

"That sounds even better. Let's get out of here."

Traffic had cleared somewhat, and the taxi ride was short. The driver let them out in front of Kat's building. Tiffany had to crane her neck to see the top. She'd never been inside a place this fancy. "Wow, how may floors is this?"

"Thirty-five."

Tiffany followed her through the beautiful lobby and into the elevators. Kat punched number seventeen. Her stomach dropped as the elevator rocketed upward. She gasped. "Oh, my God."

Kat prepared to catch her. "What?"

"I grabbed the handrail. Wild monkey sex in the ele-va-tor." Tiffany slapped a hand over her mouth.

Kat laughed. "I'm not surprised."

"Sorry. Sometimes my filter goes on vacation without me. This is why I don't get out much."

"I think it's adorable," Kat said. "And the blush is cute too."

Tiffany covered her face with her hands. "I'm so embarrassed."

Kat tugged her arms down. "Not as embarrassed as they should be." She pointed to the camera in the corner and waved before the doors slid open. "They probably play them at the holiday parties for the staff."

Great, Tiffany thought. They'll probably play that little tiddly-bit too.

Kat stepped back and let Tiffany go in first.

She squealed and ran straight for the wall of windows. "Omigod! Look at the view!"

"It's amazing, isn't it? I practically live out on the balcony. You should see it at night when the city lights up."

"How you can afford this on a journalist's salary?" Tiffany's eyes widened. "Again, sorry, filter, none, you know."

"It's okay. I don't mind. When I first moved here, I worked at Microsoft while I went to school, and I invested heavily. This used to be my uncle's condo, and because he never married, he left it to me when he passed."

"Where do your parents live?"

"They're gone too."

"Oh, I'm truly sorry."

"It was several years ago, but thank you." Kat crossed to the open kitchen. Would you like something to drink?"

"Water is fine." Tiffany sat at the granite counter on a high stool.

Kat passed a bottle over to her and then began putting together a tray. "I have fruit, crackers, several cheeses, and vegetables. I'm sorry, but I can't offer you a peanut butter and jelly sandwich."

Tiffany laughed. "Everything sounds great." A muffled ring tone sounded from her bag on the stool next to her.

Kat kept herself busy gathering food for the tray while Tiffany dug for her phone.

"Damn, missed it." Tiffany checked the caller. "Well, it's not Angel, and they didn't leave a message." She put the phone back.

"How do you find anything in that suitcase?"

"It's not a suitcase; it's a tote."

"It must weigh as much as you do."

Tiffany laughed. "I have a daughter, and sometimes when I'm working I need unusual stuff handy. I think of it as my Mary Poppins carpet bag."

"Cute." Kat put the finishing touches on the tray. "Do you want to eat on the terrace?"

Tiffany nodded. Kat loved the way her eyes lit up. Tiffany's personality was genuine and pure. It was refreshing to spend time with her and not worry if there were any ulterior motives underneath. As soon as she thought it, she felt a twinge of guilt about her own motives.

Was she being genuine with Tiffany herself? Or projecting Tanna onto her for her own selfish needs? It was a sobering question, and one she needed to answer.

Kat carried the tray to the table outside before she pulled Tiffany's chair out for her.

"Thank you," Tiffany said. "This is wonderful."

"I've never dated a clairvoyant psychic before."

Tiffany blushed. "Is this a date?"

"Isn't it?" Kat asked. "I'm sitting across from a beautiful woman I want to spend more time with. But I am wondering how fair it is if you can read my thoughts and I don't know what you're thinking."

"I can only catch traces, but nothing definitive yet. We can get to know each other the old-fashioned way. We'll talk, okay?"

Kat smiled. "Fair enough."

"And I want to leave anything related to the paranormal out of the conversation for now."

"Why?"

"I want to relax and just *be* in the moment. I'm tired of being on all the time. It's not every day I get to eat lunch in the sunshine on the seventeenth floor of a condo that looks out over the bay." Tiffany paused. "Across from a beautiful woman I want to spend more time with."

"Cheers," Kat said and raised her glass. "It's funny you said that."

"What?"

"That you wanted to be in the moment. I was thinking the very same thing the other day. Life is going so fast, and the pressures of being on all the time is weighing on me. I miss the slower pace of the south."

"Oh? Where are you from?"

"A small town in South Carolina."

"Really? You don't have an accent."

"I worked hard to lose it, but it comes back pretty quickly if I'm talking with anyone from the south. Actually, I don't know where I was born. I was adopted when I was a young child and that's where my adoptive parents lived. Funny, when I was growing up I couldn't wait to leave that place. Now that I'm older, I think about how wonderful it was."

"Did you ever look for your birth parents?"

"I tried, when I was older. Even with all the resources available to me, I never did find a trace."

"I'm sorry."

"Oh, I'm not. My parents were wonderful to me. No horror stories here. Are you from Seattle?"

"How did you know?"

Kat smiled. "You have an accent."

"No, I do not."

"To me you do."

"I was born in Burien."

"That's just around the corner."

"But farther away from this than you can ever imagine," Tiffany said softly and leaned back in her chair. "That was excellent, thank you."

"You're welcome," Kat said. Apparently, that topic was off limits as well for now. She stood to clear the small table and Tiffany got up to help. "I have this. You can sit out here and relax."

"What time is it?"

"I don't know and that's odd. I'm usually on such tight deadlines, I have almost every minute of my day planned out."

It wasn't until she reached the kitchen that she realized during lunch and their conversation, she hadn't seen Tiffany as Tanna.

She didn't know how to feel about that. Wasn't it the point that Kat get her to recognize her and remember their past life?

She wasn't sure anymore.

"We have to get you out of the sun."

Tiffany opened her eyes. She had dozed off while Kat was in the kitchen. "I'm so sorry. How long was I out?"

"Not long, but you're turning pink. Let's get you inside."

"Curse of a redhead," Tiffany said. She tried to shrug it off, but was deeply embarrassed at falling asleep. "Where's your restroom?"

"Down the hall. The door's open, you'll see it."

"Thank you." Tiffany took her black bag with her.

She braided her windswept hair, and as an afterthought quickly touched up her makeup. She was tired of running, tired of hiding. Tired of being alone. At the very least she needed to know what was going on. Anything beyond that, well, she'd just have to play it by ear.

Before she stepped out of the bathroom, the doorbell rang. She put her ear to the door.

"Detective Parker," Kat said.

His voice was too low for Tiffany to hear. She hadn't been aware that he was coming. But now that she thought about it, she did tell Kat last night they would work today. But she hadn't reminded her or said anything about him showing up. Grateful for the nap that left her refreshed, she sat on the edge of the tub and took some time to say her special prayer for protection and guidance.

When she felt prepared, she joined them in the living room. Kat jumped to her feet and looked apologetic. "He just showed up." She glared at him. "Without calling first."

"I'm sorry for the inconvenience," Detective Parker said. "I was in the neighborhood and thought I might stop in. I didn't know you'd be here." He was shuffling the glass of water with the files under his arm, and trying to free one of his hands.

She hated touching strangers. Tiffany gave him her sweetest, most polite smile and sidestepped to discourage him from it.

Detective Parker cleared his throat. "It's nice to meet you. Kat forwarded your reading, and I was impressed."

"With details from a solved case?" Tiffany wasn't mad, not really. She simply wanted him to know she knew.

Parker looked almost chagrined. "I'll apologize for that."

"You should," Kat said. "We might as well sit at the table." Kat looked at Tiffany. "Unless you want to sit in the living room?"

"Table is fine. Detective Parker, I think the wrong man was convicted in the Joy Fisher case. The killer's energy that I picked up is not from someone currently in jail."

His features hardened. "That case was solved on DNA evidence."

"I can only tell you what I see. You might want to look into that further." Tiffany could tell from his expression he would do no such thing.

Kat directed them to the dining table. "He wants to know if you can read two files for him. I told him it was entirely your choice."

"I was going to drop them off with Kat. But since we're all here, would you mind? It could be very important to a crime that was committed recently."

"Don't feel pressured," Kat said.

Tiffany noted her sarcastic tone, and smiled to herself. Apparently, she was upset at the change in plans as well. "I'll do this for you, if it will help."

"Mind if I record this?" Detective Parker asked.

"No, go ahead."

Detective Parker opened a large file. "How do you want to start this?"

"Just slide it over, closed, please." Tiffany closed her eyes for a moment. The energy off the file made her a little jittery, but she concentrated on the traces she could see in her mind's eye before actually touching the contents. "I'm getting that this one was about five years ago."

"Why do you think that?" Detective Parker asked.

"Because I feel like I'm pregnant, and for me that's an indication, a marker of time. I was pregnant five years ago." Tiffany rubbed her stomach. She loved and hated experiencing this feeling of pregnancy. She had loved being full of Angel, cherished her, but hated remembering Mark and his violent temper. She despised opening that door. She tried to concentrate on shutting him out of her reading. The victim was important here, and she wanted to make sure she kept her own fear and repulsion neutral. She refocused on the case at hand. Tiffany controlled the slight tremble in her hand as she placed it over the file in front of her. The violent energy attached to it nearly knocked her from her chair. She felt Kat place a hand between her shoulders to steady her.

"Tiffany, are you okay?"

"Oh my God," she said and snatched her hand back. She looked at Parker. "Serial killer?"

He nodded and kept his stern poker face intact.

She exhaled slowly and touched it again, but not before psychically bracing herself.

"These two victims were found together? No, wait—near each other, but at separate times. Please clarify."

"Yes. They were found in the same area."

"Thank you. Give me a second. I have to separate them. It's all jumbled together. Okay, let's start with the young woman with short hair. It's blond, light. She would have been wearing torn jeans, white shirt, and a leather jacket."

Parker leaned across the table, pulled out one photo, and placed it facedown in front of her. Tiffany flipped it over. "Yes, that's her. Hard T—Terry, or Theresa." Tiffany's heart hurt. The face smiling back at her was impossibly young, sweet. It hurt to know that the girl's life was cut so short. "Please clarify if she was at a convenience store when she was abducted, so I know it's her energy that I'm following and not the other girl."

Parker blinked. "Yes."

"Thank you." Tiffany closed her eyes. "Okay. I see her going in, and she goes straight to the counter. Um, cigarettes, red pack, Marlboros?" Tiffany paused. "I get the feeling someone's watching, watching, watching. She has no clue he's been following her. Hang on. I see a large sedan, but the windows are tinted, and it's dark outside. She goes around the side of the store, away from the light, and he hits her. The abduction is over very fast. I hear screeching tires." Tiffany opened her eyes. "Can I have a piece of paper?"

"Of course," Kat said. She handed Tiff a stack of plain white paper from the printer.

Tiffany began to sketch an aerial view of the property. "These are trees. On this side, I see old machinery, like broken dozers, dirty yellow or orange construction equipment. On this side is the road, but you can hardly see it. It's overgrown with weeds and blackberry bushes that are covering an old cyclone fence. And on this side, more trees. And here—" Tiffany drew a square on the paper. "This is an old abandoned house, gray maybe? Two stories high, broken and boarded up windows. The steps are rickety and falling apart.

"He takes her there." She tapped the paper with the pencil. "She's struggling, but he's too strong." She paused for a drink of water, taking a moment to breathe past the building anxiety. Tiffany grabbed another piece of paper from the stack and then drew another, larger square. "This is the hall, living room, and the kitchen is back here." She drew an X in a room she sketched off the back of the house. "They found her here. It's either a covered porch or mudroom."

She looked up at Parker, but his reaction was still neutral. She was aware of Kat fidgeting in the chair next her. "Please clarify."

"Yes," he said. "Please, go on."

Tiffany continued. "Which is it? Terry or Theresa?"

"Theresa."

"Thank you. I see her. *His bitch*—he thinks of her as property. He feels very powerful here—like it's his place—he feels he owns it. He knows the floor plan, and he's comfortable in it. I can hear his voice. Hang on for a second." She strained to hear.

You should have fucking listened.

Tiffany felt her heart flutter. There was something familiar about that voice. She saw a flash of blond hair a second before Mark's face intruded into the reading and taunted her. *Damn it.* She ordered herself to put him back where he belonged. Working with these killers was bringing up memories of his sadistic behavior. No wonder he kept popping up in her mind. She had to work harder at separating her emotions from the victims she was trying to help. Her problems had no place here.

"Are you okay?" Parker asked. "You've gone a little pale."

"Yes, I'm fine." Tiffany took another drink of water to stall while she refocused on the task at hand.

Kat shot Parker a dirty look. "Tiffany, didn't you tell me that you don't connect with the dark energies because it's dangerous? What's going on here?"

Tiffany blinked and felt the blood drain from her face. "You're right. I was so caught up that the killer drew me right in. It's almost as if he's aware I can see him and he's bragging." She fought the urge to shudder.

"Should we stop?" Kat asked. "We can do this another time, with Shade when she's feeling better."

Tiffany considered it and then dismissed the suggestion. *I wanted to be tougher, right?* Here was the time to prove it. "No, I can do this." She realized that Kat was trying to protect her, and she filed the detail away to deal with later. She was done hiding behind anyone.

Tiffany turned to Parker. "Shall we continue? He threw her on the floor. She's gagged, and he ties her up. He hates Theresa. Her hair is all wrong, wrong color, wrong length—and it's all her fault. His thoughts are all over the place. I'm having a hard time honing in, but I do get that he's in a rage and ends up dragging her down the hall to the small room in the back.

"He doesn't keep her alive long. He does what he did to her. You, um..." Tiffany swallowed back bile as she witnessed the violent murder and was hit with the scent of blood. "You already know the other details. I'll skip the replay and tell you I see the word *liar* cut into the skin of her stomach. He doesn't think of her as human, not at all. It's like a Christmas gift he didn't want and then broke out of spite."

She pointed to the file. "There's another energy coming in now, the other girl. Again, she's young. She has long hair, dark blond, auburn maybe? She's wearing a short plaid skirt, crop top. Can I have the next photo please?"

Parker slid the picture across the table to her. "Are you getting her name?"

"Soft H. Hailey, Harlow, Hanna? Please clarify."

"Hailey," Parker said and ran a hand over his face.

It was the first visible reaction Tiffany had seen from him yet. "Thank you. I feel led to go back to the details of her abduction. I see her making a call. She's standing on the side of the road. It feels like she's waiting for someone. She's under a streetlight. She thinks she's safe.

"He's watching her though. He's been following her for several blocks. She sees a car approach, and the window rolls down. She doesn't feel threatened. She thinks he's cute, and therefore safe. God, I hate this part, when I know I can't change anything. It's like I want to yell at her to stop, to not get in the car. It's a dark sedan, similar to one Theresa was thrown into. Hailey gets in the front of the car with him. I see her laughing, coyly almost, like she's flirting a little bit. That's giving me an indication she's not feeling threatened in any way by this man. She's very relaxed. But then he turns the car off the main road. She's starting to get nervous, but he's reassuring her."

Parker interrupted. "Can you see his face?

Tiffany concentrated. "No, I can't see him at all. I feel the presence of him in the car, but I can't see his face. It's blurry." Tiffany went on. "She's feeling scared now. The car is going faster. She tries the handle, but it's locked. She's begging him to let her out. He's telling her to shut up, shut up. He hits her in the side of the head. She's whimpering and trying to make herself small. Okay, he takes her to that same house." Tiffany drew an X in her floor plan.

"This room, the largest. It's very cold, icy cold. Her face hurts where he struck her. He tells her if she's quiet, and does what he wants, he'll let her go. If she tries to run, he'll find her and kill her. She's crying, but very quietly." Tiffany took a breath before continuing. "It's incredibly sad, but she believes him, you know, that he'll free her. He has total control of her. He's tied her up, and he keeps petting her hair. He likes her long hair. He's twisted. But we already know that. She didn't die quickly. I feel as if she were alive for a while, a prisoner."

Tiffany cleared her throat. "When he leaves, after raping her, he ties and gags her, puts her in the closet, then closes the door. He's very careful. I see him wiping surfaces—wearing those disposable blue gloves. So I feel he knows what he's doing as far as hiding evidence. He's obsessive about it. Bleach, I smell bleach.

"I can hear her humming. Her mind is going—she's here and not here. I can't tell you how long he kept her. I can only tell you that when he takes her life, she doesn't feel any more pain. And that's what pissed him off. He wanted her pain and fear. When she becomes almost catatonic, he goes ballistic. He—he—uh." Tiffany swallowed. "He ended up cutting her throat. Now I'm seeing flowers being brought in—by him. He leaves them by her body. He comes back often, makes this weird shrine to her. He hated her when she was alive, but now that she's dead, she's exonerated, saintly."

Tiffany stopped talking. "That's the killer's point of view again. I'm connected with him."

"I think we should stop," Kat said. "You've done so much already."

"No, I'll finish it. Stop fussing over me." Tiffany realized she'd snapped at her and softened her tone. "I'm fine."

"If I haven't said it before now, I appreciate what you're doing and the effort that you're putting into this," Parker said.

Kat pushed away from table and paced the room. She sat back down with a huff. She was clearly unhappy, but Tiffany tried to ignore her anxious energy. She didn't have time to deal with Kat's emotions as well as those coming from the reading. She could only handle so much at one time.

"You're welcome. I just hope that it helps you catch this bastard."

"Me too," Parker said.

"Let's get this over with," Tiffany said. "He's going back outside. I can see his back, but I still can't see his face. He's walking out to the lot, then into the trees. There's a piece of twisted metal there, and a stump that he sits on. He's lighting a cigarette. Wait, he's turning around." Tiffany held her breath. "Damn it, I could swear he's blocking me from seeing him. I'm sorry. He's looking straight at me, but I can't see his face."

Parker checked his notes. "Don't be. I have more than I had before. So far, from what you told me, the killer has a medium build, light hair, dark four-door sedan, and you think he's good-looking."

"Yes," Tiffany said. "He doesn't look like a killer. I know people always say that, but when that girl got in the car, she wasn't threatened. She was flirting."

Kat jumped in. "Then he has to be young, like the victim, eighteen to twenty-five maybe? Handsome, attractive to a young girl. He's dangerous, but fits in. He revels in the humiliation and control of his victims."

"Have you considered being a criminal profiler, Kat?" Parker asked.

"I watch *Criminal Minds*," Kat said sarcastically.

"He's definitely a sociopath," Tiffany said. "And if you haven't made the connection yet, he thinks of the victims as stand-ins for someone else. They're victims only because in one way or another, they reminded him of someone." Tiffany stretched her shoulders.

Parker stood, then shook her hand. "You have been a tremendous help. Thank you both.

"Does this have anything to do with the murder a few blocks over?" Kat asked.

"What murder?" Tiffany asked. "Oh, that's right. You said this reading might help with something recent. Do you think they're connected?"

"I'm not at liberty to say anything right now."

"I understand," Tiffany said. "Please call me if you think I can assist again."

Parker handed her a card. "And you do the same if you pick up anything else."

Tiffany nodded. "I hope you catch him before that happens again. It was a brutal slaughter that I hope not to relive. He's not done."

Kat showed Parker to the door. Tiffany got up from the table and headed toward the hallway on her way to the bathroom. Kat met her just outside the door.

"How are you feeling? That was pretty intense," Kat said.

"Drained and dirty. How about you?"

"Honestly? Tiffany, I don't know. It was rough watching you go through that, and knowing that you were reliving what those girls went through."

"It wasn't seeing the murders so much as realizing I connected with the killer. I didn't realize I had until you said something." That was worrisome. His energy snuck through Tiffany's shields without her knowing. It was definitely something that needed to be addressed.

Kat pulled her into a hug. After a few seconds, Tiffany took a step back. "I can't right now. All I can see is the murders. I need to get rid of the remnant energy and break the connection."

"I was offering comfort, not trying to seduce you."

"Oh." *Why not?* Tiffany was irked that the question even popped into her head at all. She was tired and apparently cranky too. She would feel much better in her own environment.

"Do you want to take a shower or bath?"

"Actually, I want to go home now." Kat didn't possess any of the oils or candles that Tiffany preferred to use in her cleansing rituals.

"Oh." A fleeting look of disappointment crossed Kat's features.

"You don't have to drive me. I can catch the ferry across."

"No, please. I want to. We can drive the Interstate around to Bremerton. But we might want to wait for a while. Rush hour is starting. The traffic will be insane."

"I didn't realize it was that late. Of course." Tiffany was relieved. There was no way she wanted to return home on a crowded boat after two readings. She would feel too exposed and vulnerable. Besides, she didn't have enough psychic energy left to hold any shields in place. She excused herself and closed the bathroom door behind her.

Tiffany hoped she'd given Parker something he could use, but found she was sad his visit interrupted her date with Kat, and left her with this awful feeling in her stomach.

She tried to think about what the reading was like from Kat's point of view. She'd witnessed three sessions now, but she hadn't brought up the past again. She wanted to believe her gift wouldn't destroy her budding relationship with Kat, but what if it was too late?

CHAPTER NINE

K at kept her eyes on the busy interstate but couldn't resist frequently looking over at Tiffany, sleeping in the passenger seat.

She was seriously reconsidering her interest in the cold case files if this was the result of having Tiffany work on them. She wanted to move away from the violence in the city, not dive back into it. But there was something about being able to help that still grabbed at her. She felt the same when she had been helping Jordan search for the runaways that disappeared from the streets.

She'd enjoyed her day with Tiffany, but regretted that they hadn't talked yet about Kat's visions of the past. The issue seemed to be sidestepped. She wondered if that was such a bad thing. Still, she wanted to share her dreams with Tiffany.

Kat thought it would be torturous to not project what Tanna looked like naked over Tiffany's body, to not lay her down and show her how much she was cherished. But the more time she spent with her, the more tiny differences began to show. They may look the same and have the same gentle spirit, but there hadn't been a shy bone in Tanna's body.

Then again, Kat wasn't the warrior either. Her vivid memories may stir her blood and twist her emotions, but they weren't real in this life. It was enough to drive her crazy.

Tiffany sighed and the sound shot straight to Kat's core. She shifted in her seat.

It was dark by the time she pulled into the driveway. There were no lights on in the house. Tiffany opened the door. "Thank you for the ride. I can't believe I keep falling asleep on you. Please don't think I'm rude. This is unusual even for me." She looked as if she might say more, but got out of the car.

Kat didn't wait for an invitation. She followed her up the path. Tiffany rustled in her purse for her keys. When she inserted the key, the door opened before she unlocked it. A small chill ran up Kat's neck.

"I know I locked that door," Tiffany said and pulled her cell phone out of her pocket. "I never forget."

"Wait," Kat said. "Let me go first." She opened the door slowly and then reached in to flip the hall light on. Tiffany came in right behind her.

"It doesn't feel right in here."

"Does anything look different?"

"I can't tell yet. I'll go check the kitchen."

"No, we go together." Kat reached back to hold Tiffany's hand. "Ready?"

They walked down the hall, toward the bedrooms, checked each closet, and Angel's pretty little room. There was no sign of an actual intruder, but Kat could feel Tiffany's tension.

The door was closed to the master bedroom. They stood in front of it and stared at each other. "Okay," Kat said, then turned the knob.

Tiffany pressed past her. "It looks the same as I left it, but it doesn't feel right."

Since Kat had firsthand knowledge how Tiffany's gift worked, she was more than ready to take her word for it. But she had no idea how to deal with an invisible intruder. "Can you see the person?"

Tiffany shook her head. "No." She crossed to the dresser and ran her hand along the edge. "There's just this weird buzzing. We still have the guest room to check."

Kat followed Tiffany who stopped next to the bed. "See? It looks like someone laid here." The pillow had an indentation; the covers were slightly mussed.

"Burglars don't usually hang around to take a nap," Kat said.

Tiffany walked to the window. "Look, it's unlocked. God, this is creeping me out."

Kat went up behind her to flip the lock closed. After a moment's hesitation, she wrapped her arms around Tiffany, pulling her close. She held her breath, waiting for her to draw away, but she leaned back into the embrace. Kat pressed her cheek against her hair, swaying slightly on her feet, rocking her gently. "Do you want to call the police?"

"No. There doesn't seem to be anything missing. I could be wrong. I've been so exhausted over the last few days." Tiffany laughed nervously. "If I didn't know any better, I'd say I was pregnant."

The statement hit Kat hard and deep. She hadn't considered that Tiffany would be seeing anyone else. "Is that a possibility?"

"Um, not unless somebody up there is handing out immaculate conceptions again."

The sound of rustling bushes, a cracking branch, and a loud thumping noise on the side of the house reverberated in the room and rattled the window in its frame.

Kat looked at Tiffany. "Stay here." She headed for the door and wished she had a weapon. "Call 911."

"It's okay. It's just the raccoons," Tiffany said. "We have a family of them in the neighborhood. They've been busy the last week or so."

"That didn't sound like a small animal to me."

"How would you know? They don't exactly forage on the seventeenth floor."

Kat laughed. "Touché." She returned to where Tiffany stood by the bed and drew her close again. "Still, I'd rather not leave you alone." Whether the danger was real or perceived, the thought of Tiffany being hurt sent a sharp pain through Kat's temples.

Tiffany accepted her embrace then stepped back. "I'm just jumpy, you know? It could be the violence attached to the readings. I could have forgotten to lock the door. I was in a hurry to get to Seattle."

"Yeah?" The statement warmed Kat. "I'm going to check the yard anyway. I'll be back in a minute."

"I'm going to take a bath." She turned then looked over her shoulder at Kat. "Will you be here when I get out?"

Kat's mouth went dry. "Is that an invitation?"

Tiffany smiled at her. "Help yourself to anything in the kitchen. Make yourself at home."

Kat headed for the backyard, but the anticipation she felt at Tiffany's smoldering look made her want to jump in the bath instead. But she knew Tiffany needed the downtime. She made her way to the back door, but didn't turn on the porch light when she got there. She didn't want to make herself a target. She let her eyes adjust to the dim glow of a nearby streetlight then crept around the house to look under the windows for any sign of a person. After five minutes, she felt ridiculous. She had no idea what she was doing. She lived in a concrete jungle, and the only tracking experience she thought she had came from watching television.

She sat in the porch swing and listened to the night. It was much quieter in the residential neighborhood; she was used to the high volume in the city. She could smell spring in the air, and it took her back home. Kat wondered if she could adjust to living here. She wasn't pacing, she wasn't watching television, or listening to a radio, or in any way distracting herself from her thoughts.

She didn't feel as if she were in a hurry to get somewhere, or *waiting* for anything to happen. She watched the stars and continued swinging until her phone sang on her hip.

Kat smiled. "What's up, Jordan?"

"Hey. Do you know where Tiffany is?"

"Yeah. I'm here at her house. We just got back."

"Sunny is worried. She hadn't heard from her today."

"Parker showed up at my place and asked her to read for him."

"How is she doing?"

Kat had expected Jordan to ask about the cases first, but clearly Jordan had changed more than she thought she had. "She's fine now. I didn't realize how much these readings would drain her. I'm not on board with that." Kat heard Jordan sigh.

"Sunny told me you kissed Tiffany."

"Yes. I did." *And I plan on giving her a hundred more tonight.*
Silence.

"Look," Jordan finally said. "I know you're not out to hurt anyone; it's not your style. But Tiffany is different, you know? She's like Sunny. They feel everything to the tenth degree."

"I'm learning that."

"So, what I'm telling you is—tread softly. If you don't mean to stick around, leave her be."

"I appreciate your concern, but isn't that between me and Tiffany?"

Jordan laughed. "No, it's not. If you're involved with any of the sisters, you're linked with all three of them. They're connected at the hips. And you haven't even met Angel yet. Tiffany isn't one of your career city girls. She's a single mom."

"I'm perfectly aware of that." Kat stood to pace the yard. But when she got up, she inhaled the scent of freshly mowed grass, and sat back down. "I feel different about her, Jordan. She makes me think of home." *In more ways than one.*

"Just please, whatever you do, don't hurt her."

"That is the farthest thing from my mind."

"I don't know what else to say right now," Jordan said. "I'll let Sunny know that Tiffany's okay. Tell her we called."

"I'll do that," Kat said. She disconnected and continued swinging while she looked up at the stars. For the first time in too long, she was dreaming of what her future could be, instead of what it had been.

Tiffany stood at the mirror and braided her wet hair. It had taken much longer to get into her cleansing, meditative state than usual, and she placed the blame squarely on Kat. God, the way she looked at her literally made her weak. It was hard to concentrate and put herself into a relaxing state when Kat kept appearing to her—naked.

It excited her to know Kat was waiting for her outside that door. Tiffany felt shy but looked forward to seeing where this evening was going to go. She didn't know if Kat would be gentle and soft or—

Hard and violent like Mark.

Where the hell had that come from? Tiffany grabbed the thought and shoved it back into the lead-lined box in her mind.

She settled herself by putting on lotion, and after brief consideration, some light makeup. After she was done, she looked at the final result. Two faint images appeared briefly in the mirror. Theresa and Hailey…they looked very similar to each other. Tiffany knew they weren't ghosts, just remnants of her thoughts. This was unusual. She had never had any readings leak back into her mind after she'd had her ritual bath before.

Tiffany's heart rate picked up slightly. They had the same bone structure, the same eyes.

That's really creepy, she thought. They almost look like…me. She dismissed the idea. Thousands of girls looked like her. It was only a coincidence. She lit the two white candles on the counter and drew additional white light around her to dispel the images and any more traces of the readings. She finally left the safety of the bathroom and found Kat in the living room on the couch.

"Do you feel better now?"

"Yes, thank you."

"Are you hungry?"

Tiffany watched Kat's focus travel her bare legs before looking at her face. "Starving."

Uh oh. "I can order pizza."

"Whatever you want," Kat said.

Tiffany crossed into the kitchen area where her phone and the number to a place that delivered was. "How do you like it?"

"Loaded."

"Oh, good. Me too." Tiffany called the restaurant and ordered. "Would you like a glass of wine?"

Kat stood and walked to where Tiffany stood. That flutter low in her belly reappeared and she took a quick inhale of breath before turning to find the wine and glasses. "Red okay?"

"Anything you have is fine, really." Tiffany felt the heat of Kat's body behind her and she nearly fumbled the crystal. "I've never actually used these before. I was saving them for a special occasion."

"Then I'm glad it's me," Kat said.

Her breath was so close it warmed Tiffany's cheek. She finished pouring and handed Kat a glass. Tiffany felt her nerves grow stronger than her desire. She took a step back and began to fill the silence. "I don't normally drink. I'm a bit of a lightweight."

"I'll take care of you."

"That's what I'm afraid of." Tiffany surprised herself with her quick response. She thought she was past being unsure and afraid. She looked away, and one of Angel's drawings on the refrigerator caught her eye. When she saw it, she felt her confusion drain away. That's what she was afraid of. It was nice to have a fantasy while Angel was at the beach. But in reality she had so many concerns about what could really happen if she pursued a relationship with Kat.

Tiffany didn't have it in her to have a casual encounter. Angel was everything, and nothing in the world would convince Tiffany to cause her daughter any discomfort. Angel connected with people in a way she'd never seen, and grew attached to them very quickly. What would happen if Kat came into their world then disappeared? It would leave Tiffany feeling guilty and horrible if she were the cause of any pain in their lives.

"Hey," Kat said. "Where did you go?"

"What? Oh, sorry. I was thinking. We need to talk."

Kat put her wine glass down. "After."

Tiffany wondered how Kat had so efficiently backed her against the counter again. Hadn't she been farther away? Tiffany was glad for the support when Kat cupped her face, lowered her head, and laid her lips over hers.

She tasted of wine, and it was the sweetest kiss Tiffany ever had. The gentleness in it surprised her. It wasn't the hot, heavy, I'm going to take you on the floor, kiss she'd expected. The emotions coming up for her were from a much softer place.

Kat let her kiss linger for a moment before she stood straight again, then sipped her wine. "Now we can talk. I've wanted to do that all day."

Tiffany was flustered all over again. "Um, right. Let's go back into the living room."

Kat sat near but not too close, and Tiffany appreciated it. She didn't know where to start. Did she lay her doubts on the table, or take a chance? Ask about her visions, or wait until Kat told her? This was crazy.

Kat's hand waved in front of her. "You know you have to talk to me with your out-loud voice, right?"

Tiffany laughed. The humorous remark broke the ice for her. "Yes. But I don't know where to start."

"Relax, start with your biggest concerns, and we'll go from there."

"See? That's what I'm talking about. What planet did you come from?" Tiffany asked. "You don't do anything I expect you to, then you say things that cut straight to my heart. I don't know what to do with you."

"Try me?" Kat asked.

Tiffany felt the heat in her cheeks. "Nice. But seriously. You're not like anyone I've ever been with. Let me rephrase that." She took a deep breath. "I've actually only been with one person in my life."

"Angel's father," Kat said. "So is it being with a woman that's confusing you, or is it me?"

"I'm insanely attracted to you. That's not the issue. I can't always read your thoughts, and that scares me a little."

"Why? I can't read yours either. It kind of levels the playing field."

"You don't understand," Tiffany said. "I couldn't read Mark's either."

"What does that have to do with me?"

The doorbell rang. "It's the pizza," Tiffany said.

"I'll get it." Kat stood and headed for the door.

"Let me get my wallet."

"I said I have it."

Tiffany went to the kitchen to get plates and napkins, though she wasn't hungry anymore. Kat came in and set the box on the table. "That right there is the problem."

"What's a problem? I put the pizza down? Would you rather I put it on the counter?"

"No."

Kat looked very confused. "I have no idea what you want from me right now."

The remark made Tiffany sad. "See? I don't know how to have a normal conversation. Or relationship, for that matter."

"We can start there. Tell me why you think that." Kat sat down and put a slice on Tiffany's plate then her own.

"You're so damn reasonable."

"And that's a bad thing?"

"No." Tiffany sighed. "It's completely foreign to me." She stared at her plate before taking a bite. "I met Mark when I was sixteen and he was nineteen. He was impossibly pretty and charming. I was different from the other kids, because of—well, you know."

"How old were you when your gifts began to show?"

"I was five or six when I began answering questions before they were asked or would tell a person what they were thinking. I have no idea where the ability came from. My mother didn't have any that I knew of, and her answer to all of it was to try to beat it out of me."

Kat stopped chewing and put her fork down. "That's horrible."

"I don't want to make this a long, drawn out sob story about how my mother hated me and thought I was possessed by the devil."

"But it set your foundation of who you thought yourself to be and what you might be capable of in life."

Tiffany thought that what she said was much like something her counselor would have. "So when I met Mark and I realized I couldn't read him, for some reason, I thought that was a good thing—like it was meant to be. He lavished attention on me, told me how pretty I was, how much he wanted me. It was heady stuff."

"Especially for a young girl who wasn't loved at home."

"We dated for a couple of weeks or so before Shade and Sunny finally met him. They pulled me out of the club we were in, and the three of us got in a horrible fight. I was awful to them, Shade especially. It was days before either of them would talk to me again. Shade explained she had been only trying to warn me because she sensed evil around him."

"Did you listen?"

"Yes. It broke my heart, but I broke up with him. When my aunt Darleen paid for my college, I moved back to Seattle."

"What was your major?"

Tiffany smiled. "Medicine. I wanted to be a surgical nurse. Do you really want to know all the details?"

Kat's eyes were clear and focused on her. "I want to know everything about you."

"I didn't want to be a doctor. I thought that being a nurse would allow me to use my healing gift in a more subtle way. I found a small room near campus. I loved everything about school. No one knew me, or about my home life. I felt free and brand new, you know? I missed Sunny and Shade terribly, but for once, I felt independent."

"Where were they?"

"They were attending college together in another state. I was in my junior year when I ran into Mark again at a restaurant and he asked me out. I can look back and know that when I stood at that crossroad, I made the biggest mistake of my life."

"You're being awfully hard on yourself. Hindsight is a wonderfully cursed lens to look at your past through."

Tiffany didn't know why the story was flowing so easy from her without any of the usual pain. She thought it might be the compassion Kat was showing and her incredibly insightful remarks. "I can see all the red flags I ignored. Eventually, I dropped out of school. My mother moved here to Seattle and fell in love with him. The two of them ganged up on me until I was convinced I should be *grateful* for their attention because I was so stupid and flawed. I played right into their hands."

"But you're not. You're smart and beautiful, and anyone would be lucky to have *your* attention," Kat said. "Sorry for interrupting. Go ahead and finish."

"Long story short, we were together a year before I married him. Then it got worse."

"How long were you married?"

"Three years. During those years, it was so damn hard to reconcile the man I thought I loved with the monster he became."

"Where were your friends through this?"

"I didn't want them to see the mess I'd made of my life. Especially since Shade had warned me. They begged me to leave him, but when I did, he just dragged me right back. He threatened them, you see. I couldn't let them be hurt."

Kat leaned forward, her voice barely above a whisper. "How did you get out of it?"

"One day, after a beating, I came to in a puddle of blood in the kitchen. It wasn't that the situation was unusual, it had happened before, but this time I was pregnant. I didn't know that yet officially, but I felt Angel's little light inside me. I crawled to the phone and called the police. He tried to break me while we were married, and when that didn't work, he tried to kill me."

"What happened?"

"He received a plea deal for nine years."

Kat slapped the table. "That's all?"

"I know, right?" Tiffany tried not to think of what she'd do when he got out, but she still had a few years to plan for it. For now, she was done talking about him.

"Anyway, I moved back here and had Angel. I joined Sunny's business with Shade and started over. They're all the family I need."

"I'm so sorry that you went through that horrendous situation."

"All I've done is talk about me. Now you know how damaged I am and that I make crappy decisions." Tiffany didn't know how she felt about baring her life like that, but she did feel lighter for doing so. She yawned. She may feel better, but she was tired again.

Kat kept eye contact with her but remained silent.

"Say something, please," Tiffany said.

"You got out alive. I call that amazing. I think it's tragic that the woman who was supposed to love you, didn't, and the man who promised to cherish you, wouldn't."

"I don't want to have a pity party. I just wanted you to understand where I was coming from."

Kat took their plates to the dishwasher and loaded them. Then she came back and drew Tiffany to her feet. "Oh, honey, I don't want to feel sorry for you. I want to show you what love is. What it should feel like."

Tiffany's emotional response tightened her throat, and she felt tears prickle behind her eyes. No one had ever said anything remotely like that to her before. But there was another hitch under her hope. And that was she still knew virtually nothing about Kat. If they were connected through time, how come she didn't remember this amazing woman? "We haven't talked about your dreams."

Kat took her hand. "It's been a very long day for both of us. How about we get you settled in your room first?"

Tiffany waited until they were halfway down the hall. "Kat?"

"Yes?"

She took a deep breath. "Will you stay with me tonight?"

"Yes."

❖

Kat understood now why Tiffany's circle was so strong. She was infuriated by the abuse she'd learned of, but tried to keep her temper in check for Tiffany's sake. The fact that she dove right into the homicide cases showed incredible strength. The way she came up and out of that situation to create this comfortable home for Angel was humbling for Kat.

She'd had it so easy in comparison.

As much as Tanna meant to her dreams, Tiffany was well on her way to etching herself over the memories. Kat didn't want to talk about the past anymore tonight. That was a revelation in itself. She'd been waiting to relive it, but now found herself wanting to move forward. When she came out of the bathroom, Tiffany was sitting on her bed looking down at her hands. Kat's heart filled with tenderness. She wanted to wrap her up and make the hurt go away.

She certainly didn't want to feel as if she took advantage of Tiffany when she was vulnerable. The telling of her story had to have left her feeling drained.

Kat walked to other side and took her jeans off, then slid under the comforter in her underwear. "Come here," she said. Tiffany got in beside her, and Kat wrapped her arm around her, pulling her close and enjoying the feeling of Tiffany's head resting on her shoulder.

Tiffany sighed before snuggling next to her. "Aren't we—"

"Shh. Close your eyes. Rest now." Kat kissed her forehead. She stroked her back, and it wasn't long before Tiffany's breathing became deeper. She looked down at her face and whispered softly so as not to wake her. "Sweet dreams."

Kat thought it would take a long time to fall asleep, but she felt herself begin to drift off and dream of an ancient forest.

A twig snapped behind her, and Kat turned toward the sound. She caught a flash of red tresses flying before they disappeared behind the tree on the left. She went in that direction, quiet as she could, placing each foot lightly as she stepped. She could hear her breathing now.

She felt flushed with anticipation, the thrill of the chase exciting her even as the scent of her prey heated her blood. It felt like she had waited for this night for most of her life. The rituals were nearly done, the chase was on, but the spoken vows remained. Tiffany had stayed ahead of her for hours, and the dawn was just a couple of hours away. If she didn't catch her before then, it meant that Tiffany denied her petition.

One more step, and she could pounce. She went around the tree and her heart stuttered. There in the light of the full moon, Tiffany let her white cloak drop to the grass. She stood naked, her arms raised. An offering to the Goddess, giving permission to be caught.

Kat took the last steps and dropped to her knees. She took in the sight of Tiffany's perfection and gave thanks. She'd loved her since she could remember, and now, in this moment, that love was unbearably beautiful.

Tiffany's breasts rose and fell with her uneven breathing, drawing Kat's attention to her nipples. She held herself still, but Kat felt her tremble. She'd dreamt of this night for so long. This was not the exploration of childhood, the fumbling of young girls who explored each other. This was her woman, her mate, chosen by the Goddess. This was everything. She would die for her.

Tiffany's sweet scent surrounded her, and the cool night air did nothing to lessen her lust. The pounding in Kat's heart spread until her entire body pulsed with the pure wanting of her.

"You have caught me, warrior. Do what you will."

"You humble me, priestess. It is you who has conquered me." Kat's voice hitched and she looked up at her.

Tiffany's eyes sparkled. "Love me then. Tonight is ours."

"Forever is ours," Kat said, then drew Tiffany down on the cloak beside her. Fierce love filled her heart. "I will love you until the end of time."

CHAPTER TEN

K at woke and found herself neatly tucked in and alone in the bed. She stretched and recalled her dream. She'd always loved that particular one, chasing Tiffany down in the woods. She hesitated for second. She meant Tanna.

No, this morning she could clearly recall the scar Tiffany had along her hairline that Tanna didn't have.

She wasn't sure yet how this was all going to work, but she did know that if she forced the situation into what she thought it should be, she would be selling them both short.

Kat sat up and noticed her jeans had been folded and placed on a chaise in the corner. There were a pair of large porcelain cats on the dresser, and two more in a grouping in the corner alongside a plant. She grinned. Maybe Tiffany did have some kind of subconscious thing for her. She just hadn't brought it to the surface.

She heard the sound of a cupboard door shutting in the kitchen and she smelled coffee brewing. She pulled on her jeans and walked out of the bedroom.

Tiffany looked up when she entered and gave her a sunny smile. "Good morning."

Kat stopped. The moment struck her as another important one. She wanted to stretch it out and enjoy it. Kat was still feeling the heat from her dream. "You take my breath away."

Tiffany blushed. "I don't even know what to say to that. Thank you?" She motioned for Kat to sit. "How do you take your coffee?"

"Black."

Tiffany poured her a cup then sat across from her. "Thank you for last night."

"I didn't do anything." *But I wanted to.*

"You most certainly did."

"Tiffany," Kat said. "You may be getting the wrong idea about me."

"Why do you say that?"

"I don't want to be just your friend. I'm not looking for sainthood here."

Tiffany grinned. "Oh, believe me. The things that I've thought about doing to you would have had my mother throwing holy water on me."

Kat laughed. "How did you sleep last night, sinner?" *Whew.*

"I dreamt I was being chased in the woods."

"Did you ever see who was behind you?" Kat wanted to hold her breath while she waited for the answer. They'd had the same dream and that had to mean something.

Tiffany shook her head. "It's an old nightmare that I've had off and on for years. I have to run, the urgency and fear builds until I think my heart is going to stop. I hate it."

Kat wavered. How could something that brought her such happiness bring Tiffany something completely different? She opened her mouth to say something, but Tiffany's phone rang and she got up to answer it.

"Hang on," Tiffany said. "It's one of my regular clients. I'll be back."

"It was me," Kat said softly as Tiffany went out the back door. "I was chasing you."

Someone knocked on the front door, but before she could ask Tiffany whether she should answer it, the lock clicked and Shade walked in.

"What are you doing here?" Shade looked down at Kat's bare feet.

Her snarly tone prickled Kat's temper, but she kept her cool. "Drinking coffee. Want some?"

"Where's Tiff?"

"Outside, on the phone." Kat slowly and deliberately sat back down, conveying by action she didn't feel at all threatened or feel the need to defend her position at the table. The now-familiar sensation tingled along her scalp. She put an image in her head of a gate slamming closed and was ridiculously pleased when Shade startled.

"Nice trick."

"I learned it a long time ago when I was doing a story on mind control." Kat shoved her irritation down. She didn't want to alienate her. Frankly, and Kat wasn't too proud to admit it, Shade could be a little scary.

"You don't even want to know." Shade grinned at her wolfishly and slid into a seat at the table.

Kat kept her face neutral but still felt like a small chill nonetheless. "Are we going to have a problem?"

"Only if you hurt her."

"It's not my intention."

"I know. You were a little slow on the draw."

"Then what's with the pissing contest?"

"I like you." Shade laughed. "Habit. She's my little sister, and it's my job to protect her."

"Can't fault you for that." Kat hadn't realized how much she missed having female companionship since Jordan moved away from Seattle. There were phone calls and e-mails and such, but the face-to-face, sit down and have a cup of coffee days, were few and far between. It was another check on the pro side for leaving her high-pressure job. Kat was happy to trade corporate sharks for psychics and screwed up political bullshit for clans of warrior maidens.

"What are you grinning at?" Shade said.

"It's a beautiful day," Kat said. She noticed Shade's eyes were still bruised from the attack, but the thick eyeliner worked with it. She wasn't wearing a bandage, and her hair covered the staples. "How's your head?"

"It's healing fast," Shade said. "Sunny did one of her numbers on me, and I'm hoping Tiffany can take this goddamn headache away. It's screwing with my equilibrium."

"They find the guy yet?"

Shade shook her head. "No, and Beenie's left town. Otherwise, I'd be able to find her."

Tiffany came in the back door. "Good morning." She crossed straight to Shade.

Kat saw her search for the wound and then lay gentle hands on Shade's head. Shade's eyes closed and she laid her head back on Tiffany's chest.

Kat wasn't prepared for the rush of jealousy that hit her. She held herself still and grappled with the unfamiliar emotion for a moment. She knew it was unreasonable and uncalled for. That's what made it feel worse. She got up to refill her coffee to distract herself.

Sunny came barreling in the front door with Jordan right behind her. "Why haven't you called me?"

"Ssh," Tiffany said. "I'm almost done."

Jordan winked at Kat, who tried to shake her head subtly, which caught Sunny's attention and she narrowed her eyes at her.

Way to go, Jordan. Now I'm her target. Sunny tilted her head to the right, but Kat shut the gate in her mind just as she had with Shade. Sunny lifted an eyebrow, and the corners of her mouth turned up slightly. "Impressive."

"Got any coffee?" Jordan asked and headed for the pot.

Kat looked around the room. Yes, she'd trade the newsroom for this crowd any day. "I'll make another pot."

Tiffany half-listened to Kat go over the details of the cases she'd done yesterday with Jordan, Shade, and Sunny while she opened the curtains in the living room to let the sun in. She continued through the rest of the house. She picked up a toy in the hall and dropped it off in Angel's room on her way to her own.

She bent to smooth the comforter on the bed. The room carried Kat's forest scent, and it tickled her. She stopped. It was almost the same as in her nightmare. She looked inward for the details. The smell of trees and lush greenery while she ran. The feel of loose leaves and pine needles under her feet. The sound of her heartbeat racing in her ears.

She tried to remember more, but the harder she concentrated, the more it slipped away. She must be recalling the scent because she'd been curled up next to Kat.

She certainly didn't have any reason to be scared of Kat. The moment she thought it, her heart rate picked up. Funny how desire and fear felt so similar. She'd have to think more on that later.

She heard Kat laughing at something Sunny said and finished making the bed. Tiffany went to rejoin them.

Jordan was sprawled on the floor in front of Sunny who sat on the end of the loveseat. Shade was sitting on an armchair with one leg hanging over the side. Kat sat on the sectional, and Tiffany thought she looked like she completely belonged in this happy family picture.

A cold breeze slapped at her and she gasped before turning to find the source. The conversation in the room stopped and all four women jumped to their feet.

"What is it?" Jordan asked.

"Nothing good." Shade crossed the room in unison with Kat to reach Tiffany's side.

"It's gone," Sunny said. "I caught the tail end of the energy trail, but it left immediately."

"How did it get past the protection we've set up?" Tiffany asked.

"It was strong enough to break the barrier but not stay. We'll have to reset it." Shade frowned and disappeared down the hall to the back room.

Tiffany's knees were weak and she wanted to sit down. Kat helped her to the couch. "Are you all right?"

"Yes, I'm fine. It just surprised the hell out of me."

Sunny sat next to her and took her hands before closing her eyes. When she opened them, she looked worried. "How have you been feeling lately?"

Tiffany shrugged. "Fine, why?"

"You haven't been tired or feeling drained?"

"Yes, but that's nothing unusual for me considering what I've been doing this last week."

Sunny looked at Kat. "Have you noticed anything unusual?"

"She falls asleep a lot, but I thought it was because of the stress she experiences during the readings."

As Tiffany watched Kat, she had an epiphany. She *had* been nodding off, and it began right about the time she met Kat.

"Anything else? Mood changes, the feeling of being followed?"

"Me?" Kat asked. "I thought you were asking about Tiffany?"

"Both of you."

"What do you see?" Tiffany asked. "You're kind of scaring me."

"There's dark energy around both of you, and I don't understand why I didn't immediately pick up on it. It's very subtle, but deep."

Tiffany shivered. "Why couldn't I sense it?"

"It might be because of this," Shade returned from the back of the house. She held up a small dirty box.

"What the fuck is it?" Jordan asked.

"Where did you find that?" Tiffany got up to look at it. "I've never seen it before."

"It was hiding in your closet."

"How did you know that?" Kat asked.

Shade gave her an impatient look. "I don't know, because I'm psychic and can feel dark energy?"

Tiffany reached for the box. "Here, let me see it."

"No," Shade snapped. "Don't touch it. Matter of fact, somebody please open the goddamn door."

"I will," Jordan said.

Tiffany felt Kat come up behind her and insinuate her body between the box and Tiffany before Shade took it outside. She wasn't even going to pretend that she didn't appreciate the protective gesture. She held her hand and led her back to the couch.

"Light the candles," Sunny said. "I'm going to get your sage."

Tiffany explained to Kat what they were doing while they cleared and blessed the house. Shade looked a little pale when she came back in as they all gathered again in the living room.

"What is it?" Tiffany asked. Shade swallowed, and Tiffany could see she was trying to choose her words carefully. "Please, just spit it out."

"It's a curse."

Sunny gasped, Jordan looked stunned, and Kat's expression was stoic. Tiffany looked at them and began to tremble slightly. "Did I hear that right?"

Shade looked grim. "Yes."

"How? I mean why?"

"That had to be why the door was unlocked when we arrived last night," Kat said.

"What?" Jordan stood. "Why didn't you tell me?"

"Because I told her it was nothing. I could have forgotten to lock it," Tiffany said.

"That's not like you," Sunny said. "At all."

"We will definitely come back to that, but for now, let's retrace," Shade said. "When did you first start noticing things were off?"

"When I met her." Tiffany felt Kat startle next to her. "My nightmares came back."

"You must be connected to this," Shade said to Kat.

"I don't have anything to do with a curse." Kat turned to Tiffany. "I swear."

Tiffany didn't think she did, but was still left with a seed of doubt. "I've dreamt of witches and curses for most of my life. When you first met me, you said you knew me, but we haven't talked about it yet."

"We haven't had a chance. The first time I tried to talk about it you said you didn't want to talk about anything paranormal, remember?"

Tiffany did remember telling her that at lunch. Kat had been so good to her and Tiffany hated that she'd gone pale and looked so uncertain. But she'd been snowed and misled before. She began to feel nauseated with implications.

"Kat," Sunny said. "The first time I met you I noticed an old and ancient energy, but I never did place it."

"You have gifts?" Jordan asked. "How come I don't know that?"

"Look," Shade said. "We're not going to gang up on Kat. I said she was connected, not responsible. The best thing here is to find out how she ties into it and not put her on the defense."

"That's different for you," Jordan said. "Usually you're the first to attack."

"I like *her*." Shade turned her back on Jordan. "Would you mind if we read you?"

"Not at all," Kat answered. "If it will help and put everyone's mind at rest, let's do it now."

Tiffany was unsure. "Wait. We just had negative energy blow through and found a box with a curse in it. I don't think it's smart to do this here." She was much more concerned with how the box got into the house in the first place. She was royally pissed off she didn't feel safe in her own house. That her baby could be threatened in any way caused her temper to boil.

On the heels of that thought came another, then one more. The fog of denial that had surrounded her for days began to lift just as she felt another chill.

"It's Mark."

❖

Kat looked around at the group. Everyone stared at Tiffany, frozen in place. "What's Mark?"

"The phone calls, noises outside, and the break-in."

"What phone calls and noises?" Sunny asked.

"Hang up calls, the raccoons, the unlocked door, and apparently, the cursed box."

"Why didn't you tell anyone?" Shade asked.

"I was going to, but it's been a busy week. Then with your attack—"

"Wait. Could that be related?" Jordan asked.

"It might be, but things are still fuzzy," Shade said. "I can't see it clearly."

"Okay, I'm confused," Kat said. "Isn't he in prison?"

Jordan took out her phone. "I'll find out." She left the room.

"We never could read his energy," Sunny said. "It was always foggy and unclear."

"Which is exactly how I've felt," Tiffany said. "God, I feel stupid. Why didn't we ever realize he was blocking us from seeing it?"

"Which means he's very good at it. I mean, we should have felt a trace, at least," Shade said.

"Omigod, someone slammed into me on the ferry. It was him." She turned to Kat. "Remember the dark energy in the crystal store?"

Kat stroked her back. "We don't know it's him, and I'm not going to let anything happen to you."

He'll never get through me. Kat's shoulders tightened. *No one will ever take her from me again.*

Shade looked at Kat. "Again?"

Kat wanted to tell the story, but a clear sense of danger was building in the living room. Sunny and Tiffany got to their feet alongside Shade when Jordan came back in. "He was released last week."

Kat felt Tiffany sway next to her and pulled her closer. "How come they didn't call her? Isn't there a law about that?"

"Sometimes they slip through the cracks. Let me call the department and see what we can do."

"I can't stay here," Tiffany said. "He's already been in my house." Her face paled. "Angel." She ran for her phone.

Kat began pacing the room. She didn't know what to do and had no plan other than protect Tiffany. She considered telling the group about the feeling of being followed home a couple of nights ago, but decided against it. She didn't want to scare Tiffany any more than she already was.

"Let's get some clothes for Tiffany and Angel," Sunny said. "They can stay with us until this is over."

"She'd be safer at my place," Kat said. "I'm in a high-rise with security. No one can get at them there."

"But Shade, Jordan, and I can protect her."

"I think Kat is right," Jordan said. "Would we even want to take that chance with their safety?"

Tiffany returned. "Aura just got home with Angel. They're fine."

"Everyone's arguing about whose house you're going to," Shade said. "But it's mine, right?"

"No, I don't want to put any of you at risk. We can leave town and stay at a hotel."

"That's ridiculous. You can stay with me," Kat said. She wasn't going to let her leave, and she wasn't going to take her eyes off her.

"Honey." Sunny put an arm around Tiffany. "As much as I want you to stay with me, my intuition is telling me for you to go with Kat."

"Actually, I feel that too," Tiffany said. "I'll go pack a couple of bags."

As soon as she left, Sunny turned to Shade. "What was in that box?"

Shade curled her lip. "Dirty material, small bones, and several different types of hair."

Sunny paled. "Blood magic?"

Shade nodded. "Yup. But I didn't want to tell you with Tiffany in the room."

Kat felt a cold chill run up her spine. "Why wouldn't you tell her?"

"I wanted to disarm it first."

"You make it sound like a bomb," Kat said. "Besides, don't curses only work on people who believe in them?"

"It was Tiffany's hair," Shade said. "An individual's hair holds their essence, their energy. It's a very powerful tool in dark magic when combined with blood. Now that I know it's from Mark, I'm even more worried about it."

"Wait. You couldn't read him, but now you can. How does that work?"

Sunny interrupted. "It must be some kind of spell he cast, kind of a cross between invisibility and confusion. Once we saw past the deception, it collapsed in the center."

"Would that explain Tiffany's bad headaches and exhaustion?"

"It would," Shade said. "So we're not only dealing with a sadistic stalking asshole, we're dealing with someone who knows dark magic."

Kat felt a little disoriented. Everything was happening so fast, it left her reeling. Her most important task was to keep Tiffany and Angel safe. She had no idea how to deal with the paranormal witchy stuff, so she would have to leave that in Sunny's and Shade's capable hands.

She couldn't help but flash on the day Tanna died. She never wanted to relive that pain—not in any lifetime.

When Tiffany appeared with her suitcases looking pale and a little frightened, Kat's temper spiked. She could kill him for that alone.

"I need some things from my office," Tiffany said after she shut the trunk of Kat's car.

"I'll get whatever you need," Sunny said. "Jordan and I will bring it to you at Mom's house."

"Won't you need a list?" Kat asked.

Sunny smirked at her. "Please."

"I'll meet you over there." Shade turned to get into her van.

Tiffany looked up and down the street nervously. If Mark were watching her, she didn't see anything out of the ordinary. But that didn't mean much, not really. Now that she knew he'd been released, she'd always be looking over her shoulder.

She felt her confidence slip sideways. Was she going to have to hide forever? She wanted to scream, it was so unfair. She'd done nothing wrong, yet she was the one who had to leave the comfort of the home she'd built.

She'd die fighting him before she let him get to Angel. Then it hit her. Mark hadn't known she was pregnant before he went to prison. If he was stalking her, he knew about their daughter. He wasn't stupid; he'd know she was his. Tiffany's ears began to ring as panic threatened her sanity.

"Hurry," she said to Kat. "Please, I have to get to my baby."

Kat nodded and got in the car. Tiffany looked at her house and the little yard she loved to spend time in. She hoped it wasn't the last time she would see it.

The drive to Aura's house was short, but Tiffany couldn't help but keep looking over her shoulder after each turn. The only vehicle that appeared to be following them was Shade's van. Her friends were amazing, but she was scared to death for them. All his previous threats played over and over in her mind. Mark would have no qualms about hurting them. She couldn't and wouldn't let that happen.

She looked over at Kat. It was completely unfair of Tiffany to consider a relationship with her. Although it made her very sad to think it, she wouldn't blame Kat one bit if she walked away from the drama.

"I see that look," Kat said.

"What look?"

"That good-bye look. Don't even consider it."

"Are you reading my mind now?"

"Maybe."

"You have no idea what he's capable of. I don't want to put you in the middle of this."

"Don't you see, Tiffany? That's what abusers do. They make you think that you're all alone by threatening the people that love you. It's in your nature to not make waves, not inconvenience anyone or put them in harm's way. Mark's counting on that to get to you. But you know what? He didn't count on me."

Tiffany heard what she was saying, and she wanted to believe everything would be okay, she really did. But she knew as long as he was on the street, she would never be completely safe.

She tried to keep her memory from going back to those years, but it was difficult.

"Turn left here," she said. "We'll park over there."

Kat pulled into the lot and Shade pulled up beside them. Tiffany got out of the car and scanned the area around them. There were too many people for her to focus on any one of them. Shade and Kat flanked her while they crossed the street and entered Aura's building.

"Feel anything?" she asked Shade.

"No."

Tiffany held her breath while waiting for the elevator to open and let it out when the doors shut behind them. Kat held her hand, giving her an anchor. It helped to keep her thoughts here and not let them race to the past.

Shade stood front and center when they reached the fourth floor. Tiffany could feel the intense electricity of her energy fan out, and it meshed alongside Kat's coiled tension next to her. They felt ready for a fight.

Before they got off, they each looked up and down the empty hallway then made it to Aura's door. Tiffany knew her life wouldn't be the same again.

The door opened and Aura ushered them in. Tiffany watched her stare at Kat and then wondered why she smiled knowingly, but before she could ask, Angel came streaking out of the bedroom and leaped into her arms.

"Mommy!"

Tiffany dropped to her knees and hugged Angel tightly against her. Angel's little arms wrapped around her neck in a fierce hug, and there was no other feeling like that in world. Tiffany made a vow there and then that despite bloody curses and violent threats against her, she'd kill Mark before she'd let him get anywhere near her daughter.

Angel patted Tiffany's cheeks. "Why are you sad, Mommy?"

"I'm happy that you're back," Tiffany said. "I've missed you terribly."

"Shay!" Angel squealed happily and ran to her. "What's up?"

"You are." Shade picked her up and swirled her around.

The sound of Angel's laughter rang in Tiffany's ears.

"Wait, put me down, Shay."

Tiffany watched Angel approach Kat who still stood near the door. She stopped when she reached her and her head tilted to the right before she giggled. "Hi, Kat!"

The room fell completely silent. Tiffany felt doused with ice water. "What's going on here?"

Angel turned back and pointed. "Mommy, it's Kat."

"I know, baby, but how do you know that?"

"You're silly. Don't you 'member? We all did the 'mony for you."

"What?" Tiffany felt dizzy. "What's a 'mony, sweetheart?"

"Mommy." Angel looked at her with an exasperated expression. "The 'mo-ny. We danced, played drums, and then Kat had to chase you."

Tiffany looked at Kat, who swayed on her feet before leaning against the wall. "You better come sit."

CHAPTER ELEVEN

Kat's legs felt unsteady, but she managed to cross to the couch. She was reeling after Angel's nonchalant statement. But hadn't she felt a connection when she looked at Angel's picture? Shade stared at them both. "Well now, this is interesting."

Before Kat could ask any questions, Sunny and Jordan entered the small foyer. Angel ran to them and everyone began talking at once. Kat wasn't able to decipher much of the conversation. She was still in shock. Last week, she'd been working at her desk and seriously contemplating leaving her job while using the vacation time she had coming to her. Then she met the woman she had made a promise to centuries ago but who didn't remember her. Follow that with the knowledge there was a sadistic stalker after them, and top off all of that with a statement from a four-year-old who knew who *Kat* was—in a previous life.

As open as she was to all the paranormal possibilities, there was still that part of her that was screaming for facts, something concrete she could hold on to. She felt as if she were spinning in a vortex and couldn't get her feet under her.

What sounded like a whisper in her ear had her searching for the source. From across the room, Tiffany locked eyes with her, and Kat felt the chaos of her thoughts settle somewhat. She looked just as stunned and confused as Kat imagined she did.

Fingers snapping together in front of her face brought her attention to Jordan. "What?"

"I'm talking to you."

"I'm sorry. What did you say?"

"I just told you I made the necessary calls to the authorities. But you know how that goes."

"They can't do anything unless he does something first." It completely pissed her off, but there wasn't any proof yet that Mark was stalking Tiffany. "What about the break-in?"

"I reported it, but somehow I doubt he'd leave any evidence behind."

"So we wait?" That didn't sit well with Kat at all. She would much prefer being proactive instead of reactive.

Tiffany approached them. "I'm sorry for all of the trouble this is causing."

Kat took her hand. "Don't think for even one second that anyone blames you. This is not your fault."

"I can't help but think it is."

"We'll get through this. I promise."

"Don't say anything about Mark. I don't want to upset her," Tiffany said as Angel crawled onto her lap.

"I'm sleepy, Mommy."

Tiffany looked sharply at Aura. "Does this have anything to do with—?"

"No, and I swear to you, nothing he can do will ever touch her."

"Are you worried about the—?" Kat left off the last word when Tiffany shook her head.

"It's past your naptime, baby. Let's go get you settled in." Tiffany stood and carried her down the hall.

Sunny motioned for Kat, Jordan, and Shade to sit at the table. "I'll get everyone some water."

Aura took the seat at the head of the table and waited for everyone to settle in their seats. Kat looked out the window and realized that Aura's condo had nearly the same view of the Manette Bridge as Sunny's house, the only difference being it was from the left side and a higher vantage.

"Okay, Mom," Sunny said. "You didn't go to the beach just to kick the waves."

"Very perceptive of you. And no, I didn't."

"How much of this did you see coming?" Jordan asked. "Can you see what happens from here?"

"It doesn't work that way," Aura said. "I only had a warning."

"What warning?" Kat asked. "What am I missing here?" *Besides my mind.*

Shade grinned at her. "Oh, it gets better."

"I give up," Kat said. "Could you all cut me a break here? And maybe help me make sense of this—in your out-loud voices?"

"Something that looks threatening, isn't. Another looks innocent, and isn't. Neither are what they appear to be," Aura said.

"Oh yeah, Tiffany said something about that when I was in the hospital," Shade said. "I received basically the same message."

"I knew there was going to be a shift in our lives and that it was important I be prepared to answer questions."

"Messages? Questions?" Kat wanted to bang her head on the table. "Please?"

"Can we get to the part where Angel said she knew Kat?" Shade asked. "Because that was freaking cool."

Everyone's attention turned to Kat, and the intense focus behind their eyes made her want to squirm in her seat.

"Welcome to my world," Jordan said.

"How far back can you remember?" Aura asked.

"I'm sorry," Kat said. "I'm as fascinated to know how Angel recognized me as you are, but shouldn't we be talking about Mark and how we're going to protect Tiffany and Angel?"

"Kat," Aura said gently. "It's all connected, and we have to try and find out how." She paused. "Do you think it's an accident you ran into Tiffany just when you did? That your friendship with Jordan brought you here at this exact time and place? That you're writing a book about your memories of a clan of priestesses and warriors you dreamt of as a child?"

How did she know all of that? "Well, yeah, I kind of did," Kat said. "But you're going to tell me different, aren't you?"

"I *knew* it," Sunny said. "I sensed ancient energy. I just didn't know where it came from."

Shade leaned closer, and Kat could see that her eyes were full of questions before she started to ask them. "Where? What time?"

"We didn't exactly have street signs," Kat said. "Or calendars." She waited for the skepticism and smartass comments, but none were forthcoming. "I can only tell you the village was on the shores of a river surrounded by forest. It was a society of women, a sanctuary of sorts." She looked at the receptive interest around the table and paused. "I'd rather wait until Tiffany is in the room."

"Of course," Aura said. "Let's go make some snacks, girls." Sunny and Jordan got up to help her, leaving Shade at the table, who continued to stare at her.

Kat stared right back. Since she didn't plan on going anywhere anytime soon. She was going to have to perfect holding her own in a family of psychics.

After a minute, Shade laughed. "You'll do, pup."

Kat felt something tug at her subconscious for a split second.

❖

Tiffany lay curled up next to Angel, humming softly until she knew she was sleeping soundly. She carefully got up and then stood next to the bed to look down at her. The uneasy fear she'd been holding on to all afternoon eased its way into determination. She wasn't a victim and she sure as hell wasn't going to volunteer this time around. She was going to fight until her last breath. She wondered what other secrets Angel held but didn't want to pressure her in any way. She wanted to find out as much as possible from her family first.

She closed the bedroom door gently. As she was walking back to the dining room, she heard Kat's voice and stopped for a minute. She'd thought of her as family. Was that because of the time they'd recently spent together or their past connection? She may not know the answer to that question yet, but she did know how important Kat had become to her in this very short time period. She had slid right past Tiffany's defenses.

She continued down the hall and turned the corner. She bit back laughter when she saw the look on Kat's face as she sat across from Shade and Sunny. "You look like you're facing a firing squad."

Kat smiled at her and Tiffany felt an immediate flutter in her chest. Oh yeah, she thought, definitely connected. But at this point, did it matter if it came from the past? She was much more concerned with here and now.

Tiffany crossed the room to sit next to her. "No one is going to bite you."

"That's not what I heard."

"Shut up, Shade," Tiffany said and turned to Kat. "Don't mind her."

"Can we start this conversation?" Jordan drummed her fingers on the table. "I'm dying to know the details that my *friend* Kat neglected to tell me about herself."

"Just a minute. Shade, does that box hold any more of his power?"

"Hell no. I sent that shit back to him. He's probably sleeping in an alley somewhere like the trash he is."

"Sent it back?" Jordan asked. "As in, I'm rubber, you're glue?"

Shade nodded. "Just like that."

"Sweet."

"Good," Tiffany said. "I'm ready."

"Wait, before we start, can I get a reincarnation 101 breakdown so I can keep up with you guys?" Jordan looked at Kat. "I'm sure you've done your own extensive research, but go easy on the newbie here. I've only dealt with ghosts so far."

Tiffany looked around the table. She felt a tiny shift of clarity and shivered.

"Are you okay?" Kat asked.

"Yes. That's the thing. I had one of those moments where everything just fits. Jordan, we'll let Aura give you a rundown."

"I thought you told me you did the past life stuff," Kat said.

"Yes, but I learned from Aura."

An expectant hush filled the space in the circle around the table as Aura began talking. "The old matriarchal religions teach that dying is just an intermission. Our lives are a cycle. As the seed grows into a flower, blooms, then dies, it is the natural order of the universe. In the spring, the plant blooms and repeats the life cycle again. That too, is irrefutable truth. Our natural state is spirit, and each life provides lessons that are designed for the soul's personal growth and are needed in order to evolve. These challenges are chosen before a soul reincarnates."

"I have a hard time believing I chose my mother," Jordan said.

Sunny bumped her with her shoulder. "Look where you ended up."

"Yeah, the payoff for that was pretty great."

Shade fidgeted. "Can we get on with this?"

Tiffany pressed her thigh against Kat's under the table while she reached for her hand. She was being very quiet. Kat's warmth seemed to travel through Tiffany, and she let herself lean against her. Tiffany loved listening to Aura. She remembered hundreds of afternoons sitting at her feet while she taught the girls how to use their gifts.

Aura gestured while she talked, and the silver bracelets she wore emphasized her words with the sound of tiny ringing bells. "Some souls," she continued, "reincarnate for various reasons. It could be that they feel cheated by death and have unfinished business, or they lost someone they loved, and continue to return until they've found them."

Tiffany felt the muscles in Kat's leg tighten.

"When they come back, the new child could be filled with a sense of urgency, dream of events, or have a great sense of purpose to find the one they lost."

"So that fits my experience," Kat said. "I've also read that recent studies have been done on children who have night terrors, some of which report they're reliving their death while sleeping."

"Angel has never had nightmares," Tiffany said. "Yet, she remembers Kat. How come I don't?" She didn't want to feel left out, or broken in any way, but she did.

"Tiff," Aura said. "I've noticed our newest generation has the oldest souls. They don't always relive their deaths, especially if they had a good life and were satisfied with it when they passed. They bring forward great gifts and show a mastery of them way beyond their years."

"I still don't know what your memories are," Tiffany said and faced Kat. "Or how I fit in them." She felt sad knowing that. The time they'd had together had been so focused on working for Parker and Tiffany's problems, she hadn't taken the time to really *look* at Kat's soul, her innate spirit. The protective bubble she lived in may have protected Tiffany, but it also kept others out.

"Soul mates connect on all levels," Aura said. "Physically, mentally, and spiritually. Their experiences together carry forward through time."

"So why doesn't Tiffany remember me?" Kat asked.

"I want to, I really do. But every time I've tried to do a past life reading on myself, I run into a black wall." Tiffany didn't mention that it also filled her with terror and anxiety. She'd had enough of that to deal with after Mark went to prison and she began the long road to healing.

"A death that was very traumatic could permanently imprint itself into our consciousness," Shade said. "I have clients who address that."

Tiffany recalled her recurring nightmare of the horseman and his bloody ax approaching her in slow motion. She must have really been in denial, as she'd never made the connection before.

Aura continued. "Relationships are not accidental. Everyone we meet is for a reason. That too is universal. As individuals, we draw people to us that have something to teach us. You know the individuals that you meet and either know on the spot or are repulsed by? By knowing that, we can assess which relationships need to be healed and transformed. We will continue to meet these individuals in *each* life until we master what we're supposed to learn or right some karmic wrong from the past." Tiffany recognized that in herself. She'd been attracted to Mark because she had unfinished business with him. And if her nightmare was any indication that he would continue to terrorize her through time, this was the time to change it. Break the pattern once and for all. Kat began to fidget and her leg began to bounce.

"We also have soul groups that reincarnate together. A good analogy that I can use is how kids start kindergarten and stay with the same people until they graduate, which in this case, would be to cross over."

"Can we get to Kat's memories now?" Jordan asked.

Kat shook her head. "Excuse me. I need a minute." She got up from the table then left the room.

"I'll go." Jordan stood.

"No, please," Tiffany said. "I'll talk to her."

Kat splashed cold water on her face. She was feeling a little overwhelmed, and right this second, she didn't much care about the theories of reincarnation or soul groups. She already believed in them. She was more invested in how best to protect Tiffany.

There was a soft tap at the door, and Kat turned off the water. She opened it and Tiffany stood on the other side, looking worried. Kat pulled her arm to bring her inside then shut the door.

"Ssh. Let me hold you for a minute."

Tiffany wrapped her arms around Kat's waist and rested her head against her chest. "I can feel your heart beating," she said.

Kat swallowed a small lump in her throat. "If it's all the same to you, I'd rather not share our story for the first time with the entire group."

Tiffany looked up at her. "Of course, but may I ask why?"

Kat took a step back to lean on the counter, bringing Tiffany with her so they kept contact. "Because it's so personal for me. I've had this story locked up inside me for years, and it's very special to me. I don't want it dissected in the middle of the table."

"I understand that. I'm also sorry it appears that we're ganging up on you."

"No, I don't feel that. It's just that it's very important to me that *you* don't emotionally link your traumatic memories with my treasured ones. I wanted to share them with you first. Is that bad?"

"No, but I want you to know that I can't help which ones are prevalent for me. What I got out of the conversation at the table was that I'm supposed to serve Mark a big fat karmic hamburger."

"Good one." Kat chuckled. "Okay, I'll give you that. Maybe I'll just admit that I'm tired, and it's been a very long couple of days."

"Are you leaving?"

"I thought you were coming with me," Kat said. "Isn't that what we decided?"

"Yes. I thought you meant—never mind." Tiffany ducked her head.

"I am not going to run away from you. Not now, not ever." Kat lifted Tiffany's chin and kissed her gently. "We'll get through this. We may not get through exactly how we imagined, but we'll get by." Kat was used to an orderly life. It may have been chaotic at times, but she'd always had a clear path in front of her, one that provided answers and a direction. But right now, while she held Tiffany in her arms, she didn't much care if the road ahead wasn't paved yet. Kat only knew that she wanted to cut through it with Tiffany and Angel.

"Hey! Get a room, you two." Shade pounded on the door. "I have to use the bathroom."

Tiffany looked up at her. "Let's start the good-byes now because it'll take another hour before we get out of here."

When Kat pulled the car into the underground garage, Tiffany felt her shoulders relax a little. The ride to the city had been torturous for her. She had to keep conversation light and airy to keep Angel occupied with small talk that didn't involve how serious their situation was. They sang songs along with the radio, and it surprised her that Kat joined right in.

Tiffany appreciated the way Kat tuned in to her own energy so seamlessly. She didn't feel alone when she was with her, and she imagined this was what a normal family would feel like—full of unspoken compassion, and the intelligence to know what was appropriate for a young child.

Angel hadn't said any more about knowing Kat, and Tiffany refused to bring it up again until she did. She wanted her to come out with it as naturally as possible. Asking her questions about it could insert false memory.

Kat pulled into her spot and turned the motor off.

"Are we here?" Angel asked.

"Yup," Kat said. "Your castle awaits, princess."

Tiffany got out of the passenger seat and turned to help Angel out. Kat got their bags out of the trunk before they turned to head toward the elevator.

"Mommy!" Angel screamed and ran back to the car. Kat dropped the luggage as Tiffany's purse fell, and they sped after her.

Angel was folded over herself and kneeling on the cement in front of the car. Tiffany reached her and wrapped her up in her arms. "What, baby? Are you hurt?"

Angel hiccupped and began wailing. "No, Mommy, no."

Tiffany's panic at hearing her daughter scream stifled her psychic probing, but she ran practiced hands along Angel's body to search for wounds.

"What do you have in your hands, munchkin?" Kat asked. "Can I see?"

Angel held out her hands, and cupped within them was a tiny kitten that couldn't have been over five weeks old, covered in oil and dirt from the parking garage. Its head hung at an odd angle. Tiffany reached for the little body, knowing before she even touched it that the spark of life was very dim.

"It's broken, Mommy. You can fix it, right?" Angel's trusting eyes implored her to make it better.

"Oh, honey," she said to Angel. "I don't think I can." She stared at Kat. Her mouth was set in a grim, tight line, and Tiffany knew that she'd come to the same conclusion she had.

Mark had been here first.

Angel's crying became more anguished. "No. We have to save the kitty. Please, Mommy. Help me."

"We have to get upstairs, now," Kat said. Tiffany picked up Angel who had a death grip on the kitten, and then they retrieved their bags before rushing to the elevator. They didn't run, but walked quickly to Kat's door.

When they locked the door behind them, Tiffany put Angel down in the foyer before she tried to take the small body from her.

"Honey, I think the kitten is going to die." Angel's pain shot through her own body. Tiffany would spare her from it if she could. She gently cupped her hands under Angel's. "Angel, let me have it, okay?"

Angel kept her hold on the tiny ball of fur, closed her eyes, and began to hum softly. The notes had a haunting quality, almost eerie, and it gave Tiffany chills from her neck down to the base of her spine. She had never heard it before. A small breeze sprang up between them, barely stirring the air, caressing her cheeks.

Tiffany became aware of the warmth spreading through Angel's palms beneath her own, and transferring to the kitten's body. She felt a tingling sensation and heard Kat's sigh of wonder behind them. Angel's tiny face was drawn as she concentrated, and Tiffany could swear her skin was lit from within. Tiffany felt a barely perceptible flutter in the kitten's chest, followed by another. Fascinated, Tiffany held her breath and watched Angel's face. The kitten's heartbeat, faint and weak, grew stronger until it regulated itself under her palm.

The kitten mewed and moved its head. A tiny pink tongue licked the air. Tiffany was shocked. Did her daughter just bring the kitten back to life? Or was she mistaken in the fact she thought it was dead?

"Look, Mommy! See? I knew we could do it."

Tiffany didn't have any words. Even if she did, she wouldn't have been able to speak. Joy filled her even as a tiny trace of uncertainty remained. Where had Angel learned that song? Tiffany knew she would never forget that melody as long as she lived.

"That was awesome," Kat said. "How?"

"I'm not sure. I'm still in shock."

"Let's give her a bath," Angel said. She curled the kitten to her neck, looked around the foyer, then headed to the kitchen. "Bring a chair, Mommy."

Tiffany slid one over to the sink and lifted Angel onto it. She'd always known Angel was incredibly gifted, but this had her reeling.

Often, Tiffany would hear her laughing or having one-sided conversations in her room. She'd never figured out why she couldn't connect with Angel's ethereal companions. She'd grown used to it and put the worry out of her mind when Aura told her Angel would reveal her gifts in her own sweet way eventually. But Tiffany had never imagined she would have a healing gift of this magnitude.

She turned the faucet on low and adjusted the temperature. Tiffany kept her voice calm despite the adrenaline pounding through her system. "So what do you want to name it?"

"Airmitt," Angel answered without hesitation. "Mitt."

That's different. "Air-mitt?"

"Uh, huh."

"Where did you come up with that name? I've never heard it."

"The pretty lady over there told me it was her name," Angel crooned softly and continued to gently wipe the kitten, which didn't appear upset at all and was, in fact, purring up a storm.

"Oh? I didn't see her. Is she still here?"

Kat stood at the door, and her eyes went wide. Tiffany stifled a chuckle. In spite of all her problems right now, the spark of life filled her spirit and lightened her heart. Maybe it was a sign to pay attention to the miracles.

"Airmid," Kat said.

Angel beamed. "Uh-huh."

"You know her?" Tiffany asked Kat.

"Keeper of the Spring, one who can regenerate life. She's also known for bringing back the, uh, dead."

Tiffany's arms broke out in goose bumps under the warm water. She grabbed the towel Kat had put on the counter and reached to take the kitten, but Angel insisted she could do it. "Put me down now, please."

Angel's hands and shirt were covered in grease and dirt. "Okay, but now we have to get you cleaned up as well."

Kat returned to the foyer and picked up their bags. "I'll show you to the guest room."

Tiffany followed her down the hall and wondered how much more she could take before she broke down. None of the challenges of the last week had any resolution. She'd had a gorgeous stranger recognize her from a past life, suffered vivid nightmares of her own death, felt the emotions and fear from three murders, discovered an ancient curse, and, oh yeah, her murderous ex-husband was on the loose.

And ostensibly, her daughter could raise the dead.

Where did she go from here?

Kat helped Tiffany put their things away. "My neighbor's cat had kittens a few months ago. I'll go and ask her if she has anything we can borrow for Mitt. If not, I'll go to the store and buy them."

"I can," Tiffany said.

"Absolutely not. You will stay here."

Tiffany felt her shoulders stiffen at Kat's bossy tone. Evidently, she had more backbone than she thought she did. She deliberately stood straight, to prove to Kat, and herself, that she stood on her own two feet. "I won't have you telling me what to do."

"It's for your own good." Kat crossed her arms over her chest.

"So now you're going to go all controlling on me and dictate how I can come and go?"

"Jesus, Tiffany!" Kat said then immediately lowered her voice for Angel's sake. "I'm not Mark, and I'm not trying to keep you a prisoner. I'm trying to keep you safe."

"No fighting, Mommy." Angel was sitting on the bed with Mitt wrapped in her arms. "Be kind and gentle."

Tiffany's temper deflated and she sighed. "I know that. I'm sorry." She moved to where Kat stood and put her arms around her. "I appreciate it. I really do." She stood on her toes to kiss her lightly on the lips.

Kat returned the kiss, but her arms stayed at her sides. "I'm going to Lizzie's to see about the kitten."

"Okay." Tiffany was a little hurt. But really, could she blame Kat? Tiffany had been nothing but hot and cold since they'd met. She couldn't read Kat to gauge her feelings or thoughts. Maybe she had decided Tiffany was too much trouble to pursue.

Tiffany couldn't blame her at this point.

"Lock the door behind me. I'll take the deadbolt key."

"All right." Tiffany followed her and did as she requested.

Angel called from the other room. "Mommy!"

"I'm coming." Tiffany took a deep breath, then went to draw Angel a bath.

❖

Kat juggled the box in order to unlock the door. When she entered, the sound of Angel's laughter echoed down the hallway. She was struck with a rush of emotion, almost as if she'd reached for that brass ring and touched it. But the circumstances that currently surrounded them prevented her from swinging on it. The longing for that missing piece ached in her soul, making her stomach ache.

The sound of splashing water told her that Tiffany had Angel in the bath. She wanted to run to them and join in the family interaction, but instead she went to the kitchen to unpack the supplies.

Tiffany had told her she didn't want to pressure Angel for details, and Kat agreed with her, but she also felt the conversation was long overdue with Tiffany. She couldn't just keep herself on the edge, waiting for the perfect opportunity to tell her of her childhood memories. It was so difficult to act as if she weren't in love with Tiffany already.

Did it matter anymore where the love started? Whether it was a thousand years ago or last week? She didn't think it did.

It was time to sit Tiffany down and let her know how she felt. Kat was only human, and it was getting harder and harder to withhold her actions and reactions to honor Tiffany's request that they progress slowly.

She started toward the bathroom when Angel ran naked, wet, and giggling out of the bathroom and toward Kat's room.

"Angel, you get back here! You're not dry yet, honey."

The mural.

Tiffany was quick to follow, looking a little harried. Kat stood where she was and waited for them to come out. When they didn't, she took small steps to the bedroom to join them.

She stood in the doorway and watched Tiffany and Angel staring at the painting in awe.

Angel laughed and pointed at the warrior. "Kat!" She also said several other things, but as she was speaking toddlerese, Kat only understood a few words, one of them being, Mommy.

Tiffany looked at Kat. "It's so beautiful."

"Thank you."

The kitten appeared and wound herself around Kat's ankles. Angel ran over to pick Mitt up. "Look," she said. "That's where you're from too."

It was almost too much. Kat made her way to the end of the bed and sat. She didn't know what to say, which questions she should ask, or in what order. All her journalistic skills were gone in an instant.

She was so used to burying how she felt and not talking about the secret she'd kept for decades. But she'd been dropped in the midst of a gaggle of women who not only assumed her visions were possible, they shared knowledge of them. Her entire paradigm had shifted completely in the last week. It wasn't a bad thing, just a big one.

Tiffany wrapped Angel in the towel that was hanging over her shoulder. "I'll be back. Let me get her pajamas on, and I'll set her up in the guest room with her portable DVD player."

"I'll meet you in the living room. Do you want me to pour you some wine?" Kat knew that she needed a glass.

"Sure."

Kat went back into the kitchen and set up the litter box and food for the kitten. She put some warm milk in the cat food and carried it to the guest room. Tiffany was brushing Angel's hair. There was something so comforting and normal about the scene, she felt some of the day's strangeness leave her.

"Thank you," Angel said.

"You're welcome, honey." Kat left to find the wine. She wondered briefly if she had anything stronger in the liquor cabinet but decided against drinking any of the hard stuff. She wanted to keep her head during the conversation.

She poured the wine and took the glasses out on to the deck. She realized they hadn't eaten dinner yet so she left the glasses on the small table. She hoped pizza two nights in a row was okay, because she didn't have anything quick in the kitchen.

She had no idea of what Angel liked so she included cheese sticks and wings into the order.

The large yellow moon was making its appearance in the early evening sky when Tiffany came out to lead her into the living room. "Here, let's sit on the couch."

Kat grabbed the open bottle and poured herself another glass before she complied and handed Tiffany the one she'd already poured.

"Thank you. God, what a day, right?"

"It feels like a week."

"I know and I'm sorry."

"What are you sorry for? Please stop saying that. You are not a bother, not a burden."

Tiffany stared at her, and Kat could see the shadows under her eyes due to the stressful situation. She imagined her own eyes had a couple of shadows as well.

The silence stretched, and neither said a word. Kat would have, but didn't know where to start. When she realized Tiffany wasn't going to talk, she began. "You know," Kat said conversationally, "I'm usually very charming and charismatic."

"Are you now?" Tiffany raised an eyebrow. "Tell me more, please."

Kat grinned, appreciating her light-hearted tone. "But from the moment I've met you…"

"I've been nothing but trouble."

"That's not what I was going to say."

"Sorry."

"Stop that."

"I'm sorry. I can't help it."

Kat put down her glass then took Tiffany's from her and put it on the coffee table. Then she tackled her and began tickling her.

"Stop it! What are you doing?"

Kat laughed at Tiffany's giggles. She attacked her again until they were both out of breath from laughing. When they were lying still, Tiffany's hips began a slow roll underneath her and Kat instantly heated with lust.

Kat stopped and let herself roll off into a sitting position. Angel was in the other room.

She helped Tiffany up from the position on her back and whispered in her ear. "I want you so bad, Tiffany. I ache with it. I want to make love to you under the moonlight. And when we're done, I want to do it again."

She heard Tiffany's sharp inhale of breath, and Kat felt the sound travel directly to her core. The pressure between her legs began to build, and she tried to steady herself but wasn't having much success with it.

Kat moved back on the couch so she wasn't touching Tiffany. It didn't help much. Her scent was moving through Kat's system, curling around her, far more intoxicating than the wine.

"Okay," Tiffany said. "Give me a second. It seems like all we've done with all of this attraction is a push-me, pull-you dance."

Kat began to protest. "But—"

"I know that's on me. I'll own that. But oh, woman, you kiss me breathless. You make all my reasons, all my justifications, and more importantly, all my arguments feel flimsy and invalid."

"I'm sorry?" Kat asked.

"Touché. But I very much want to, what do the kids say now? 'Get busy' with you?"

Kat laughed. "Really, Tiffany? You are so freaking adorable."

"We both know Angel is in there, and I have more problems than I know what to do with right this minute."

"I know how to be responsible."

"Oh, I know that. I didn't think you'd take advantage of that. My argument is this: You deserve, *we* deserve, my entire attention."

"If you say it's not you, it's me, I'm going to flip you over and tickle you again until you cry uncle."

Tiffany laughed. "I'm not finished yet. I deserve to know your whole story before I do anything else. Your connection with my daughter has me a little bewildered. I need to know all of it."

"I'll tell you." Kat paused. "From the beginning."

"Would it be easier if I hypnotized you?"

"You can do that?"

"Yes. Do you trust me?"

"Of course. But why would it be easier?

"Because I can reach and talk to Kat in the past, in the first person, without your memories or thoughts getting in the way."

"Jesus. That's amazing. I don't think I can be hypnotized."

"They all say that, honey." Tiffany laughed. "We're just going to get you relaxed. You'll be safe. I promise."

"You're not going to make me take my clothes off and cluck like a chicken are you?"

"Not this time. Maybe later."

Kat picked up her wineglass and emptied it in two swallows. "Ready."

"Sit back, close your eyes, and relax your shoulders. Let's start with letting down your defenses. Breathe in and out. Slow, even breaths, and visualize the walls around your mind and memory coming down brick by brick."

Kat did as she asked. It was more difficult than she imagined. They'd been built up so long. The years since she'd shared the story with anyone only served to make the mortar between them thicker and harder. She concentrated on Tiffany's soft voice.

"Now imagine the bricks at your feet, crumbling down into the earth where green grass sprouts from the rubble, growing, growing, until it's an emerald carpet at your feet. Now imagine it spreading out in all directions and stopping at the edge of a forest. We're walking down the tiny path that curves in and around the trees. You can hear the water bubbling in a nearby stream. Can you hear the birds singing?"

"Yes."

"Good, now focus on the sights and smells of your surroundings while you're moving at a gentle pace through the woods. You turn a corner and see something in the distance. Can you tell me what it is?"

Ahead of her, Kat saw the roofs of the village huts. The large sacred hall, along with smaller circular huts, scattered over the hillside and near the river. The sun was warm on her face, and she was filled with a sense of peace.

"I see you smiling. What do you see?"

"Home." Kat heard the dreamy quality in her own voice as if she were standing outside herself.

Time appeared to have folded, twisted in on itself. Kat stood with one foot in the past and one in the present. The feeling was surreal. Kat snapped her eyes open.

"What's the matter?" Tiffany's concern was evident in her voice.

"Nothing. Give me a second." Kat stood and reached for Tiffany's hand. "Come with me."

Kat took Tiffany to her room and stood before the mural. "This is where I went. I was there, in that place."

Tiffany touched the canvas lightly. "I can see you painting every detail and each blade of grass. I feel the emotion and pain that sparked the creation."

"What else do you see?" Kat had hoped that Tiffany would connect with Tanna.

"I see a woman that looks like me."

"Tanna. We were six when we met and grew up together along the shores of the river in a place known as Sanctuary run by the elders and priestesses of the Goddess Danu. We were inseparable and never spent a day apart."

"The women you captured in your mural look to be in their early twenties. That's a lot of memories to hold of someone."

"I have years of journals that I wrote about those. It's what I'm basing my novel on, my life with you."

"Do you remember the last dream you had of this place?"

"Vividly." Kat backed away from the wall until she sat on the bed. Tiffany followed and held her hand. "I was nineteen. I had foolishly thought if they stopped, it meant that you were near, and I would meet you in this life. You, I mean Tanna, died in my arms. That was the last time I saw you, her."

"That makes me sad, because it's so unfair."

"How is it unfair? I *loved* you."

"I'm not Tanna. I don't have her memories of you. I am me—here and now. You can't expect me to just fall in line, to live in the past with you, or to fall in love with you simply because I'm supposed to. That doesn't give me any say in it at all."

"Let me finish," Kat said. "That's how it was when we first met. Since I've spent time with you, worked with you, touched you, I don't see Tanna anymore when I look at you. I see you—Tiffany."

"I want to believe you, I really do. But right now, I'm going to ask you for more time. I don't want to have to wonder if you're seeing her when you look at me."

"But I just told—"

Tiffany held up a hand. "I have to feel it, Kat. I have to know without a doubt that I'm not a stand-in or substitute for her. I don't want to compete against her memory." She pointed to Tanna.

Sorrow dropped onto Kat's shoulders and chest like a rock. She'd wanted nothing more than to share the whole story with Tiffany, but before she'd barely started, she'd taken two steps back. "I'm asking for a chance."

Tiffany cupped Kat's face with her palms. "Until I sort all of this out, and get through the nightmare going on with my ex-husband, we'll have to not do *this* anymore." She kissed Kat on the lips gently before she stood.

Kat reached to draw her back for another one when the intercom buzzed. Kat sighed. "What is it with the timing of the pizza deliveries?"

"Again?"

"I couldn't think of anything else on such short notice."

"I love it. So will Angel."

Yes, but will you both love me?

CHAPTER TWELVE

They had all gone to bed early after dinner, but Tiffany lay awake next to Angel, who was cuddling the kitten between them. Her mind raced and she wasn't having any success with meditating.

She was livid. Anger at the situation she was in boiled inside her, festering in her spirit. Tiffany was going to have to get out of the bed. She didn't want to poison the room Angel was sleeping in with her negative energy.

She threw a robe over her pajamas on her way out. Maybe sitting on the deck for a while would help. She tiptoed down the hall and realized she didn't even know if Kat was a sound sleeper. She would have to be extra quiet just in case.

Kat had left a small lamp on in the living room, but Tiffany wouldn't have needed it. Seattle's nighttime skyline was spread before her outside the wall-sized windows.

It was a stunning view for a sanctuary. She paused and wondered how long she'd be a prisoner in a glass cage. That she even thought of Kat's beautiful place as a jail ticked her off. It had taken years for her to feel safe, and months of counseling to learn her own worth. How dare he come back and terrorize her?

She slipped out the sliding doors then walked to the railing. She looked over the side and wondered if he were looking up. She wouldn't have been able to see him anyway. Was he down there plotting how he was going to kill her? Worse, was he planning on hurting her family? Her instincts told her that it was Mark who planned the attack on Shade. He would have known that she was the greatest threat.

Hell no! It was her naiveté and choices that put them all in this position. This fight was between her and Mark.

Tiffany opened her arms to the wind and began to draw on strength she hadn't known she possessed. Power began to surge through her body until she was nearly trembling with the force. The moon was full and bright above her, and she prayed for strength and courage. Several minutes later, she relaxed her arms and knew she'd made her decision.

She was going to put a stop to this.

Alone.

With her mind made up, she went inside to the kitchen counter where she'd left her phone with the sound turned off. Twenty-two missed calls. *Bastard.* Now that he knew they were aware of him, he'd stopped any pretense of secrecy. He was flat-out in the open and full of blatant arrogance.

She would have to be very careful. She wouldn't be able to talk to Sunny, Shade, or Aura because they would immediately know she was up to something. Kat probably wouldn't let her out of the house because she would want to protect her.

If anything happened to Tiffany, her chosen sisters would raise Angel. There was already an airtight will and custody agreement in place. Grief stabbed her heart, and her resolve wavered. She didn't want to leave her beautiful baby. She tried to tell herself they would find each other again in the next life, as they clearly had in this one, but that was small comfort.

If she didn't force a resolution, he would never give up, and he would always be a threat to Angel and the others she loved.

She recalled Kat's story and the emotional pain she'd felt when Tanna died. Tiffany was so damn sorry she didn't feel their connection in the past. She did care deeply for Kat and wished they'd had more time together. She had no doubt that those pieces would eventually have fallen into place, and they'd have been happy together.

Tiffany realized she was thinking of herself in past tense, and although it disturbed her, she wasn't going to change her mind. Besides, she didn't plan on losing. She reached into her Mary Poppins bag and felt around for the secret compartment that held her insurance. Tiffany abhorred violence, but after Angel was born, she'd bought the .22 pistol for protection. Maybe it was because she subconsciously knew it would come down to this one day. Satisfied with her decision, she pulled out a notepad and began writing letters to her family.

Just in case.

When she was done, she glanced at the clock. It was only ten p.m. She reached for her phone, and it vibrated in her hand before she could redial the number she now knew by heart.

"Mark."

"Coming to your senses? Can't hide up there forever. You know that."

"Oh, I'm done hiding." Tiffany took a deep breath. "Here are my terms."

"You're not in any position to negotiate, bitch. Get your ass down here."

Fear began trying to crawl up her spine before she shut it down. It was nothing more than a reflex. "How long do you think you can wait out there? Days, months? Because I have everything I need in here. You can't keep watch forever." She echoed his words back to him.

"I'll stay as long as it takes, and in the meantime, I'm going after everyone that's helping you. I'm going to make your life a living hell."

"Don't you think I know that? Here's the deal," Tiffany said. "I'll meet you somewhere, but you leave my family out of this." She didn't really believe he'd leave them alone if she left with him. But she also knew he was full of rage and wanted to get his hands on her. He would agree to her terms for that reason alone. If he killed her, then he'd go back to prison. If she killed him, she would be free to live her life. Either way it went, there would be resolution and Angel would be safe.

"So if I agree to leave the bitches alone, you'll come out?"

"Yes." Tiffany heard a door open down the hall. She relayed the address and time into the phone and disconnected. She quickly put the notebook away and turned to see who was coming.

❖

"Couldn't sleep either?" Kat asked. She opened the fridge to pull out a bottle of water.

Tiffany shook her head. "Come here for a minute." Tiffany wrapped her arms around Kat's waist. "I have something to tell you." Kat's heart thundered beneath Tiffany's cheek.

"Mmm?"

"I don't want to be just your friend." Tiffany kept her eyes open and stretched to lay her lips against Kat's.

Kat's eyes held secrets and hints of power. Tiffany felt it ripple against her skin like a caress and shivered while a fire lit deep within her. She felt both wonderful and desperate at once. She pulled her closer and her tongue entered her mouth, stroking with heated passion until Tiffany moaned with the sheer pleasure of it. Kat broke the contact. "Are you sure?"

Tiffany nodded because she didn't feel as if she could speak. She had a moment of awe, realizing how much Kat had been withholding for her sake.

"Thank God." Kat took Tiffany's hand to lead her down the hall, into her bedroom. Tiffany stopped by the bed while Kat continued to the window to draw the drapes.

"No," Tiffany said. "Love me in the moonlight." She pulled her shirt over her head, lowered her pajama pants, and stood in the soft glow wearing only her bra and panties.

Kat's eyes narrowed. Tiffany watched her breathing increase and the deep sigh coming from her made Tiffany feel sexy and powerful. She reached behind her to unclasp her bra and let it slide down her arms to the floor. The cool air and Kat's gaze hardened her nipples into sharp, aching points.

Kat kept eye contact with her as she undressed on her way back to the bed. Tiffany knew Kat had a slamming body, but when she was naked, she was magnificent. Her lean muscles transitioned into soft curves. Tiffany's body grew hot, and she felt wet desire on her thighs. Her knees were weak, and she turned to crawl onto the bed. Just as she got on her hands and knees, one of Kat's hands splayed across her lower back and pinned her while the other pulled her panties down to her ankles in one quick motion. Hot lips kissed her tailbone before Tiffany moved to the center of the bed and turned over. She wanted to see every inch of Kat.

For one endless moment, Kat held herself above her, watching her face. The moon was framed behind her and their breath mixed, while their hearts beat in tandem.

Then Kat's hand was in Tiffany's hair, sweeping it to the side before she pressed her lips against the pulse in her throat and sighed. That last gesture tripped Tiffany's heart. There was nothing between them but skin, yet Tiffany wanted to be closer still. The emotion took her to a place she'd never been before, but knew she'd never want to leave. A tiny voice inside her told her it was selfish for her to make love with Kat knowing she might not come back. But was it so wrong that she wanted this moment and this experience to take with her? Couldn't she want something for herself, just once?

When Kat's hand molded to her breast, all thoughts and questions flew away. She cupped her softly, reverently, while she came back to Tiffany's mouth. Softly at first, then increasingly urgently, she nipped at her lip before sliding her tongue along Tiffany's. Kat's hips rocked against her own, and Tiffany began to tremble with need. When Kat bent down to lick her nipples, Tiffany cried out and increased the pace.

"You like that," Kat whispered.

"Yes." Kat's sucking motion nearly put Tiffany over the edge. The sensation traveled straight down between her legs and returned in waves. "Don't stop."

"I'm not going anywhere. Tell me what you want."

"You," Tiffany said, "I want you."

"You have that already." Kat's hand slid along her side, then between her thighs to cup her sex. Tiffany could feel the thunder of her pulse beat against Kat's palm as she rose to meet it. Kat increased the pressure until Tiffany thought she might burst, reaching higher and faster until she felt frantic with the need to keep riding the crest until she reached it.

"That's it, baby. It's mine, give it to me and fly." Kat's demands whispered softly against her lips. Tiffany drew her tongue into her mouth, suckled it.

Tiffany's sighs increased until the sound was a continuous sound for release. Nothing else mattered; nothing else existed but that primal pounding between her legs. Liquid pooled beneath her on the slick sheets, but it wasn't nearly enough. This wanting felt desperate and urgent.

Kat entered her with long, slender fingers and stroked in time with Tiffany's hips. Higher and higher she flew until her body stiffened, her legs straightened, her toes curled almost painfully. Her fingers dug into Kat's shoulder and she gasped for breath as her orgasm swept through her, body and soul.

"I can't breathe. Oh God, I can't breathe."

"Ssh. I got you. I'm here." Kat stroked her hair. "I'm right here."

Tiffany's eyes closed and her heart thundered in her ears. Gradually, she became aware of Kat's gentle motion. She moved slowly and lightly against Tiffany's thigh. She was still holding back. That she was so considerate of Tiffany's feelings made the guilt resurface.

"Kat," Tiffany said. "I won't break." She drew up on an elbow to look at her face, and found caged lust burning in her eyes. "Get on your back."

Tiffany straddled Kat's stomach. She inched her body down until she felt soft curls between her thighs, and then she gripped Kat's hips and ground her clit against Kat's soft flesh. Kat's fingers dug into her ass, taking control of the motion.

"Yes," Kat said, the word drawing out into a long hiss. "Ride me, Tiffany." Kat's hands came up to Tiffany's breasts and pinched her nipples. The sensation sent shock waves from the top of her head to her toes and she leaned over, offering them to Kat's mouth.

Tiffany's long hair curtained Kat's face, creating a private cocoon where only they existed. Where they depended on each other's breath for life, where they were one with each other and the universe.

The look on Kat's face went straight to Tiffany's heart. The love she saw mirrored there tripped her pulse. She slid further down Kat's body. Her fingers trailed down Kat's tight stomach muscles, registering the strength behind the soft, silky skin. "Open your legs for me."

Kat immediately obeyed and never took her eyes off Tiffany's. That this strong woman yielded herself so willingly humbled her. She was completely vulnerable and trusting. It was a heady feeling.

"Inside me. I need you inside me."

Kat's sex was swollen and slick and she began to tremble under her.

"Please. Tiffany, please."

Tiffany entered her with two fingers and felt Kat tighten against them, drawing her deeper. She thrust slowly, allowing Kat to set the pace. "Like this?"

"Just like that. I love you inside me."

A surge of protectiveness washed over Tiffany, along with fierce possessiveness. She had no idea where the feelings came from, but she acknowledged the truth that the revelation brought her.

She'd never been so aggressive in her life. It felt good, this righteous strength, this need to take Kat and make her writhe in passion. She began thrusting firmer and deeper, watching her face. "Give it to me, it's mine." She mirrored Kat's own demands back to her in a whisper. "Come for me under the moonlight."

"I'm yours," Kat said. "I've always been yours."

Tiffany kissed her, her gentle lips a direct contrast to her firm thrusting. She straddled one of Kat's thighs and matched her rhythm. Her stomach muscles contracted with each whisper and sigh.

Kat's orgasm shook Tiffany to the core. The tenderness in her arms as she held and kissed her moved her deeply. Her throat closed with emotion. But she couldn't decipher whether they were from unrepressed joy, or the guilt of betrayal from what she was about to do.

Kat ran her thumb along Tiffany's lower lip. "I've dreamt of you for so long, I know how you taste. And yet, the memory can't compare with how you feel right now, right this very moment."

"I'm overwhelmed with it." Tiffany kissed her softly and then got out of bed.

"Where are you going?" Kat asked. "Stay here with me."

"I have to use the bathroom, and then check on Angel." Tiffany tucked the sheet up around her. "I'll be back."

"Okay." Kat turned back onto her side. "I'll be waiting."

When Tiffany came back to check on her fifteen minutes later, she was sound asleep. She quietly closed the door.

"I'm so sorry," she whispered. "That I didn't have more time to love you. We would have been amazing together." She hoped that if something bad happened, Kat would find her again in another life.

Tiffany stopped outside Angel's door. She could not—would not—go back in. If she did, she wouldn't be able to bear the grief of leaving.

She stopped in the kitchen to turn off Kat's phone in case Aura, Sunny, or Shade called to warn her. They didn't always see what was coming, but she wanted a head start. Tiffany took out the small pistol from her bag and put it in her coat pocket. She also grabbed a baseball cap to cover her hair, and she was ready.

Stepping out the front door was excruciating. She had every intention of making it back, but prepared herself for the worst.

She laid her hand against the outside of the door. "Good-bye, my loves."

Tiffany made her way to the elevator. After sending her senses into the dark, she slipped out the side exit of the building, keeping to the shadows. She kept herself close to a small group of people walking out of a restaurant and hoped she blended in. When she'd made it six blocks or so, she hailed a taxi.

Tiffany had the driver drop her off three blocks from her destination and made it to the meeting place a full two hours before the scheduled time. She'd picked this spot because she knew a little bit about the area, having lived there with Mark when she was married to him. She hoped the small neighborhood park was still there, since she hadn't been here in almost five years.

She breathed a sigh of relief when she saw the tall trees that ringed the perimeter of the playground. The streetlights lit the small area and the trees cast giant and twisted shadows.

A couple of teenagers were on the swings. She hadn't even thought of the possibility there would be people around. She scanned the area for a place to hide from them as well as to find a good vantage point to spot Mark when he approached.

Tiffany listened to her intuition when she came upon some thick brush on the far side of the property. It was far enough that the teenagers wouldn't spot her, but close enough that she felt she could surprise him.

Strangely, she wasn't scared. It was a liberating feeling for her. With each passing moment, her senses became clearer and her focus narrowed to keeping her breath slow and even.

She refused to think about anything other than Mark. Tiffany looked to her memory and took out every humiliation, every painful blow he ever gave her, and drew strength from them for what she was about to do. She'd lived her life doing the best she could in any given situation, she took her spirituality seriously, and she never thought she would consider hurting someone on purpose. But that's exactly what she was going to do. The implication of how easy the decision was for her would be handled later.

That is, if she made it through the confrontation.

An hour later, the teenagers left, and she was alone in the park. One hour to go.

After twenty minutes, Tiffany shifted her position because her legs were falling asleep. She willed the pins and needles sensation away. She didn't want it to affect her range of motion, and she would need to be quick.

She looked to her left when she heard a small rustle in the bushes. Of course, he would be sneaking in, she thought, but he would never have thought Tiffany would, or have the guts to do so.

The sound grew louder then faded as he moved off around the perimeter. Tiffany tracked him. She would need the perfect opportunity to catch him off guard. She hadn't shot the pistol in over two years when she took her defensive training class, and there hadn't been time to practice when she learned he was out of prison.

She would only get one opportunity to surprise him.

The park grew quiet, and Tiffany didn't know where he was. Several minutes ticked by and she sat very still. Then she heard it. A small branch broke behind her and she leapt to her feet to swing her arm around to shoot the gun.

The blow hit the side of her head, and the last thing Tiffany saw was the ground coming up to meet her.

CHAPTER THIRTEEN

Kat woke and found she was alone in the bed. She got up to use the restroom, and when she was done, she peeked down the hall. The guest bedroom door was closed, and she assumed that Tiffany got back in bed with Angel. She didn't think too much about it; they were in a new place and Angel may have been scared. Tomorrow they could talk about where they went from here. Maybe Kat could talk Tiffany into taking a trip to the East Coast. She didn't imagine that Mark would have any means to follow them there. They could lie on the beach and watch Angel play in the waves. The nights would be for making love.

The room was cold, and Kat pulled on a pair of flannel pants and T-shirt before getting back into bed. She felt wonderfully sated, full of hope for the future, and had no problems falling quickly back asleep.

She dragged herself another foot through the mud and leaves before she flipped onto her back. Her body began to shiver from shock. Her teeth chattered painfully behind swollen lips.

She steeled herself to look at the wound that slashed across her abdomen. Her leather shirt gaped where the enemy had stabbed her. She was afraid to look because she felt the blood seeping through her fingers. The warmth of it was a direct contrast to the icy rain.

She felt heavy, exhausted with the effort to reach home.

Blood, there was so much blood. She grew languid as she stared at the sky. The noise of battle faded, then stopped.

She felt as if she were floating, but that was an illusion. The constellations slowly swam into unfamiliar patterns, blurring beyond recognition. She began to hum the lullaby her mother had taught her when she was a child.

She knew she was dying. Her heart ached with loss. She was too young; there was so much she hadn't done yet. She cried out to the Goddess for help.

Her lover's beautiful face swam amongst the stars. She had that smile on her face. The one she had after making love in the sacred forest grove under the light of a full moon.

She had to find her. She forced herself to her knees and began to crawl toward the sickly red glow over her village.

She didn't want to die alone.

"Ow!"

Kat's arms were tightly wrapped around a little body. She opened her eyes and saw Angel staring right back at her. Kat didn't feel Tiffany behind her so she didn't quite know what to make of the situation. "Good morning."

Angel patted Kat's face. "I had a bad dream too."

Kat kissed her forehead. "I'm sorry, honey." She could still feel the smoke burning in her lungs from the nightmare. The unimaginable loss she'd just relived again was tearing her heart into shreds.

"No Mommy. Where is she?"

Kat's blood turned to ice in her veins as she tried not to panic. She didn't want to show Angel how scared she was. She hoped her voice was calm and steady. "Let's go find her, okay?"

Angel nodded and held her arms out for Kat to carry her. Kat picked her up and held her close while they left the room. She knew something was horribly wrong.

❖

The horse galloped toward her in slow motion. Flowers burned at her side, and small sharp stones cut into her knees. Screams rent the air, echoing through her mind repeatedly. Steel glinted in the glow of a dozen fires, and blood ran in small rivers in front of her.

The thudding grew louder until she was aware only of the whites of the rider's eyes and her breath. The sword arced into the air and then sliced downward. She closed her eyes against the impact.

Tiffany became aware of a woman weeping in the darkness. Helpless keening filled the air with despair and hopelessness that wrenched her heart. She wished someone would help her, do something to quiet her anguish. She fought to come out of the nightmare, tried to open her eyes, but something was wrong with them. They felt fused shut. She could only manage to lift them a few millimeters, enough to know there was no outside source of light in the room.

Panic began beating in her chest that had nothing to do with the dream. Her heart thudded against her ribcage. What was even more horrifying was realizing that the sobbing was her own. She fought to control it, tamped it down to small whimpers.

The more aware she became, the more her body racked with pain.

She moved slowly to try to sit up and gritted her teeth against the sharp pain in her ribs the motion caused. Fear and blind terror permeated the air in the space, stifling her attempts to question where she was. She couldn't remember how she could have gotten here.

Darkness closed in around her, and she had a fraction of a second to be dimly aware she was going to lose consciousness again before she fell back.

"Maybe she went to the store, munchkin." Kat stroked her hair and tried to soothe Angel's worry. "To buy something for Mitt."

"No," Angel said. "The Rider has her."

Chills threatened to overtake Kat's composure, and the beating of her heart escalated until her blood pounded in her ears, but she knew she had to keep calm for Angel's sake. "What can you see, sweetheart?"

Angel clutched the kitten. "It's dark and scary." Her little face twisted, and she began to cry. "I want my mommy."

"I know you do. I do too." Kat held her tight and carried her to the kitchen where she left her phone. "How about we call Nana and the aunties?" Kat desperately wanted to go out and search for her, but she couldn't leave Angel alone. All her fighting instincts were turned on, and she wanted to move, do something *now*. But she had no idea where to start. *What happened?*

"Okay. Can I feed Mitt the bottle now?"

"Yes, let me get it ready for you. I'm going to put you down on the couch, okay?"

Angel nodded and settled in the corner of the sofa with Mitt, who was purring softly. Kat was relieved that Angel seemed to be distracted.

She picked up her cell phone and was dismayed to find ten missed calls, all from Tiffany's family. She checked and noticed the sound had been turned off.

Oh, sweet Mother of God, she left on purpose.

The intercom next to the front door rang, and Kat ran to answer the call from the doorman. "I have four distraught women who want to see you."

The gratitude and relief she felt nearly knocked her to her knees. "It's fine, James. Please send them up." She left the front door open while she went into the kitchen to make the kitten a bottle.

She'd never felt so helpless in her life.

Aura walked in the door and headed straight to Angel. "I'm going to take her in the other room," she said. "What do you have there, baby?"

"Her name is Mitt. I found her. She's mine."

"And I can tell she's very special too. Show Nana your room, okay?"

"Are we going to find Mommy?"

"Of course we are. Come on. We'll let the aunties take care of that, okay?" Aura nodded to Kat. "Call me if you need me."

"Why the fuck are your phones turned off?" Shade stomped in.

"I didn't do it. Tiff did." Kat was numb. Sunny walked over to her, but it was apparent she wasn't at all stable either. She was pale, and black mascara tracked dark tears down her cheeks and onto her white shirt.

"Listen to me," Sunny said. "She's alive. I would know if she weren't."

Kat looked into her eyes. Sound and space appeared to narrow down to a small box. Sunny was trying to give her hope, but she was having a hard time breathing against the thought of losing Tiffany. There was nothing in that box but grief, shards of glass that cut into her heart and twisted, leaving bloody pieces behind in its wake. She didn't know how to survive it again.

Kat forced herself to continue looking into Sunny's bi-color eyes, focusing first on the blue, then the green. Breathe. Again. Concentrate on the tasks and not the probable result. Gradually, the red in her vision cleared and the pounding of her pulse slowed enough for her to think.

She saw Jordan on the phone and knew she had to be talking to the authorities.

"She left her bag," Shade said and dumped it on the counter. "We can look for clues."

Sunny pulled out the blue notebook from the pile and flipped through it. "She wrote us good-bye letters."

Tiffany came out of the darkness once again. This time she had better command of her heavy limbs and managed to put her hands to her face. She took an inventory. Her lips and cheeks were swollen and her nose felt off center. She knew without looking it was broken. The copper smell of blood nauseated her, and she felt her stomach roll.

The small room's only window was boarded up, but a small sliver of light traveled through a crack, and fractured across the room to illuminate just two inches around her. She was in the corner, on cold concrete. Her fingernails were broken and dried rusty stains covered her hands. There wasn't an inch of her body that didn't hurt. She lay there for a moment and then slowly began the task of sitting up.

She finally managed to shift her leg but found she was held in place. She reached down and felt the rope around her ankle. She struggled with the knots, but they were too tight.

She was trapped.

In a basement.

Her skin began crawling. Tiffany forced herself to take a deep breath, and when she did, she almost passed out from the white-hot pain that stabbed her ribcage. Death permeated the air, and she struggled to breathe around it. All her senses were screaming there was evil here, real and definable malevolent intentions.

She closed her eyes. Suddenly, she knew exactly where she was and why she was there. She patted her sides and realized her coat had been stripped from her. She leaned to the side and heaved repeatedly.

Tiffany inched her way back from the mess to lie down. She fought to stay awake against the dark wave of pain, but when she blinked, her swollen eyes refused to reopen, and she went under again.

"Tiffany! You get over here right now."

"No, please. I'm sorry. I won't do it again. I promise."

"Spawn child. You know what happens when you break God's Law."

"No, Mommy."

Her mother stood at the top of the stairs to the basement and pointed into the dark hole of the entry. "Get! When you're down there, get on your knees and beg the Lord for forgiveness for your wicked ways."

"But there are spiders down there!"

The slap sent Tiffany through the doorway and onto the landing. The door shut, clicked, and she was alone in the dark.

Kat watched Shade approach, fierce determination carved into her features. "Where would Tiffany's energy be the strongest here?"

She thought of the love they shared last night. "The master bedroom, at the end of the hall."

"We'll set up back there," Shade said. She picked up Tiffany's hairbrush and her own black bag on her way out.

Kat wasn't psychic, and she felt helpless with this plan. "Shouldn't we be out there looking?"

"We are going to search, Kat," Sunny said. "With tools far different than the police have."

Forty-eight hours, wasn't that the general rule for finding a murderer? What about missing persons? How many hours before it turned into a homicide? As soon as Kat thought it, the ticking of a clock started in her mind. She would work under her own set of rules.

Her skin burned with the need to rip something apart, the desire to pummel someone for answers, but she needed a direction to go in. So for now, she would take Sunny and Shade's lead, see what they were capable of, and decide what to do from there.

But when it was time to unleash, when she had a target—God help anyone who got in her way. There would be no mercy from her.

Tiffany was drowning. She beat her hands against the tub, aware of the pressure on the back of her head, the pain of her hair being pulled back. She felt the air hit her face and gasped before coughing up water. She was thrown onto the floor to her side.

She opened her eyes as much as the swelling would allow. A muscular man hovered over her. Her vision was blurry, but she managed to see well enough to know his head was shaved and covered with tattoos. She would have never recognized him like this.

"Wake up, cunt."

The instant she heard his voice, her old fears crashed down around her.

"Surprised, Tiffany? Prison changes a man."

She had no doubt of his intentions. He was going to kill her this time. Tiffany attempted to curl up into a ball to protect herself, and then folded her arms over her head. She pulled a vision of Angel's face close to her. Her heart shattered at the thought of never seeing her baby again, never smelling the sweet spot on her tiny neck, never feeling her little arms come around her in an embrace.

"Did you think I wouldn't see through your pathetic attempt to ambush me?"

Tiffany shook her head and felt hopelessness crush her spirit. It was as if the last five years had been turned back and she was lying in a puddle of blood on her own kitchen floor.

A roaring sound filled her ears. She could see his mouth moving but couldn't hear the words.

Mark grabbed her chin painfully. "Listen to me when I'm talking to you, bitch."

Tiffany tried to shake free, but his grip tightened and he twisted her face painfully.

"It's time to pay for what you've done. You stole five years of my life."

Wait a minute. The absolute absurdity of his statement kindled a flame in her. It was tiny, but steady. How like him to blame her for his actions. How could she ever have thought she loved this monster? She searched his face for clues. What had changed between them?

A small very faint voice inside her answered.

"You have."

Mark stood, and pain exploded in her back where he kicked her in the kidneys. Her head began swimming again and she saw telltale black dots that told her she was going to lose consciousness again. Tiffany sent out a silent plea.

Help me, Mother!

"I can't just stand here. I have to *do* something." Kat paced in the middle of her bedroom. She was so scared for Tiffany, she felt as if she were having an out of body experience. Five paces to the left, turn, eight to the right, turn again. She could still smell Tiffany on her skin and in the room, rich rosemary and earthy scents of the forest. The reminder spurred her to greater agitation. "What the hell was she thinking?"

Both Sunny and Shade looked up from their position on the floor where they held hands over a white candle's flame. "Sacrifice," they said in unison.

Kat's helpless rage exploded. "Where are the fucking cops, Jordan?"

"We don't have a crime yet, but I pulled some strings. They're sending someone over."

"We're going to find her," Sunny said firmly. "There is no other alternative that we will accept." Her eyes filled. "Please, Kat, I'm trying to keep it together here. She's our best friend and we love her. I can't deal with your anger right now."

Kat's heart skipped a beat, then another. The pain in her torso threatened to fold her in two. How could this happen? God, it was the past overlapping with the present. She couldn't let this play out again. She focused on the steely determination in Jordan's eyes, and beat back the fear. Tiffany needed her. It was time to draw on the warrior she knew lived in her, through her. This was not the time to focus on the helplessness—it was the time to be fierce. She took a deep breath and stood straight.

"I can't find her," Shade said.

Sunny's tears were falling freely. "I can't either."

"Try harder," Kat said. "Please." She had the utmost respect for Sunny and Shade and what they were trying to do, but she found it impossible to continue to sit here in this room while they appeared to be looking at nothing and listening to voices Kat couldn't hear. It was driving her crazy.

"Would you please," Shade said, "quit fucking fidgeting?"

"Sorry," Kat said. "I can't help it."

"Then leave the room."

Angel padded into the room still wearing her pajamas with the kitten tucked in her arms.

Kat crossed to her then crouched to her level. "What do you need, munchkin?"

"I only left her for a second," Aura said, coming in behind her. "Come on, baby. Let's go eat breakfast. Nana will see what's in the kitchen."

Angel continued to stare at Kat, who began to squirm under the intensity of her blue eyes. It felt like she was being stripped of all her ego and her soul was stripped from her and laid bare on the floor.

Kat felt Shade and Sunny shift behind her. The moment was heavy, as if time itself had stopped and everyone was waiting for it to start again before they could take another breath.

"That which was written in history, will be again."

Did that mature voice just come out of Angel? Kat felt every hair on her body rise to attention. She looked around to Sunny and Shade who were both staring with their mouths open in surprise.

She fell from her crouch to sit on the floor. "Angel?"

"The Dark Rider seeks to destroy us once more."

Kat felt as if she might faint. She knew that voice.

"Mother?"

Strong arms tried to pull her from the mud. Tiffany heard a primal scream, and the anguished notes of it seemed to pierce straight to her soul. She was fading, but aware of being shaken. Who was yelling at her? She was tired, so tired, but the screams persisted. She tried to open her eyes, but they were heavy, too heavy. A hand brushed her face and gently moved the wet strands of her hair.

Salt from the woman's tears fell on her lips to mix with the coppery taste of the blood that filled her mouth.

"Don't leave me!" The voice again. Tiffany tried to smile but didn't feel her muscles make the motion. She felt like she could float away on a cloud of peace.

She'd been so incredibly blessed by the Goddess. She'd been loved beyond measure by her warrior lover, and she wanted to take that feeling with her on her great journey home. In the corner of her vision, a small dot of light grew larger until she was encompassed by the glow.

"Daughter. It's time now." The feminine voice was more prevalent than the screaming, and Tiffany latched onto the sound. Now she felt the corners of her mouth lift slightly. Home.

The pain that filled her stopped when she reached for the Goddess's hand. She floated to stand beside her but was deeply aware of the emotion behind her. The rain fell in sheets, but not a drop hit her or the Goddess. She turned and was surprised and a little shocked when she realized the body on the ground was her own. The person wracked with grief and rocking her dead body was Kat.

There was so much blood, but floating outside her body, she was detached from the horror of it. Wait! She wanted to see more, to try to understand. Tiffany turned back to the Goddess, but before she could protest, the light grew brighter, erasing the scene before her.

"You will remember her, child. I promise you will find each other again. It's not her time yet. You have been faithful and devoted to me. Do not doubt, or take my vow to you lightly."

The Goddess smiled, and Tiffany was filled with a sense of well-being, homecoming, and utter harmony. "I will remember," she whispered. The light held and comforted her at once. Joy and love swam through her soul.

A harsh slap to her face brought her out of the vision she so desperately wanted to hang on to.

"Wakey, wakey."

"It was *you*," Tiffany said. "The rider was you."

Mark's high-pitched giggle gave her chills.

"How could I have not known that?"

"You've always been stupid, Tiffany."

What was he saying? Her head ached and her thoughts were muddled from the beatings.

"Don't remember?" Mark sat on the cement floor in front of Tiffany. "Let me tell you a beddie-bye story. Listen carefully, because I'm nearly done with you again."

Tiffany closed her eyes and then opened them when he pinched her.

"Pay attention." He laughed. "It's a good one."

Tiffany didn't have a choice. She tried to focus.

"Once upon a time," he started sarcastically, "in a land far, far away and long ago, there lived a king. He had several wives of course, but it was the red-haired witch that was his favorite. She could see things that helped the king smite his enemies and brought him untold riches. Now, this king and witch had a daughter."

Mark giggled again and poked Tiffany in the chest. "That's you. Anyway, this young girl proved to have, let's say, special gifts as well. One of the other wives had a son born from another man before she married the king."

He pounded himself in the chest. "That's me. Can you see where this is going?"

Tiffany shook her head slightly. She listened carefully, hating that she was fascinated with his story when she knew how it ended. But knowledge was power, and she needed him to continue.

Mark cuffed her head. "See? I'm telling you. Stupid. The other wife was jealous of the witch and her daughter. She went to a sorcerer and brought to the castle some magic of her own. Dark magic. She put a spell on the king to murder the witch so she could take the girl, and promised her to her oldest son. But something went wrong, you see. The witch and her brat got away. The entire clan at the castle searched and searched, but they didn't find them. They hid very well. The woman, who was my mother in that life, created a powerful spell and sealed it with the blood of young, innocent women. One that would ensure the girl, that's you, was tied to us throughout time."

Mark's eyes were full of rage, and spittle sprayed from his mouth as he talked. "But you wouldn't come back with me when I found you."

Tiffany heard buzzing in her ears. The sound of madness. Hadn't she heard that recently? God, she couldn't think.

"It took ten years that time, but I fixed you. I fixed all of you bitches. Yes, I did." He jumped to his feet. "But you don't know the very best part yet!"

Tiffany gagged. *No, don't say it.*

Mark clapped. "Guess who *your* mother is this time around."

❖

The intercom buzzed in the hall, but its harsh sound didn't break the stunned silence in the room. Kat continued to stare at Angel, whose features had shifted somehow, and she looked like someone much older.

"The curse was cast a thousand plus two moons ago, and it must be broken."

Mitt stirred in Angel's arms and mewed. She looked down to comfort the kitten, and when she looked back up, her face was once again that of a young child.

Kat exhaled and heard Sunny and Shade do the same.

No one said anything until Aura took over. "Honey?"

"Yes, Nana? Is breakfast done now?"

"Let's go and see." Aura took one last look over her shoulder before disappearing.

Jordan walked in. "The police are here, along with Detective Parker."

Kat's legs had fallen asleep, and she took the time to get her circulation going again. She looked at Sunny. "Did you—?"

"No clue. Wow."

Kat was finally able to stand. "Try to find her again. I'll go out there with Jordan. Don't give up. We have to find her." She was frantic with worry but still had the ability to feel the otherworldly moment she'd had with Angel. At least she had something to focus on, if not a direction yet. Now she had to figure out how to find Tiffany and break the curse.

She walked down the hall and was almost surprised to see how pretty the day was turning out to be. Somehow, she thought it would be raining and storming, like the day when Tanna was killed. *Hell no.* She couldn't allow herself to go there at all, but how could she mend the threads of grief and anxiety torn within her when she was faced with a horrible situation much the same as the first?

Kat had to keep positive or she'd fall apart. Angel was eating on the patio with Aura, and she felt her heart fill with a fierce sense of hope, love, and belonging. This event may have been set in motion over a thousand years ago, but they would finish it in their favor this time. Besides, if they didn't have a chance, why was everything coming together in just this way? It would be too cruel of the Gods and Goddesses to take everything away again. They would win this.

Or she would die trying.

Hang on, Tiffany. I'm coming for you, love.

❖

"My mother? How does she tic into this?"

"Well," Mark said. "She was *my* mother back then, and she bargained with the dark sorcerer. There is always a price to be paid. She went quite mad you know. The curse cost her a tiny bit." He held his fingers an inch apart. "She promised the sorcerer things she couldn't deliver for his services. He couldn't have cared less about you, the child; he wanted the red witch for himself. When the bitches couldn't be found, he revealed a clause she hadn't known existed in the original spell. In the event he didn't get paid, the curse would go back onto my mother, and she would have to search throughout time for the witch until she delivered her unto him."

"But you said I was the child."

"Ah, but I had a deal with him myself where you were concerned." Mark nudged Tiffany with his foot. "Guess who my daddy was. Guess!"

Tiffany closed her eyes. "The sorcerer."

"See? You're catching on. Well then, my daddy scried for you in his crystal ball. It took him years. We'd almost given up. Imagine our surprise when we actually found you, and you had married *another* in my place. Another bitch at that. I couldn't let that pass, oh no. You stained my honor and I was duty bound to kill you for it."

"But I didn't know I was promised to you," Tiffany said. "I was six years old when we left."

Mark ignored her, and she knew she wasn't going to change his mind about something that happened so long ago with a simple declaration of innocence. He wouldn't believe her anyway.

"I took my marauders with me and gave explicit orders for them not to touch you. And we burned that fucking sanctuary down to the ground."

And with that statement, Tiffany thought, the missing pieces fell into place. "Why did you kill everyone? Why not just me?"

"Because it was fun."

Tiffany's blood chilled as the realizations occurred one after another. Her mother's hatred, the recurring nightmares of dying, why she had been so blind where Mark was concerned, and Kat. *What had happened to Kat?* She refused to think or ask about how Angel fit into this nightmare. He hadn't mentioned her yet; she wasn't going to remind him. So far, his sick obsession had only included her. She managed to block her pain, and her head cleared slightly.

"Mark, how many times have we relived this?" She kept her voice small, trying not to set him off.

"That's the thing, *Tiffany.*" He spit her name out spitefully. "When we murdered the women, one of my men was too excited and accidently killed the red witch. I went to the largest hut, and the older women had been slaughtered like pigs while they held on to each other and prayed to a Goddess who never came to their aid."

Mark's eyes lit with evil glee. Tiffany knew that look well and attempted to shrink back from him, but her back was already to the wall.

"Needless to say, my father was pissed off at me."

Another missing piece clicked and she felt a surge of power when she received the information. Tiffany couldn't help it. "Oh, that's rich. You were cursed to search and search for me until you could make me marry you."

Mark rolled his shoulders and cracked his neck. "Are you laughing at me, *Tiffany?*"

She put her arms up to block the blow, but her head snapped back from the force, and hit the bricks.

Kat sat at the table and joined Jordan, along with the two officers in uniform, and Parker. "I'm sorry," she said then gestured toward the newspaper and folders stacked in front of him. "Why are you here again?"

"I can't really say for sure," Parker said. "I was sitting at my desk, going over the files for the umpteenth time, and felt the need to come right away. Something in my gut said I would find the answers I was looking for here."

"But your gut didn't tell you Tiffany wasn't here?" Kat regretted the comment the instant she'd made it. "I'm sorry. I'm not angry with you."

Parker nodded once. "What do we know?"

Jordan cleared her throat. "Nearly two weeks ago, Mark Blasier was released from prison. There must have been a problem with the paperwork, as no one called Tiffany Curran to notify her the man that tried to kill her was free."

Kat felt wave after wave of anger flow over her skin, but she kept her mouth shut. These people were not at fault and had nothing to do with a data entry error. She focused her rage toward Mark, concentrated on sending her hatred for him into the ether, and hoped it found its target.

"There were instances over the last week that no one thought much about until we compared notes."

"What happened?" Parker asked.

Kat interrupted. "I could swear I was being followed. Tiffany began receiving strange phone calls, and there was an intruder outside her house."

"Yesterday," Jordan continued as one of the officer's took notes. "We found a strange box in Tiffany's house."

"What was in it?"

"Old bloody rags and bits of hair."

One of the officers snickered and Kat glared at him. "Regardless of what you're thinking, it proves he was inside her house."

"Do you still have the box?" Parker's face paled.

"Shade does."

"Can I see it?"

Jordan nodded. "Yes, let me finish first. Last night, Tiffany came here to Kat's with her daughter, Angel, because of the building's security. But she disappeared sometime during the night."

"So she left of her own free will?" One of the uniformed officers stood. "This doesn't prove anything, and there's no proof

that Blasier kidnapped her." He turned to Jordan. "I'm sorry, but you know how busy we are. There's no crime here."

"But…" Kat wanted to smack him. "You know how this will end. I know there's nothing you can prove until the crime has already been committed. But what about being proactive for once? Can't you do that?"

The other officer stood to join his partner. "I really am sorry, Jordan, Kat. Call us after the forty-eight hours, or if…" His face turned red as he stammered. "We have to go."

Kat didn't bother showing them to the door. She knew she wouldn't be able to refrain from slamming it.

"Kat," Jordan began. "It's not their—"

"I know." Kat turned to Parker who sat back in his chair.

"I'm still listening," he said.

Kat put her head on the table and heard footsteps in the hall and Shade's voice. "I told you, she went this way."

She looked up to see Sunny walk onto the balcony and say something to her mother. Kat left the table to see what she was saying and if they had managed to find a clue about where Tiffany might be. When she had gotten as far as the glass doors, Angel ran to her and lifted her arms to Kat. She nearly lost her fragile hold on her composure. She felt so damn helpless and insignificant in the face of Angel's absolute faith in her. She should be out pounding the pavement, asking questions, something other than talking in circles.

Angel patted Kat's cheek. "Don't cry."

Kat didn't trust herself to speak so she nodded instead.

"Mommy will come back."

"Of course she will, munchkin."

"We're going to the pet store for 'plies."

"Supplies," Aura translated. "We'll replace what she's already used from your neighbor and buy her own."

Kat nodded again and reached for her wallet.

"No, I have this."

"Are you two going to be safe?" Kat didn't want them to leave and disappear as well.

"I wouldn't be going if I thought we weren't."

"Are you always cloaked in enigma?"

"Pretty much. Listen, Kat, it doesn't matter what you do as long as you love our Tiffany. This was her choice and battle. It's hers to win or lose. You can't fight it for her."

That is so what I don't want to hear. Kat's jaw tightened. Aura put a hand on her shoulder, and she felt warmth spread from the tension in her neck and stomach muscles. She didn't want to give in to the relaxation. She felt as if she had to be wound up like a spring and was ready to bounce at any second. "I'm so confused. Aren't you afraid of what might happen to her?"

"Terrified." Aura looked at Sunny, Shade, Jordan, and then back at Kat. "But I think all of my girls can handle whatever comes their way."

"Nana! Come on."

"Go on," Aura said to Kat. "They need you at the table." Her skirt rustled as she swept past her on the way to the door.

"Bye." Angel held up a little hand and waved. She held up Mitt's tiny paw and whispered to the kitten. "Mitt says see you later."

"See you soon." Kat wanted to believe Aura so badly. It was so hard to put her heart and faith into something and someone else. She wanted to believe they had it handled and all would be well, but they hadn't lived through the grief of losing Tiffany before.

Had they?

She had no time to think about that now. Damn it, she needed a plan.

CHAPTER FOURTEEN

This time when Tiffany regained consciousness, she was alone. She was thirsty and had no idea what time or even day it was. She also had little illusion that she was going to live through this encounter.

She sat up and was surprised when there was little pain with her effort. She closed her eyes and became aware of a low-level frequency of energy in the room. The question was whose was it? She cautiously sent her senses out to see if she recognized the signature it contained, but pulled back when she didn't.

Tiffany realized that she had either healed herself somewhat in her sleep, or someone had psychically done it for her. Her first thought was Sunny and Shade must have found her, but she negated that when she couldn't connect with either of them. She didn't dare probe any further because she had no idea how powerful Mark was psychically. He had hid it the entire time she'd known him without anyone ever knowing about it.

Who was here with her?

The sound of heavy boots descending sounded on the wooden stairs. Tiffany lay back down quickly. She wouldn't let him see she was feeling better. It was better that he think she was still helpless. She turned her head toward the wall and willed her body to heal more.

She must be doing a good job of playing possum because she heard his boots pacing the room aimlessly. He mumbled something repeatedly, but Tiffany couldn't make out the words.

The buzzing began in her head again, growing in volume until she bit her lip to stay quiet and still. She let out a breath when she finally heard him leave again.

A plan, she needed a plan.

❖

Kat did as she was told and closed her eyes while she held hands with Sunny and Shade. Jordan and Parker sat out of the circle.

"I know you're here," Shade said. "I saw you."

"Who?" Kat asked.

"Ssh." Sunny squeezed Kat's hand. "Can you tell us your name?"

Parker cleared his throat. Kat could just imagine how he felt about this whole séance thing. But to his credit, he stayed where he was and didn't say anything.

She was willing to try absolutely anything at this point, but she wasn't going to lie to herself about being a little weirded out that Shade said there was a ghost in her home.

"I hear crying," Sunny said.

"Is it Tiffany?" Kat's stomach tightened.

"No, I would know if it were her. Please, help us. Why are you here?"

"Got her," Shade said then inhaled sharply.

"What's wrong?" Kat asked.

"She's covered in so much blood I can't tell what she looks like."

Kat's palms tingled with energy from their clasped hands.

"Oh, there you are. Thank you." Sunny let Kat's hand go. "Yes, I see you now."

Parker whispered a question to Jordan.

"It's the way they work. Shade sees them as they looked when they died. Sunny sees them as they want to appear. Tiffany sees them as they actually looked in life."

"Can you help us?" Sunny asked. "We're looking for our sister."

There was a pause while Sunny appeared to be listening.

"Wait, there are additional women here now," Shade said and then choked up a little. "They all look brutalized. One of the women had died very recently. She's confused and wants to go home. Hold on while I try and get her name. She's scared of me."

Kat watched Shade's eyebrows furrow as she concentrated. She must have been talking to the spirit in her head, because she nodded a few times before she opened her eyes. "Sylvia. She says she died a couple of blocks from here." She paused. "In a fucking Dumpster."

The room was already chilled, but Kat rubbed her arms when the temperature dropped even further.

"She's a little scary," Parker said to Jordan.

"You don't know the half of it."

"The woman to my left is Joy," Sunny said.

"Oh come *on,*" Parker said.

Kat ignored him. "Could they still be here from the readings we did with Parker?"

"No, they keep showing me hands linked together. Together in death is what they're telling me." Sunny's eyes widened. "She says he knows where Tiffany is."

Kat locked eyes with Shade who nodded, then turned to look at Parker. "Where did you find the bodies?"

When he didn't answer right away, Shade shoved her chair back. She advanced on him. "Where did you find the fucking bodies of these women?"

❖

Tiffany could almost feel her wounds healing. Her ribs still ached, but there wasn't any pain when she took a breath.

She sat up and looked at the knots around her ankle again. She didn't know how long Mark would be gone this time, but she refused to just lie here and wait for him to come back and kill her.

The past might already be written, but the future was fluid. While she attacked the knots, she became aware of spirit energy and the smell of copper beside her. The signature was familiar. Once you'd connected with it, the pattern remained.

"Hailey?"

In her mind's eye, Tiffany easily brought forward Hailey's image and then another joined her. "Theresa." It was a statement and not a question. She knew she was right.

"What are you doing here?"

The word came from far away and echoed forward toward her in increments until it reached her ears.

Trapped.

"Here?" Tiffany knew she should be shocked, but things always came full circle. She thought of how she met Kat and how everything snowballed from that moment to this. Details revealed themselves to her from hindsight—the buzzing of madness, how the girls resembled her, why she couldn't follow his energy trail. He'd taken great lengths to make sure she couldn't.

"It was Mark who did this to you."

Hailey answered with a sigh, and Tiffany felt the chill and her anguish. Hailey showed her three boxes, almost identical to the one Tiffany had found in her house, complete with blood and hair. "He kept you here with these? Who's the third?"

Joy.

The rope on her ankle fell off. Tiffany shoved to her feet and then ran for the stairs.

No! He's coming.

Tiffany tried to think past the adrenaline that flooded through her system. Where did he put her coat? She spied the blue fabric and raced over to it. The pockets were empty. Frantic, she looked around the basement for a weapon. Then she saw it.

A baseball bat leaned against the cinderblock wall. She grabbed it and gagged when she felt the energy it emanated from Hailey's and Theresa's murders. Oh shit, she was here in *that* house. She forced herself to tighten her grip and ducked behind a stack of boxes.

It wasn't much as a hiding space, but it was all she had.

Mark began whistling on the landing before he descended.

The sound stopped when he reached the bottom. "Where the fuck are you? I know you're here. I can smell you."

Tiffany tightened the grip on the bat and sent up a silent prayer. She would only get one shot at this.

"You come out right now."

Not a chance, asshole.

Tiffany took a deep breath and held it. She brought to mind every move she'd learned in her self-defense classes.

"Face me now, bitch, or it will be worse on the little girl."

Tiffany's blood ran cold and the rage built inside her until her entire body was shaking with the need to kill him.

Three more steps to the left, that's all she needed from him.

Two.

One.

Tiffany exploded from her hiding place swinging the bat in front of her. She felt the satisfaction of hearing the thump against his skull and kept at him.

Mark wrestled the bat from her and backhanded her. But Tiffany was full of righteous fury and came right back at him with fists, nails, and teeth. "You will never touch her."

He opened his mouth to laugh, but a cold wind came up between them, spinning so fast the cardboard boxes on the floor flew up into the vortex it was causing.

The distraction allowed Tiffany to pick the bat up once more and she fought against the wind to get closer.

Mark smiled at her and raised his arm.

He had her gun.

Tiffany laughed. "You have no power over me anymore!" Tiffany felt no fear, no regret, just freedom. "Go ahead!" she shouted to be heard over the gale.

Then she swung for the fence.

"Can't you go any faster?" Kat yelled.

"I'm trying," Shade said.

"Jordan is going to be so pissed at us."

"Yeah, so?"

"Turn left. He just turned left." Kat heard sirens coming up behind them. Parker had ordered them to stay away, but there was no way that was happening. "Now turn right!"

Parker's car screeched to a halt in front of a dilapidated house. He left his door open as he exited the car and hit the ground running.

Kat and Shade were right behind him, ignoring his shouts to stay back. Kat entered the house behind him and saw him disappear around the corner, presumably down the hall.

"The basement door is open." Shade pointed in the opposite direction.

The primal scream that sounded from the floor below curdled her blood and made Kat's ears ring. "No!"

She raced through the door and took a step down the stairs before she fell down the rest of them. When she landed, she looked quickly around the room to find Tiffany. *Please don't let me be too late.*

Tiffany stood straight with her arms stretched up to the sky. She screamed again, and the hair rose on Kat's neck. She looked magnificent in her triumph. A body lay at her feet.

Kat felt her blood heat and her heart began pounding. An ethereal hand appeared in front of her and she looked up. Maeve stood in front of her in full battle gear and helped her up. "Go on, little sister, go to her."

Shocked, Kat felt her mouth open, but no words came out. She blinked a few times, and then saw Shade wink at her.

"Kat!" Tiffany ran straight for her, covered in blood.

"How bad is it, baby?" Kat tried to search for injuries. She held her so tightly, she gasped for breath.

"It's not mine. It's his."

Parker took the stairs two at a time, and took in the scene in front of him.

"Get upstairs," he said to Shade and Kat. He looked at Tiffany. "Emergency services are on the way."

He tried to help her up the stairs, but Tiffany shook him off.

"Tell them to take their time. He's not going anywhere."

When she reached the hall upstairs, Tiffany went into one of the bedrooms. Kat was on her heels. "What are you looking for?"

Shade went into the closet and pulled up a floorboard. Underneath it were three wooden boxes. She nodded to Tiffany. "Now it's over," she said.

Parker was right behind them. "What are those?"

"Inside them, you'll find the victim's blood and hair mixed with his own. There are your clues, evidence, and DNA."

"Trophies?" Parker's expression hardened as he took them with gloved hands into evidence.

"If calling them that makes you feel better," Shade said.

"What do you mean?"

"They're curses, made with very old, very dark magic. It's like the one I have in the back of the van from Tiffany's house. I'll get it for you."

Parker turned to Tiffany and Kat. "You have to leave the basement, go outside, and wait for me. It's a crime scene."

"I know. I have one more thing to do," Tiffany said. "I'll be right behind you."

Kat followed Tiffany into the derelict living room where she stopped and closed her eyes.

"What are you doing?" Kat asked.

"I'm thanking Joy, Hailey, and Theresa. Now I'm going to send them to the light where they belong."

Kat gave her own silent thanks, to the women both past and present that brought her to this moment with Tiffany.

Where she belonged.

Then, now, and forever.

CHAPTER FIFTEEN

Tiffany was tired of people fussing over her. If it wasn't Kat, Sunny, Shade, or Jordan, it was the nurses and doctors.

She was fine. Better than fine, she was free.

No charges were to be filed against her as Mark's death was clearly a case of self-defense. Tiffany doubted that the official report would include any mention of the murdered women's ghosts, but that was okay too.

Jordan had read her the riot act about leaving the house with a gun, as she could have been charged with all kinds of things if she'd shot Mark with premeditation. But Tiffany knew she was only talking for form's sake.

Tiffany struggled with the fact she'd killed another human being. She figured there would be some work to do around that emotional issue, because it wasn't in her nature. It went against everything she stood for. Then the coin would flip, and she would be flooded with memories of what he did to her, and the other women. The only reason they'd died was because they resembled Tiffany in Mark's twisted brain. There would be some part of her that would never get over that.

When the guilt of killing him reared its ugly head, Tiffany could make it go away entirely when she reminded herself that he'd threatened Angel. And when she remembered that, she wanted to kill him all over again.

Then she remembered how Kat had stayed with her all night, despite the nurses trying to kick her out.

As if her thoughts summoned her, Kat walked into her room. "Hey. Ready to go?"

"Absolutely." Tiffany stood up from the chair. "Kat?"

"What, love?"

"Do you think we could find it?"

"Find what?"

"The river with the waterfall at the edge of the forest."

Kat's smile lit her face. "We already have."

"No, really. I'm being serious."

"We can try."

"Wouldn't it be awesome research for your book?"

Kat nodded. "It would. Is that the only reason you want to go?"

Tiffany sighed. "No, that would be secondary. What I really want would be to kiss you under the full moon where we met for the first time."

"Sounds like heaven to me. I'm still trying to wrap my head around the idea that Angel was my mother in that life."

"Or that Mark's mother was *mine* here. It's enough to drive you crazy thinking about it."

"Do we have everything straight now?" Kat shook her head. "Because you could have knocked me over with a feather when I found out Shade was my warrior-teacher, Maeve."

"I know, right? What about when we figured that Parker must be the king, trying to undo his past wrongs? Or that—"

"Come here," Kat said, then pulled her against her body. "How about when Kat and Tiffany find each other and live happily ever after?"

"There is that," Tiffany said. "Let's go home."

"Which one?" Kat asked. "I love your family and all, but can we spend some time alone? We've been overrun for a week now. God, Tiffany, I almost lost you. I nearly went off the edge at the thought…"

"You were going to say, again."

"That's the thing," Kat said. "You think that I can separate how I felt for Tanna from how I feel about you. Love feels like love. You make me happy, Tiffany. You're beautiful, sexy, loyal, funny, and sweet. What's not to love about you?"

"Well, according to you, nothing."

Kat smiled. "Let's go home, baby."

Tiffany's cell signaled a text message. "Apparently, the odds are in your favor. The aunties took Angel to the Puyallup Fair."

Kat put her arm around Tiffany as they headed for the elevators.

When the doors slid open at the parking level, they gasped in unison.

Dark green forest filled the large garage, and birdsong filled the air. In the distance, a waterfall could be heard tumbling over the rocks and into the river.

"It's beautiful!" Tiffany said.

And with her spoken words, the illusion was broken. They walked to the car.

"Kat," Tiffany said.

"What, love?"

"I'm so glad you caught me."

EPILOGUE

Three months later

Tiffany was curled on the couch with Kat beside her. Shade was telling one of her stories, the kind that gave most people nightmares, but it wasn't fazing Kat in the least.

"Wow," Kat said. "That's fascinating. Can I use some of this stuff in my next book?"

"You haven't finished the first one." Tiffany laughed.

"Of course you can, my young friend," Shade said. *"There are more things in heaven and earth, Horatio, than are dreamt of in your philosophy."*

"Did you just quote Shakespeare?" Tiffany was flabbergasted. She'd never heard Shade do that before. "Besides, Kat is older than you."

"This time." Shade grinned and launched into another tale of darkness to entertain her audience of one, Kat.

Tiffany smiled because loving Kat was so damn easy. They just stepped right on into it and everything seemed to fall into place. Kat had moved her personal items from the condo and taken over the guest room for her new office, where she spent the days writing her book about Sanctuary.

Her condo in Seattle remained unoccupied, as Kat hadn't decided whether to sell it or rent it out.

Angel didn't bring up the past again, and Tiffany didn't push her. Kat moving into their home hadn't fazed her in the least. She welcomed her new mother figure and called her My-Kat. Tiffany was so happy, sometimes she would lie awake at night and worry about when the other shoe would drop. She wondered if it all could be taken away as fast as she received it. Then Kat would turn to her in the dark and make love to her. She kissed away the anxiety and soothed Tiffany with her warm presence.

Shade must have finished her story, because the room fell silent for a moment. Tiffany was happy to see her so relaxed lately. She had become a regular fixture at their house, and they both enjoyed having her.

"So did you see the new receptionist at SOS yet?" Kat grunted when Tiffany elbowed her. "What?"

Shade's expression immediately shut down and her voice was clipped and short. "I've met her. Which reminds me, the Bristol Terrace investigation has been rescheduled for next month."

Tiffany nodded but wondered what that was about. The new receptionist, Raven, was beautiful and charming. Why the snappy reaction?

"Mommy!" Angel's scream echoed down the hall.

Tiffany, Kat, and Shade, ran toward her room where they found her sobbing on her bed. Tiffany scooped her into her arms and began soothing her. "What, honey?"

"The rider! He says I have to go with him. I don't want to leave."

Her blood turned to ice and her scalp began crawling. "You're not going anywhere. I've got you."

Kat paled and looked at Shade. "How? I thought you cleansed the spot where he died."

"I can feel him. There must be a trace left here." Shade crossed to the closet, turned on the light, and then dropped to her knees to begin moving various toys and boxes out of it.

"I hadn't even thought of that." Tiffany was livid. "Why did I not think of that? I do this for a living."

"He's right there," Angel said and pointed to the corner of the room.

"I know, baby. Auntie will take care of it as soon as I find what I'm looking for."

Angel stopped crying and nodded toward the empty wall.

"What's he saying?"

Kat sounded as hysterical as Tiffany felt. She stood with Angel in her arms, intending to leave the room when the door slammed shut in front of her.

"No, Daddy," Angel said. "You have to go to the light."

"Leave her alone, you bastard!" Tiffany screamed. "Get out!"

Angel didn't flinch at the volume in Tiffany's voice. Instead, she continued to stare at the area where Shade was frantically searching for what must be another blood curse. "But if you don't feel good, the light will make you better. I promise."

Kat moved quickly to put Tiffany and Angel behind her, trying to protect them from something that Tiffany knew she couldn't see.

"I can't go with you now." Angel paused. "Next time, maybe."

"Oh God," Tiffany said. "Shade?"

A cold wind blew out of the closet. "Found it." Shade got up from the floor. She was holding a small box against her chest. "I'm leaving with it. I'll take care of it."

Tiffany nodded. "Please hurry."

"It's okay, Mommy," Angel said. "Daddy says he won't bother us anymore. He's almost done."

The doorknob clicked and turned before Shade reached it. Tiffany felt Kat shudder slightly. She walked in front of her and Angel.

"Be careful," Kat said when she opened the front door.

Shade turned back to look at them when she was halfway down the walkway. "Good-bye, guys. I love you."

Tiffany felt that her tone and choice of words were off somehow. She wanted to call her back, but a sharp pain in her temple kept her from voicing her concern. She wanted Angel as far away from the damn box as she could get.

She blew Shade a kiss when she got in her van. "Love you too."

Kat waved as she closed the door. They had only taken two steps toward the hall when a bright orange flash illuminated the room an instant before the glass in the picture window shattered inward, and an explosion rattled the entire house.

Tiffany screamed. "Shade!"

About the Author

Yvonne Heidt's first book, *Sometime Yesterday*, was a 2012 Lambda Literary Award finalist in lesbian romance and a 2012 Golden Crown Literary Award winner. She is also a bronze medal Rainbow Award winner for Debut Author. Yvonne was born a fourth-generation San Franciscan, but is currently living in Texas with her partner and their four dogs, where she channels her inner rock star on Friday nights. Writing is her passion and she considers herself blessed beyond measure that she and her muse get along so well.

Books Available from Bold Strokes Books

The Quickening: A Sisters of Spirits Novel by Yvonne Heidt. Ghosts, visions, and demons are all in a day's work for Tiffany. But when Kat asks for help on a serial killer case, life takes on another dimension altogether. (978-1-60282-975-6)

Windigo Thrall by Cate Culpepper. Six women trapped in a mountain cabin by a blizzard, stalked by an ancient cannibal demon bent on stealing their sanity—and their lives. (978-1-60282-950-3)

Smoke and Fire by Julie Cannon. Oil and water, passion and desire, a combustible combination. Can two women fight the fire that draws them together and threatens to keep them apart? (978-1-60282-977-0)

Asher's Fault by Elizabeth Wheeler. Fourteen-year-old Asher Price sees the world in black and white, much like the photos he takes, but when his little brother drowns at the same moment Asher experiences his first same-sex kiss, he can no longer hide behind the lens of his camera and eventually discovers he isn't the only one with a secret. (978-1-60282-982-4)

Love and Devotion by Jove Belle. KC Hall trips her way through life, stumbling into an affair with a married bombshell twice her age. Thankfully, her best friend, Emma Reynolds, is there to show her the true meaning of Love and Devotion. (978-1-60282-965-7)

Rush by Carsen Taite. Murder, secrets, and romance combine to create the ultimate rush. (978-1-60282-966-4)

The Shoal of Time by J.M. Redmann. It sounded too easy. Micky Knight is reluctant to take the case because the easy ones often turn into the hard ones, and the hard ones turn into the dangerous ones. In this one, easy turns hard without warning. (978-1-60282-967-1)

In Between by Jane Hoppen. At the age of 14, Sophie Schmidt discovers that she was born an intersexual baby and sets off on a journey to find her place in a world that denies her true existence. (978-1-60282-968-8)

Secret Lies by Amy Dunne. While fleeing from her abuser, Nicola Jackson bumps into Jenny O'Connor, and their unlikely friendship quickly develops into a blossoming romance—but when it comes down to a matter of life or death, are they both willing to face their fears? (978-1-60282-970-1)

Under Her Spell by Maggie Morton. The magic of love brought Terra and Athene together, but now a magical quest stands between them—a quest for Athene's hand in marriage. Will their passion keep them together, or will stronger magic tear them apart? (978-1-60282-973-2)

Homestead by Radclyffe. R. Clayton Sutter figures getting NorthAm Fuel's newest refinery operational on a rolling tract of land in Upstate New York should take a month or two, but then, she hadn't counted on local resistance in the form of vandalism, petitions, and one furious farmer named Tess Rogers. (978-1-60282-956-5)

Battle of Forces: Sera Toujours by Ali Vali. Kendal and Piper return to New Orleans to start the rest of eternity together, but the return of an old enemy makes their peaceful reunion short-lived, especially when they join forces with the new queen of the vampires. (978-1-60282-957-2)

How Sweet It Is by Melissa Brayden. Some things are better than chocolate. Molly O'Brien enjoys her quiet life running the bakeshop in a small town. When the beautiful Jordan Tuscana returns home, Molly can't deny the attraction—or the stirrings of something more. (978-1-60282-958-9)

The Missing Juliet: A Fisher Key Adventure by Sam Cameron. A teenage detective and her friends search for a kidnapped Hollywood star in the Florida Keys. (978-1-60282-959-6)

Amor and More: Love Everafter edited by Radclyffe and Stacia Seaman. Rediscover favorite couples as Bold Strokes Books authors reveal glimpses of life and love beyond the honeymoon in short stories featuring main characters from favorite BSB novels. (978-1-60282-963-3)

First Love by CJ Harte. Finding true love is hard enough, but for Jordan Thompson, daughter of a conservative president, it's challenging, especially when that love is a female rodeo cowgirl. (978-1-60282-949-7)

Pale Wings Protecting by Lesley Davis. Posing as a couple to investigate the abduction of infants, Special Agent Blythe Kent and Detective Daryl Chandler find themselves drawn into a battle over the innocents, with demons on one side and the unlikeliest of protectors on the other. (978-1-60282-964-0)

Mounting Danger by Karis Walsh. Sergeant Rachel Bryce, an outcast on the police force, is put in charge of the department's newly formed mounted division. Can she and polo champion Callan Lanford resist their growing attraction as they struggle to safeguard the disaster-prone unit? (978-1-60282-951-0)

Meeting Chance by Jennifer Lavoie. When man's best friend turns on Aaron Cassidy, the teen keeps his distance until fate puts Chance in his hands. (978-1-60282-952-7)

At Her Feet by Rebekah Weatherspoon. Digital marketing producer Suzanne Kim knows she has found the perfect love in her new mistress Pilar, but before they can make the ultimate commitment, Suzanne's professional life threatens to disrupt their perfectly balanced bliss. (978-1-60282-948-0)

Show of Force by AJ Quinn. A chance meeting between navy pilot Evan Kane and correspondent Tate McKenna takes them on a roller-coaster ride where the stakes are high, but the reward is higher: a chance at love. (978-1-60282-942-8)

Clean Slate by Andrea Bramhall. Can Erin and Morgan work through their individual demons to rediscover their love for each other, or are the unexplainable wounds too deep to heal? (978-1-60282-943-5)

Hold Me Forever by D. Jackson Leigh. An investigation into illegal cloning in the quarter horse racing industry threatens to destroy the growing attraction between Georgia debutante Mae St. John and Louisiana horse trainer Whit Casey. (978-1-60282-944-2)

Trusting Tomorrow by PJ Trebelhorn. Funeral director Logan Swift thinks she's perfectly happy with her solitary life devoted to helping others cope with loss until Brooke Collier moves in next door to care for her elderly grandparents. (978-1-60282-891-9)

Forsaking All Others by Kathleen Knowles. What if what you think you want is the opposite of what makes you happy? (978-1-60282-892-6)

Exit Wounds by VK Powell. When Officer Loane Landry falls in love with ATF informant Abigail Mancuso, she realizes that nothing is as it seems—not the case, not her lover, not even the dead. (978-1-60282-893-3)

Dirty Power by Ashley Bartlett. Cooper's been through hell and back, and she's still broke and on the run. But at least she found the twins. They'll keep her alive. Right? (978-1-60282-896-4)

The Rarest Rose by I. Beacham. After a decade of living in her beloved house, Ele disturbs its past and finds her life being haunted by the presence of a ghost who will show her that true love never dies. (978-1-60282-884-1)

Code of Honor by Radclyffe. The face of terror is hard to recognize—especially when it's homegrown. The next book in the Honor series. (978-1-60282-885-8)

Does She Love You? by Rachel Spangler. When Annabelle and Davis find out they are both in a relationship with the same woman, it leaves them facing life-altering questions about trust, redemption, and the possibility of finding love in the wake of betrayal. (978-1-60282-886-5)

The Road to Her by KE Payne. Sparks fly when actress Holly Croft, star of UK soap Portobello Road, meets her new on-screen love interest, the enigmatic and sexy Elise Manford. (978-1-60282-887-2)

Shadows of Something Real by Sophia Kell Hagin. Trying to escape flashbacks and nightmares, ex-POW Jamie Gwynmorgan stumbles into the heart of former Red Cross worker Adele Sabellius and uncovers a deadly conspiracy against everything and everyone she loves. (978-1-60282-889-6)

Date with Destiny by Mason Dixon. When sophisticated bank executive Rashida Ivey meets unemployed blue collar worker Destiny Jackson, will her life ever be the same? (978-1-60282-878-0)

The Devil's Orchard by Ali Vali. Cain and Emma plan a wedding before the birth of their third child while Juan Luis is still lurking, and as Cain plans for his death, an unexpected visitor arrives and challenges her belief in her father, Dalton Casey. (978-1-60282-879-7)

Secrets and Shadows by L.T. Marie. A bodyguard and the woman she protects run from a madman and into each other's arms. (978-1-60282-880-3)

Change Horizons: Three Novellas by Gun Brooke. Three stories of courageous women who dare to love as they fight to claim a future in a hostile universe. (978-1-60282-881-0)

Scarlet Thirst by Crin Claxton. When hot, feisty Rani meets cool, vampire Rob, one lifetime isn't enough, and the road from human to vampire is shorter than you think... (978-1-60282-856-8)

Battle Axe by Carsen Taite. How close is too close? Bounty hunter Luca Bennett will soon find out. (978-1-60282-871-1)